FROSTBITE

CAMBRIA HEBERT

FROSTBITE

1

Bellamy

I cried myself to sleep. When I woke, the room was still just as dark as when I'd succumbed to grief. Automatically, I reached for Liam, but the space where he normally slept was cold and bare.

Feeling slightly disoriented, I pushed into a sitting position and glanced over at the clock. Seeing that I'd literally only been asleep for an hour made me deflate faster than a cut balloon. Sudden nausea rolled over me as if I were a passenger on a boat at stormy sea. Gagging, I nearly fell out of the bed, racing into the bathroom where I emptied my already empty stomach. I was only a few weeks along, and already I'd puked more than I had my entire life.

After cleaning up, I went back into the bedroom, standing in the center of the dark room, just staring at the door.

God, it seemed like a lifetime since I'd seen Liam. The longing I felt to even just lay eyes upon him was enough to send me quickly toward the door. I didn't open it, though. Instead, I leaned my forehead against it, palm flattening on the smooth wood.

What he must be going through.

Out there. Alone.

I shut myself in here, thinking it was what he wanted, that it would be easier for him. His father was dead, and I was the reason.

I wanted to go to him, to offer comfort and whisper it was going to be okay. I held back, regardless of the itch in my palms, the tug in the center of my chest.

Cold air drafted beneath the door, making my bare toes curl under.

I gasped quietly and shoved back.

My God! Liam was out in the living room. The very place where two men were killed and his own father had been mortally wounded. The back door was broken, the frigid air rushing in.

The blood… *Dear God, the blood.*

Without another thought, I rushed out into the hallway, my bare feet slapping against the cold wood floor. It didn't matter anymore that this was all my fault.

It didn't even matter if he was going to shun me.

I had to try.

I have to fight.

I had to at least offer comfort to the man I loved. I wouldn't let him deal with this alone. I knew what it was like to be alone with grief so dark you couldn't even see in front of you.

He was standing at the window, staring out into the black night as though there were something infinitely interesting and not just night so deep it shrouded everything.

My feet stuttered, my heart clutching at the sight of him. He looked as he always did: strong. But I knew better, and it caused everything inside me to scream with pain.

Liam must have heard me charging down the hall, because at the same moment I halted, he spun and looked in my direction.

I teetered on tiptoe, my body wobbly from the force of my stop. Liam's eyes flashed but then quickly moved down toward my feet, his entire face darkening.

I followed his gaze, realizing that I stopped just shy of the blood still pooled thickly on the floor. In fact, my toe was mere centimeters from it. If I moved just a fraction, I would be touching someone else's death.

I was so very weary of death.

I glanced back up, noting Liam still drilling holes into the puddle at my feet. Pushing away the queasy feeling inside me, I hopped over the stain, moved a few feet, then had to hop over even more blood.

It was grotesque that this was our home, the place I once cherished and felt safe in. Now it was a crime scene. A murder den.

Liam watched me move. When I got within arm's length, I prepared for him to stiffen or tense or for his body to turn away.

He didn't do any of that. Instead, his eyes, so silvery and bleak, latched onto mine and held. His expression was partly blank, frosty like the outdoors.

It didn't stop me.

I rushed forward and slid my arms around his neck. In that moment, all the obstacles that lay between us didn't matter. I loved him, and he was in pain. Everything else would have to wait.

I pressed close, straining to my full height, trying to match his size just a little bit more. I wished I were bigger, more solid… something greater to hold on to.

Tell him. My mind urged. *Tell him it isn't just you holding him, but his child, too.*

Liam's vise-like arms came around me and squeezed. The feel of him, the scent of him chased away everything else. I clung harder, pressing close, holding him so tight my arms and shoulders ached. We clung to each other in the middle of the cabin stained with blood, scented with death, and filled with the bite of winter's air.

My face pressed into the side of his neck. I would have crawled beneath his skin if I could. I didn't know what to do. How to apologize for everything I'd cost him. There was no making up for this. The loss he was served tonight would haunt him for the rest of his days.

Against me, his arm quivered a bit, and I realized what I was doing. Gasping, I wrenched back, my eyes flying to the bandage covering the bullet wound in his shoulder. The shoulder I'd just been clinging to.

Liam's fingers clutched, keeping me upright as I moved.

"Your shoulder!" I stressed.

He shook his head once. "Is fine."

Only two simple words came out of his mouth, but it was like a downpour of rain in the middle of a desert. I soaked them up, the deep timbre of his voice, the slightly scratchy way they ripped from his throat.

Emotion rushed up inside me, tightening my chest and making it hard to breathe.

"I w-was squeezing y-you," I stuttered, trying to get control of my wits.

"Were you?" he said, turning back to the window. Turning away from me. Even though he whispered, I heard him speak. "It sort of felt like you were holding me together."

My teeth cut into my lower lip, and I stepped forward. I reached out, my hand hovering in the distance between us. Hunger so severe ached inside me. I thought maybe the pain would never go away. I wanted to touch him again.

I was afraid.

Fight.

I went forward, curling my fingers around his bicep. He stiffened, and I froze. We stood like that as the sound of whirling wind whistled through the broken door. He didn't yank away, and I couldn't convince myself to either. Still, I didn't move any closer, afraid he would flinch away and afraid it would shatter me.

Still resolved to be there for him, I realized maybe it wasn't my touch or comfort he wanted, but there were other ways I could fight.

I let go and headed toward the kitchen. Pulling out a bucket and disinfectant, I turned on the hot water and started to fill it up. I found a rag and a mop and set it close by. When it was full, I carried it toward the living room where the worst of the blood was.

Liam moved like the athlete he was and appeared soundlessly. Startled, I sloshed water over the rim of the bucket and over my foot.

"What do you think you're doing?" he intoned.

"Cleaning this up," I answered. "I don't want you to see it."

He growled as though he were angry and ripped the mop from my hand, throwing it across the room. It landed with a clatter on the other side of the fireplace.

"You *will not* clean up the blood of the men who tried to kill you."

"They killed *your* father," I whispered, hollow.

His shoulders fell, and the breath inside him hitched. Glancing up, I noticed for the first time the smears of blood all over his shirt, how it was ripped around the place he'd been shot. His hair was a wreck, and his eyes were bloodshot.

There were smears of blood on his neck and cheek.

I made a sound and went forward, forgetting all about the way he reacted the last time I'd reached for him. "You're covered in blood."

"It's probably Dad's."

My chest caved in just a little. When I reached for his hand, he didn't flinch or pull away. "Your fingers are like ice," I murmured when we entwined.

"Come on," I said, soft, tugging him back down the hall toward our bedroom. I felt him hesitate just a moment on the threshold, but by the time I glanced over my shoulder, he was moving again.

This was a new kind of pain for me. Here I thought I'd already met most kinds. Turns out the pain I'd known in the past didn't compare to the pain of knowing the man I loved most hurt. All I could think about was soothing him, easing him, at the very least, taking just a fraction of it away.

Tugging him through the bedroom, we went into the bath. I released him so I could turn on the shower and grab some towels. "C'mon. Help me," I whispered, tugging his shirt up over his good shoulder.

Liam removed it the rest of the way, and I reached for his jeans. When he was completely undressed, I reached for my own clothes. Partway through pulling them off, I realized he wasn't helping, and I also felt his stare.

Pausing, I sought him out, the sound of water falling behind us and thick, warm steam rising toward the ceiling. "I'm going to help you, okay? So you don't get your shoulder wet."

He nodded, eyes sliding over my body, goose bumps raised along my skin with the caress of his eyes.

I gestured for him to go first, guiding him to the back of the shower, out of the reach of the spray, then stepped in. Positioning myself between him and the water, I angled his body so his wounded shoulder was facing away.

Grabbing the loofah, I began squeezing water over his chest and arm. Liam's eyes slid closed and his throat worked. I continued the ministrations, working up to soaping him down and then painstakingly rinsing him off a little at a time.

When I was finally done with his body, I grabbed a cloth, saturated it, and went to work on his face. A small purring sound drifted to my ears. I glanced up, but his eyes remained closed.

The air in here was thick with the humidity from the hot water, but also from the emotion welling up around us. Sorrow was heavy, and regret was impenetrable. I caught myself several times blinking back tears and swallowing down the worst of my pain.

When I was nearly done with his face, Liam caught my wrist, his fingers gentle.

Dull silver eyes focused on mine, and water pelted us from the side. "Why are you doing this?" he whispered.

"Because I'm in love with you."

Life flared in the silver, making it glitter. My heart kicked up a little faster when he grabbed me. Liam lifted me, my legs clamping around his waist as if they knew that's where they belonged. Water droplets clung to my lips and cheek, damp strands of hair heavy on my back.

He moved so I was plastered against the wall farthest from the spray, his body pinning me in place. Between us, I was surprised to feel the strength of his cock.

"I know I shouldn't," he said, resting his forehead against the wall right beside my ear. "But I want you. I want you so badly I can't even see."

Grasping his face between my palms, I forced him to look in my eyes. "I'll give you whatever you want."

He didn't say anything. He just moved. With one thrust, his rigid length speared me, and my head fell back against the wall. Even though his eyes rolled closed, Liam reached up, sliding his hand between my head and the wall so it was pillowed against him and not the hard surface.

That was where his gentleness ended.

The minute my body stretched around him and I sighed contentedly, he began to move with fierce desperation. He thrust into me over and over again at an unrelenting pace. Pleasure poured over me. I bathed in it, far more thoroughly than I ever had in any water. For long moments, the shattering pain I knew was dulled, and all that remained was Liam moving inside me again and again.

The sounds he made echoed through the steam. His fingertips bit into my hip as he slammed up into my body, a pleasant kind of discomfort. The hand at the back of my head tightened in my hair, and my back slid along the tile wall with every single thrust.

I don't know how he kept up with it, how he didn't succumb to the intense bliss bursting between our bodies. I cried out, practically crumpling toward the floor, when an orgasm ripped through me. Even as I quaked, Liam held me up, keeping up the pace. I shouted his name over and over, and he growled as though hearing me yell for him were a basic need.

Soon his body stiffened. His hands bit into my hips and pulled my body down so I could feel his throbbing head deep in my womb. Liam's shout filled the bathroom, and then his teeth sank into my shoulder as his body continued to spasm with pleasure.

I held him close, clinging to him, offering up every last ounce of energy and comfort I had inside me. The only way we could beat back death was with life, and feeling him inside me was the most alive I would ever be.

Liam collapsed against the wall, both of us gasping for breath. The water was starting to cool, so once I recovered enough to stand, I very carefully washed his hair and made sure every last trace of blood was gone. Once he was clean, I moved fully beneath the spray to wash myself.

Liam watched every move I made. I didn't feel the rapidly cooling water because the way he looked at me kept me warm.

He didn't touch me, something I severely wanted, even though he'd just been inside me. Usually, his hands were everywhere; he couldn't keep them away.

Today, though, I washed myself as he stared, a desperate plea in his eyes but his hands firmly at his sides. The animalistic way he'd fucked me was gone, replaced with an odd sort of loneliness even though we stood here together.

The second the water was off, I patted a fluffy towel over his chest and arms. I shivered, and he frowned, took the towel from my hands, and wrapped it around my shoulders. It was already damp from the water I'd mopped off his skin, but I didn't care.

After handing him the extra towel, I stepped out of the shower and dried. I avoided looking at him as I worked, though not looking at him made it even harder to forget he was there. Finally dry, I tucked the towel around me and reached for the brush. My hair was tangled and knotted. I lacked the patience to brush it without tugging.

Liam made a sound, and the next thing I knew, the brush was in his hands and the heat from his body curled around my back and caressed my shoulder blades. I glanced in the mirror, but it was too fogged up to see him.

My eyes slipped shut when he began brushing, using all the patience I simply didn't have. His movements were so gentle compared to the way he'd just made love to me. The contrast between these two moments brought tears to my eyes.

"Bellamy," Liam whispered, and something about the way he said it pierced my heart. Fear skittered along my spine because I just knew what was coming.

I knew he was about to say what we'd just done was a mistake.

Swallowing, I allowed him to pull me around. The brush made a light snapping sound when he laid it behind us on the counter.

Our stares bounced between the other's, measuring, trying to talk without saying a single word. The air around us shifted, his broad shoulders rose, and I braced for whatever it was he was about to say.

A muffled ringing broke the moment.

Liam stiffened. Then worry filled his eyes. Grabbing his pants, he yanked the cell out of the pocket and answered instantly.

"Mom?"

I couldn't hear what she said on the other end. Liam didn't look at me when he listened. It was as if he forgot I was there.

"It's okay, Mom," he said, his voice gentle yet pained. "I know."

He was silent again. Then he spoke. "We'll be right there."

More silence.

His eyes slid to me, then away.

An odd feeling squeezed the back of my neck, and my stomach clenched. Swallowing back the bile rising in my throat, I reached around and grabbed the counter as an anchor.

"Okay. Yeah." He spoke softly and then disconnected the call.

I had to clear my throat twice before I could speak. "Is she okay?"

Avoiding my gaze, he replied, "No. She's not."

I nodded. I couldn't even imagine how she must feel. I glanced at the bandage covering Liam's shoulder, remembering the agony that ripped through me when I saw him fall after being shot. I remembered the way it felt when I left the resort over eight years ago and thought I'd never see him again.

Finally, I thought of the way he'd just looked at me as he was on the phone.

Maybe I could imagine. At least a little.

"You should be with her," I whispered. "She needs you."

I felt his eyes, but I didn't look up. Instead, I focused on the floor and the single drop of water still clinging to the top of my foot.

"Get dressed," he said, heading for the door.

My head whipped up, and something that felt a hell of a lot like relief opened up inside me. "You want me to come with you?"

He stopped in the doorway. The way his shoulders nearly hit his ears was all the answer I needed. Without turning back, he robbed me of the sight of his face. "I'll take you to Alex's," he replied, then disappeared into the bedroom.

I stood there and stared at the empty space he'd occupied. That little bit of relief I'd experienced shriveled up and died inside me.

It didn't matter that we'd just made love. Maybe it hadn't been love at all. Maybe it had been clinging to life after a night full of death.

Whatever it was, I knew.

I know.

Liam and I had just reached the beginning of the end.

2

Liam

Alex lived in a cabin not far from mine. Rarely did we drive between places because we usually had a board or skis strapped to our feet, but tonight was different.

The first rays of the sun were beginning to crest over the mountain, turning the night sky into a peach-hued dawn. Stars still dotted overhead, and the massive amounts of snow the blizzard brought in covered everything.

My truck drove as though the snow wasn't even there, the headlights bouncing off the wooden A-frame exterior of his place when I pulled up. I barely had the truck in park when Bellamy reached for the door handle.

We hadn't spoken at all. There was an awkward charged silence between us, having only disappeared when I was inside her in the shower.

I knew I shouldn't, but her body had just been too hard to deny. The comfort I found in her was the only thing that tethered me to sanity.

"I'll be back as soon as I can," I said, voice gruff.

She paused, her body leaning toward mine even though she didn't glance around. "You don't have to rush."

The muscle in the side of my jaw ticked. "She just needs a little time…" My voice drifted away.

Breath whooshed out of her, and with it came words. "She blames me, Liam. I wouldn't want to see me either."

My eyes closed, hands gripping the steering wheel tight, when what I really wanted was to reach for her. "Bellamy."

"It's okay," she said. "Go be with her. She's your family."

My eyes snapped open and head flew toward where she sat. She wasn't looking at me, though, but out the windshield. A small sound ripped from her throat, and the truck door flung open, ripped out of her hand by the winter wind.

"Charlie!" she cried and scrambled down from the cab.

Alex was standing in the door of his place, loose sweats covering his frame. The dog bounded off the porch, barking, and beelined for Bells. They met at the front of the truck, the headlights creating a spotlight on the pair as they reunited.

Bellamy flung her arms around the giant dog's neck and buried her face in his fur. Charlie's tail beat so hard against the snow it drifted up around them.

Bellamy's shoulders shook a little beneath her coat, and my throat constricted. I couldn't even imagine what she'd gone through last night.

And here you are leaving her with your best friend.

She pulled back from the dog, and he lapped her face with his slobbery tongue. Bellamy wiped at her cheeks, and I knew it was tears she swiped away, not the dog drool.

Alex called out, and they both looked up and started to the porch.

His lips moved when she drew close, and her head bobbed. Alex unfolded his arms and pulled her in, tucking her body against his.

Through the windshield, our eyes met and held. Even from this distance, I saw the sorrow in his face, the solidarity he represented. He'd been close to my dad, too. We were all grieving right now.

Still holding on to my girl, his stare stayed on me. Slowly, he nodded with promise of watching out for her while I was with Mom.

Why did I always feel so torn? Torn between Bellamy and everything else.

The truck reversed with ease. Snow blew around a bit, and a few branches wobbled under the weight of the white. Alex stayed in the doorway, Bellamy bundled in his arms.

The second I put the truck in drive, I saw her body flinch, as if me leaving caused her physical pain.

Instantaneously, I slammed the gear in park. The Extreme wobbled a little as I threw open the door and jumped down. My shoulder throbbed, but I kind of liked the pain. It kept me grounded to the here and now.

The several feet of snow underfoot was of no consequence. It certainly wasn't enough to keep me from making a beeline right for my girl.

Alex leaned down and whispered something beside her ear, and she jerked away from him to spin around with wide eyes. When she saw me stalking forward, emotion broke over her face and she started to run. Bellamy rushed across the deck, and I held out my arms, gesturing for her to come home.

Without a single moment's hesitation, she leaped off the top step as I rushed forward and caught her around the waist. Her thighs clamped around my body, her arms around my neck.

"You're my family, too," I said, rough.

"Even still?" she asked, her eyes searching mine.

"Oh, baby, even still."

Tears fell, creating glistening tracks down her cheeks. I wiped them away, feeling some of the distance between us crumble.

"I'm coming back for you." I vowed. "We're gonna talk this out."

Chemistry and unspoken thoughts and feelings ebbed and flowed around us, the emotion swirling so raw and tangible I could practically taste it.

"Don't give up on me," I rasped, the plea bubbling up from the darkest fear inside me.

"I won't ever," she whispered.

I filled my hands with her ass and leaned up. She met me halfway, our lips brushing in a tender kiss. Everything inside me went quiet for long, precious moments. Relief made me go slack. My lips fell away, our foreheads pressing together.

I knew I should say more, but the words were lodged in my throat, and no matter how many times I swallowed, I couldn't unstick them.

I loved her so goddamn much. She deserved better than me. Better than a man who couldn't protect her.

Reluctantly, I pulled back. "I have to go."

"I know."

Instead of putting her down, I walked a few feet, carried her up the stairs, and then placed her on the deck.

Alex shifted in the doorway. I glanced over her shoulder at my best friend. Lightly, he tapped the center of his chest with his fist.

I returned the gesture.

It hurt when I left her standing there on the porch. I felt her stare as I left.

I would come back for her. We would talk this out...

I just wasn't sure if words would be enough.

3

Bellamy

I felt like a battery with no life left in me at all.

Walking through Alex's cabin, I didn't even notice my surroundings or realize this was my first time at his place. I walked into the sunken living room and curled up on the end of one of the leather couches. Charlie jumped up beside me and lay down, his big head covering my side. His fur was soft and warm, a comforting sensation to contrast the intensity of my feelings and thoughts.

Alex stepped in front of me, dragged the coffee table behind him close, and lowered so he was sitting right in front of where I was curled.

"How you doing?" he asked, his voice hushed.

"How do you think?"

"Want to talk?"

I shook my head, adamant.

He fell quiet, but his eyes never left me. I wondered how I looked to him then, pathetic and weak or like a tornado of havoc destroying everything in my path.

After a while, he started to get up.

"Alex…"

He dropped back down and covered one of my hands with his. I tightened my fingers around his, clinging on as if I just realized how badly I needed an anchor.

We stayed like that a long time, me staring off into space and him holding my hand. The curtains were all drawn so the room remained dim, no sunlight intruding. It still felt like night regardless because, really, I hadn't even been to bed.

After a while, my voice startled me, as if my mouth spoke without consulting my brain. "Alex?"

"Yeah?"

"I killed someone today."

"He deserved worse."

"You've killed before, haven't you?"

He didn't react physically, but the energy in the room changed. "Liam told you?"

I shook my head and looked up from the arm of the sofa. "No."

The piercing light blue of his eyes stared at me, maybe recognizing something. "I have."

Behind us a fire crackled in a large stone hearth. Charlie had all the warmth of a blanket, and Alex's strong presence made me feel a little brave. "Do you ever feel guilty?"

He studied me for long moments, almost weighing his words. "Truth?"

I nodded.

That calm, deadly exterior fell over him, the one I saw before. I realized then I only saw that piece of him when he allowed me to. "No. Some men don't deserve to live."

I nodded again. His honesty made me feel better because the admission didn't change the way I felt about Alex. The fact that he killed without guilt didn't make me look at him any different than before.

Alex wasn't a bad person, and that meant neither was I.

Then why do I feel like one?

His long fingers reached out a little later, pushing away some of the hair falling into my face. "You're blaming yourself hard, aren't you?"

I puzzled his words. "If I hadn't killed Spidey, he would have killed all of us."

"Not Spidey. Ren."

The mention of Liam's father brought a rush of tears to the surface and a piercing pain through my chest. "It's my fault," I whispered.

Alex made a sound, dropped off the coffee table, and hit the floor right in front of the couch. His fingers squeezed mine. "Ren's death was *not* your fault. Liam said you tried to push him out of the way."

"I was too late."

Alex's mouth flattened. "No one blames you for his death."

"Liam does."

"No, he doesn't," he retorted.

"His mom does."

He sucked in a breath, knowing I was right. I was here with him because Liam's mother couldn't bear the thought of looking at me. After pausing for a few heartbeats, Alex said, "I think she gets a pass for tonight. She just lost the love of her life."

But what happens when she still hates me tomorrow? I didn't say it out loud because I was weary of talking.

Allowing my eyes to drift shut, I replayed the moment I shared with Liam before he left. How he looked bursting out of the Extreme and rushing toward me. How right it felt when his lips brushed over mine.

Even after everything, the pull between us was undeniable.

Still, he left anyway.

Liam

"I'm sorry to call you over here like this," Mom said when I stepped in the door.

She was wrapped in a thick robe, dark circles shadowing her red eyes.

I shut the door, then hugged her. I was bigger, so she fit against me easily. "You don't need to apologize."

"This place is just so empty… I never realized how big it was until tonight."

"Dad had a large presence," I remarked, glancing around.

"Yes, he does." She pressed her lips together. "Did."

Tucking an arm around her shoulders, I led her upstairs.

"How about some tea?" she said, moving ahead into the kitchen.

I followed along, agreeing to the tea I didn't want. "Have you slept at all?" I asked.

"I don't think I could."

"You need to try, Mom. You have to take care of yourself."

She was good at redirecting the conversation. "How are you? How is your shoulder?"

"It's just a few stitches."

She rushed across the kitchen and wrapped her arms around me again. "Oh, if I'd have lost you, too…" Her voice quivered.

"You might have if Bellamy hadn't been there."

She stiffened and then jerked away, going back to the tea.

I didn't know why I said that. It was a dick thing to bring up, and I should have known better. I was just so damn angry.

About everything.

I felt like a pot on high simmer, rapidly approaching full boil and about to spill over.

"Mom," I said, remorse thick in my voice.

She sniffed. "You wouldn't have been in that position at all if it weren't for her." She spun, a tea bag swinging between her fingertips. "Your father would still be alive!"

He was dying anyway.

I sucked in a breath at the thought. Thank Christ I had enough control left in me to not spew that. My God, what the fuck was I thinking?

"She didn't want Dad to die. You have to know that. She was trying to push him out of the way, just like she had me."

Her shoulders slumped, and she turned back to the tea kettle that was beginning to whistle. Silence filled the house as she poured the tea and added honey to both mugs.

"She killed the man who killed Dad, you know." I went on after a few strained moments. "Bellamy picked up the gun and emptied and entire clip into that asshole."

"Why are you telling me this?" Mom whispered.

I thought back to the shower, to the words Bells whispered to me. "Because I'm in love with her."

She turned, eyes meeting mine. "You could love a woman who killed your own father?"

I flinched, feeling as if she'd smacked me. She saw it so black and white… Maybe I would too if this wasn't Bellamy.

If this wasn't the girl who'd gotten away and then come home.

"She loved Dad just like we do."

Her voice was shrill when she snapped, "*No one* loves him like me!" Her anger dissolved into weeping, and I felt about two feet tall.

My footsteps ate up the kitchen tile, and I pulled her into a hug. She clung to me and cried, her wrenching sobs finding a piece of me that had yet to break and snapping it in two.

Talking about this right now was a shit idea. My mom couldn't handle anything except the next moment in front of her. Convincing her that Bellamy wasn't at fault was a waste of time because her feelings were her own. As were mine.

Who are you trying to convince, Liam? You or your mom?

The front of my shirt was damp as I led her out of the kitchen, away from the forgotten tea, and into the living area where I guided her to sit on the sofa. She tucked her legs beneath her and leaned her head on my shoulder. Her cries had quieted, but she fidgeted with a used tissue in her hands, occasionally dabbing her face.

"What am I going to do without him?"

I was wondering the same thing.

"It was too soon," she murmured. "He wasn't supposed to die this soon."

"We could have had forever, and it still wouldn't be enough." I agreed, the lump in my throat threatening to choke me.

"I'm glad the man who shot him is dead," she said a short while later, after some of the grief settled at our feet.

I squeezed her a little tighter, offering more comfort that I didn't feel.

I supposed it was something she was willing to admit that Dad hadn't died directly because of Bellamy.

But really…

Spidey might have shot my father, but was he the one ultimately responsible for his death?

Perry Crone claimed ownership of that nefarious deed, so in my eyes, the man who killed my father was still alive and breathing.

Bellamy

Two days.

It had been two days since Liam dropped me off on Alex's porch and two days since he said I was still his family.

The more time that passed, the more I was able convince myself he'd only said that in the moment, and the minute he'd gotten some space, he realized just how bad I was for him.

I slept most of the days away. Grief, exhaustion, and I think probably the pregnancy left me extremely lethargic and feeling ultravulnerable. I was mad at myself for it, too. I wasn't this girl. I was the girl who managed not to lose it while my father was murdered. I was the girl who hid from the mob and had enough guts to put Perry Crone in prison. I gave up my entire life and went into witness protection.

More recently, I was the woman who emptied an entire clip into a man who'd terrified me for weeks.

I was most definitely not the girl who cried at the drop of a hat, got sick at the mere sight of food, and chose to sleep away life because it was easier than living it.

Renshaw Mattison did not give up his life for yours so you could squander it this way.

The scolding thought made me jolt up into a sitting position. Blankets fell down to my waist, and Charlie looked up, his tail wagging.

Automatically, I reached for one giant, fluffy Charlie ear and scratched. He made a groaning sound that elicited a half smile to form on my lips. "Everything is such a mess," I told him.

He licked my hand, then nudged it for more scratches.

I obliged and stared off across the room. Alex absolutely insisted on me taking the bedroom. I told him to stuff that idea.

He backed down because I started crying (*again, who was I?*)—until I fell asleep on the couch, and he carried me back here and put me in bed.

The jerk face.

I hadn't argued again because it was easier to hide in the mountain of pillows and blankets at the back of his cabin and not speak to anyone at all.

I'd heard the phone ring a few times. The first couple times, I'd lay against the mattress with bated breath, expecting Alex to come in and say Liam wanted to speak with me.

He never came.

Eventually, when I heard the phone or the door, I didn't even hope.

The familiar feel of my stomach about to toss up everything inside it sent me rushing toward the bathroom. My knees hit the tile, and my body was already heaving. Nothing came up, and the sheer attempt to vomit made me hurt.

When I was done, I sat back on my haunches and sucked in some deep breaths. Charlie whined from the door, and I reached out to pet him.

This stops now. I could still grieve and mourn. I could even feel sorry for myself, but lying in bed, sleeping, and not taking care of myself was over. I might not feel worthy of life, but dammit, Ren thought I was, and my baby…

My baby deserved everything.

Putting a hand to my belly, I glanced down. There was a piece of Liam inside me, a piece counting on me to take care of him. Liam might need his space right now, but even if he wasn't here, I was still close to him because of this little peanut.

I left the bathroom and bedroom and followed the sounds into the kitchen where Alex was burning himself, trying to use the toaster.

"GD-mother—"

"Need some help?" I asked, cutting off his very inappropriate language.

"Agh!" He jerked around and pressed a hand to his heart. "First this toaster tries to attack me, and then you do!"

My lips twitched. Lifting my hands, I said, "I come in peace."

Smoke literally started rising out of the toaster behind him.

My legs felt wobbly when I moved forward and pushed him out of the way. "Step aside. You need an intervention."

"What I need is a new toaster."

I laughed.

"Knew I'd get one of those out of you sometime."

I paused and glanced over my shoulder. Warmth pierced me, and it was sort of like stepping in front of a fire after being out in the cold all night. "You mean you ruined this toaster to make me laugh?"

"Hell no. That toaster tried to kill me."

I made a rude sound and unplugged the appliance. Then I dumped the black bread into the sink. Along with it, about ten tons of breadcrumbs fell out. "How long has it been since you cleaned this thing out?"

"You have to clean it?"

I abandoned the toaster with a grimace. "How about some eggs?"

"I think I have one pan left in here that hasn't tried to kill me."

Tried to kill him = he ruined it trying to cook.

Bless his heart.

"You need a girlfriend, Alex."

"I think relationships are more complications than anything."

I paused at the fridge, feeling his words all the way into my heart. "Maybe you're right." I agreed.

"I meant for me, not for you."

I gave him a withering glance. "How's the couch treating you?"

He made a face. "Point taken."

I busied myself whisking some eggs and prepping some bacon for the micro. I would have put it in the oven, but it was faster this way. Charlie laid at my feet and was working on a nice puddle of drool for me to step in as I worked.

In no time at all, I had a plate of cheesy scrambled eggs and bacon in front of him. There was a familiar foil-wrapped item on the counter, and I pointed to it.

Alex nodded.

"Sharon was here?" I asked as I unwrapped the banana bread.

He nodded. "Yesterday. Everyone here is pretty shook up."

I swallowed, cutting off a thick slice. "I can imagine."

Alex tucked into his plate, and after a few bites, he glanced up. "You eating?"

I didn't want to, but I nodded and filled a plate of my own, reminding myself that I had a baby to think of.

As I ate, I fed Charlie too much bacon and a hunk of bread. The silence between us was comfortable even though I knew we were avoiding the giant elephant in the room.

Liam.

He was almost done with his plate when he said, "The funeral is in the morning."

"Already," I murmured.

"Tomorrow will be three days."

"I know how long it's been," I replied, sad.

Alex set down his fork with a clink and reached for my hand. Charlie thought he was offering him some bacon and tried to eat his fingers.

Alex made a sound and pulled back. "I ain't got nothing for you!" he said, offended. "You already ate more than me!"

"Poor baby," I crooned and gave the dog some more bacon.

"When that dog has the shits, you're going outside with him." Alex threatened.

I held out another piece to him. He looked between me and the crispy slice, then snatched it up to shove half in his mouth.

"You need to eat more," he said, nudging the side of my chair with his foot.

I took another bite, and my stomach nearly revolted.

Alex frowned when I replaced the fork and chewed with a smile that probably looked more like a grimace.

"You know everyone at the resort and in Caribou thinks what happened to Ren was an accident."

"What's the official story?" I asked, reaching for my water to force the food down my throat. The cool wetness of the drink felt good, and I took some more.

"Some asshole guest at the resort targeted Liam because he's Mr. Olympic and a snowboard celeb and tried to rob his place. You all showed up and interrupted, and things went south."

Leave it to the FBI to invent some kind of highly believable story. I frowned to myself. Speaking of the FBI, I'd barely had to talk to them. "Has the FBI been here?"

Alex shook his head.

"Chief of police stopped by. I told him you were sleeping."

"You could have gotten me up."

"I was beginning to think you were becoming one with the bed," he cracked.

My eyes filled with tears. "I'm sorry," I whispered.

God. There I went again.

His chair made a horrible sound when it scraped across the floor. "Hey now, I was just playing."

Sniffling I tried to smile. "I know. I just—" My voice cracked, and that's as far as I got in explaining how much of a mess I felt.

Alex cursed and reached out to hug me. I went into his arms, though it was Liam I really wanted. Alex held me tight, shifting in his seat so I was leaning between his legs. He rubbed up and down my back vigorously, almost as if I were wet and he wanted to dry me off. If I wasn't so emotional, I would have giggled.

"Don't you have a sister?" I asked against his chest.

He pulled back a little, swiping a tear off my cheek. "I got two now."

More tears fell, and I pushed my face against his chest. Suddenly, the way he hugged was perfect.

"I only said that before because I wanted you to know no one around here blames you. You don't have to worry when you step out the door that people will be whispering and talking. No one knows the real story."

"She's not going to want me there, at the funeral."

But my God, how could I stay home? How could I not go and pay my last respects to a man who literally gave his life for mine?

"That's exactly why you're going," Alex remarked, pulling back to stare at me.

I furrowed my brow.

"To pay respects to the man who gave his life for yours," he explained as if he realized my brain was working slow.

"I said that out loud?"

He nodded. "Holly won't cause a scene. She's too classy for that. And Liam is going to need you there."

I sat back and wiped at my face. "He hasn't been here in two days."

"He's called."

"He hasn't asked to speak to me."

Alex glanced down at his empty plate.

"I should get a room at the resort," I announced.

His eyes whipped up. "What?"

"I'm an employee here now." I paused. "Unless I'm fired for not showing up to work in a few days."

"You still have your job." His words rang with authority.

My eyes widened. "You called Chef?"

"Not me." He spoke meaningfully, his eyes conveying a lot more than his words.

Liam. Liam called and saved my job? He did it even as he was grieving? Even as he blamed me for his loss?

A spark of hope flickered to life inside me. I grabbed it and held until it burned my chest.

Clearing my throat, I continued. "As an employee, I probably get some kind of lodging discount. I'll get a room. You can have your bed back and—"

"Stop talking."

I glanced at him, incredulous. "What?"

"You're not moving out."

"I haven't moved in."

"About that… I'll take you to get some clothes from your place. You need something besides that shirt you've been wearing since you came here."

I blanched. I hoped I didn't smell!

He grinned. He had bacon in his teeth. "Good thing you cook good."

I groaned.

A few seconds later, Alex turned serious. "Look. Give him a few more days, okay?"

I debated, then nodded once. Truth was I didn't want to be alone. "I'll take the couch."

"No." His voice was hard.

"This is why you're single." I observed coolly.

He barked a laugh. "I'm single because I want to be. Women are nothing but trouble."

"You sound like you speak from experience," I goaded, interested.

"We should probably head over to your cabin before it gets dark."

I made a face. "Hearing about your problems might make me feel better about mine."

Alex got up and dumped his plate in the sink. "I left my problems exactly where they belong—in the past. Now finish eating so we can go. I'll take out Charlie while you finish."

"I thought you said I had to take him out."

He made a scoffing sound. "Like I'm gonna send a girl out in four feet of snow to take her dog to pee."

I watched him pull on a coat and boots as I chewed a piece of bacon. Charlie danced around in excitement as he moved, and it was a good distraction from all the whirling emotion inside me.

"Hey, Alex?" I said when he put his hand on the door to leave.

He glanced back around, his piercing eyes so easy to find even with all his winter gear piled on. "Yeah?"

"Thank you. For being here, for letting me be here. For everything."

"It ain't no thing," he quipped, then opened the door. Charlie charged out in a blur. Alex stepped out but then stuck his head back inside. "You're welcome."

I finished up what I could of my food, which admittedly wasn't much. But at least it was something. I did drink down the rest of the water, which honestly made me feel pretty proud.

As I worked on picking up the kitchen, the reality of where we were going began to sink in.

I was going back to the cabin… the place where Liam and Ren were shot. The place where I'd killed a man.

The blood had probably stained everything by now, and inside was probably ice cold from the hole in the door. Seeing it all again would be like reliving a nightmare.

I jumped about three feet in the air when Alex and the dog burst back into the kitchen. Catching myself on the counter, I fell back, pressing a hand to my heart.

"What's wrong?" Alex asked, narrowing his eyes.

"You scared me." I gasped.

He relaxed. "Sorry."

I shook my head and went on unsteady legs to my shoes and coat. I couldn't remember the last time I'd felt steady. It was a fleeting feeling these days.

By the time we pulled up to the cabin I shared with Liam, I was worked up in a frenzy of nerves. My teeth were chattering, and I told Alex it was because it was so freaking cold outside. I didn't know if he believed me, but he didn't say otherwise, so I took it as a win.

When we trudged onto the back deck, Alex moved cautiously, keeping an arm out so I stayed behind him as he took in all our surroundings.

It was then that I realized this probably wasn't even over. My God, would it ever be?

I might have killed Spidey, and Spidey might have killed the other guy who'd come after me, but there would be more. Crone wasn't going to stop.

"Alex, we should go," I said, suddenly panicked.

He glanced around. "Why?"

"What if they've come back?"

He stalked back to where I was, sweeping all our surroundings before glancing down at me. I felt small standing near him. Both Liam and Alex towered over me. "No one's here."

"The door is broken," I said, afraid. "The house isn't even locked up."

I stepped around to point at the busted door and frowned.

"It's not busted anymore," I murmured.

Alex walked up and turned the handle. "It's locked." Reaching into his pocket, he produced a key. "Good thing I have a key."

"You knew the door was fixed?" I exclaimed.

"Yeah…" he said and swung it open.

I marched forward, right past him and into the house. Bracing for the blood splatters, the rivers of red on the floor, I nearly flinched when I looked around.

It was all gone.

The house was spotless.

All traces of murder completely wiped away.

I stared in awe, then slowly turned toward Alex. "It's all gone."

His brows lifted. "You thought I was going to bring you here with the place looking like an episode of *CSI*?"

I rushed across the room and smacked him in the stomach. "Do you have any idea how sick I was at the thought of coming here and seeing it all?"

"My bad." He crossed his arms over his chest and glowered. "I'm offended you thought so low of me."

"You cleaned all this up?" I asked, sweeping my gaze around the room again. I thought he was at the cabin the entire time I was…

"Not me," he said in the exact same tone he had back at his house.

I swung around to meet his eyes. "Liam cleaned this up?"

Alex's voice was very quiet when he answered, "Just because he ain't been around doesn't mean he don't care."

Quickly, I turned away, swiping privately at the freshly falling tears.

I know. How the hell did I have any left?

You'd be surprised how many the body can make when life is an utter mess.

"I'll just get my things," I said, watery, and rushed down the hall.

Once my bag was packed, I hauled it out into the living room where Alex waited near the windows. I had a sudden flashback of the way Liam stood there staring out right after…

Hearing me, Alex turned. "Ready?"

I nodded, and he took the bag, tossing it over his shoulder as though it were weightless. "Let's go."

"Can I just have a minute?"

Alex seemed to weigh the request carefully, then nodded. "I'll wait right outside the door."

I nodded, knowing that was as alone as I would get.

The second he was outside, I turned back to the place. To my home.

It didn't feel like home anymore. It felt like the shell of place that once was filled with love. The blizzard that blew through crammed this place with icy air, and now everything in this room had the burn of frostbite.

Even though the mess was clean and all the blood was gone, I still saw it as if it were burned into my retinas. I tried to see past it. To the couch where Liam and I made love. To the first place he'd slid inside me without a condom, the very place our baby was probably conceived.

Placing a hand over my stomach, I looked back at the fireplace where we'd spent a night roasting marshmallows and burning almost every one. To the kitchen where I made breakfast and coffee and we made out on the island.

So many memories here, so many happy times.

Tainted.

Stained.

Frosted over.

I didn't think I could ever be here again and not be reminded of that fateful night when everything changed.

Glancing back to the floor, I recalled how it had pressed into my shoulder blades as the man sat on me, forcing me to the floor. I remembered the hollow look in his stare when he pointed the gun directly at my head.

I flinched, hearing the echo of the gunfire, and bit my lip when I saw the river of red draining from his body and reaching toward mine.

With a gasp, I spun, forcing myself out of those memories. Shaking my head, I noticed Charlie's favorite red ball lying near the window. He probably missed it.

When I bent down to pick it up, something sticking out from beneath the couch caught my eye. It was a crumpled piece of paper. It didn't look familiar, but as I stared at it, an odd prickly sensation climbed along my neck and spine.

I scooped it up and stared down at it, wondering what it was and where it came from.

Tucking the ball under my arm, I reached for the paper, meaning to smooth it out and look it over.

"Yo!" Alex said from the doorway. "My balls are literally turning into ice cubes out here."

"Coming!" I called out and shoved the paper into my jacket pocket.

I'd have to look at it later.

39

6

Liam

I barely ate. I barely slept.

I thought too much.

Arrangements had to be made for Dad. Mom wanted to do it, but then it became too much and I had to step in to make sure everything she wanted got handled. People called. People brought food. People cried and said they were sorry.

Their grief was heavy, and the more that stopped by, the more weighed down by it all I felt.

Between it all, I hired out cleaners for the cabin and a locksmith for the broken door. The image of Bellamy about to clean up the blood of those fuckbags still haunted me.

The fact she was doing it so I didn't have to look at it was worse.

I called the kitchen where she worked so Chef knew not to expect her in. I dealt with the police and their fifty million fucking questions. I almost came to blows with asshole Frost—aka Agent Frost of the FBI. The idea that they should haul Bellamy in for briefing and God knew what else made me murderous.

These guys had no sense of humanity at all. After everything she'd been through, after everything I hadn't been able to protect her from, they thought I would allow an interrogation?

Fuck them.

Over my cold, dead body. I told them that, too.

They backed off. I didn't give them a choice. I handled most of their questions, and I knew eventually they would talk to her, but it would be when she was ready and not a moment sooner.

I missed her.

My hands trembled with it. My ears turned to new voices every time they carried close by, hoping one was hers. The more time quickened by, the tighter all the knots in me became, the closer the darkness in me grew until it tinted the edge of my vision.

Despite the constant demands on my time, it was her I thought of beneath it all. Her I kept going for. If I couldn't be with her, the least I could do was shield her.

Especially since I'd failed so hard at that before.

I fought myself a thousand times a day in my desire to go over to Alex's and pull her close. I didn't allow it. For several reasons:

1) I was afraid it would send my mother over the edge. I was a breathing link to my father, and taking that away seemed cruel.

2) There were so many things to deal with. Every minute of my day was overfull. For those who thought death meant the end, for those left behind, it was only the beginning.

3) I was scared. Scared I wasn't good enough for her. Scared I would fuck up again and hurt her even worse.

And…

4) Denying myself the one thing that truly gave me any sense of peace was fitting punishment.

All the arrangements were made. Flowers were on nearly every surface of this house. The fridge was so full it barely closed. After locking up the place, I went upstairs and shut myself in the bathroom, rubbing my hand over my eyes. They felt dry and gritty. My jaw hurt from clenching my teeth for days, and I felt if I didn't get some real sleep, I wouldn't make it through the service tomorrow.

After splashing some freezing-cold water on my face, I stared in the mirror. Taking in the bloodshot eyes, untrimmed beard, and wild hair, I turned away. My eyes fell on the closet, where I moved without thought.

Wrenching open the door, I stared at the organized racks, zeroing right in on all the orange bottles with white lids.

Dad had been dying.

This cabinet was stocked with pain pills.

I closed my eyes against the lined-up prescriptions, but all that did was allow my other senses to remind me of the haze of indifference a few pills could offer. The way they could offer solace from a mind as tumultuous as mine.

With a soft sound, I snatched a bottle from the shelf and dumped some of the tablets into my palm. I stood there staring at them for a long time, a war raging inside me.

Take them.

Don't take them.

Doo it.
You're better than this.

"Liam?" Mom called from the hall.

I replaced the bottle and shoved what I had poured out into the pocket of my jeans. "Right here," I answered, leaving the bathroom.

"I think I might take one of those—" She faltered and glanced at me. Then away. Then back again. "I'm pretty exhausted. It's been a long few days. I think I'm going to turn in, try and get a full night's sleep before tomorrow."

"You can say you're taking a sleeping pill, Mom. That's why the doctor gave them to you. For rest."

I was the biggest fucking hypocrite just then. The damn pain pills I'd just stolen from her cabinet tripled in weight and threatened to choke me even from the pocket of my pants.

"How about you, Liam? Have you had the urge to… take anything?"

"No." I straight up lied.

She nodded, accepting the lie as though I'd fed it to her on a baby spoon. "I'm so proud of you," she said, coming forward to hug me. "Your father is, too."

I'm sure he'd be real proud of me for lying.

"Thank you for being here these past few days." She went on, still hugging me. "I don't know what I'd have done without you."

"You can always count on me, Mom," I rasped.

I thought of Bellamy in the moment. Wondering what she'd been doing without me.

God, I missed her.

She pulled back and smiled. "Well, I'm off to bed. I'll see you in the morning."

"Sure." I agreed and watched her slip into the bathroom.

I stood in the kitchen and listened to her moving around. Once she shut herself in the bedroom, I waited for her light to go off, and then I stood at the window, looking out into the night.

The pills in my pocket seemed to vibrate. Seemed to sing some kind of siren's song.

I was at my breaking point.

I was attending the memorial service for my father tomorrow. What was left of him would sit on the mantel or wherever my mother chose to put him.

I wanted Bellamy.

Taking care of her from afar sucked. The way I saw it, I had a choice: take the pills and float away until the sun rose or go to the only true peace I knew.

It wasn't hard to slip out of the house silently. Hopefully, Mom was already asleep and wouldn't even notice I was gone. I didn't even try to talk myself out of it as I climbed into the truck and backed down the driveway.

This was about survival. This was about getting something that was as essential as air.

Alex opened the door almost the second I pulled up. I jogged up the back steps, my heart fluttering erratically in my chest. Nervous energy coiled beneath my skin, nearly making me twitch.

"How is she?" I asked by way of greeting.

"She looks about the same as you," Alex said, studying my face. "Worse than shit."

Impulsively, I reached out and hugged him. Since my father passed, we'd been communicating regularly via phone. I checked up on Bellamy more than she realized.

But this was the first I'd really had any face-to-face time with my best friend.

Alex hugged me back instantly, patting my back with his palm.

I pulled back, and we moved into the house. It was dark and quiet. I went into the living room, expecting to see her curled up on the sofa. She wasn't there.

"Where is she?" I asked, turning back.

"In bed."

I bristled. "In *your* bed?"

"I'm taking the couch." He gestured to the mess of blankets.

"Right," I said, deflating. "I'm sorry, man."

Alex chuckled. "Minor," he quipped.

"So minor it doesn't even need an apology," I said, a ghost of a smile haunting my face.

"You remembered," he said, placing a hand over his heart as if he were touched.

"High school wasn't that long ago, dick."

He chuckled, and I started moving.

"Don't be getting it on in my bed," Alex called out behind me, keeping his voice low.

I gave him the finger and kept going.

Truth was sex wasn't even on my mind. Just touching her, just breathing the same air as her would be enough.

I slipped into the dark room. Charlie began growling before the door was even closed. I still didn't know how he ended up at the resort the other night, but I knew it was likely because Bells was trying to protect him.

"Charlie," I whispered, and the growling stopped. He leapt off the bed and jumped at me, putting his paws near my shoulders, and dragged his large, super-sticky tongue up my face.

I scratched his ears and felt the first sense of relief loosen my tight muscles.

"Good boy," I told him quietly. "Good boy for keeping watch over our favorite girl."

Moving past Charlie, I crept toward the bed. Bellamy hadn't even moved since I walked in. It took a moment to find her small frame in the blankets, but once I did, I didn't look away.

Kicking off my shoes and tossing the shirt on the floor, I crawled over the mattress gingerly, slipped beneath the blankets, and moved toward her.

Her breathing was even, her body relaxed against the mattress.

With no hesitation, I slipped my arms around her, tugging gently to bring her entire body against mine. I folded around her, trying to touch every inch I possibly could. In inhaled deeply, taking in her familiar scent and letting it act as balm to the worst of my wounds.

She stirred then, still partly asleep but awake enough to register she wasn't alone.

I waited for her to stiffen and push me away. If she did, I would go.

Her small, graceful arms slid over mine, her fingers wrapping around my wrist and holding on. A gentle, relieved sigh filled the silence of the room, and her body pressed farther back into mine.

Just like that, everything inside me quieted. The pills in my pocket were completely forgotten. For the first time in what felt like forever, everything was okay.

I was home.

7

Bellamy

I don't know what time it was when he slipped into my bed. The second he touched me, all concept of time faded away. Even though he was cold from being outside, I melted against him as if he were the sun.

He didn't say anything.

Neither did I.

Being in his arms was enough.

When I woke the next morning, he was gone. The space where he lay had gone cold.

I might have thought it had been nothing but a blissful dream if not for the evidence he left behind.

There in the center of the bed was something powerful enough to chase away all traces of comfort and hope I'd found last night in his arms.

There in the center of the bed, lying against the pale-blue sheets, was a small, white tablet.

I closed my fingers around it and cried.

8

Liam

Everything was a sea of black. And not because the darkness tormenting me rimmed my vision. No, that dark halo around my sight had vanished with the sleep I'd gotten while spooned around my girl.

The black I referred to was the color everyone was draped in.

There were so many people at Dad's memorial service they wouldn't have fit into a single church in the entire town of Caribou. There were even people from the neighboring towns because my father had just been that kind of man.

Everyone knew him. Everyone respected him. Not even the four feet of snow just dumped on us kept a single soul away.

Because of the massive turnout, his memorial service was held at BearPaw, which, in my mind, was perfect because this place had been where he lived. The largest conference room we had was filled with chairs, flowers, and a podium for the minister to speak from. There was a giant wall of windows that overlooked some of the mountains, bringing inside some his loved terrain.

Because Dad was cremated, there was not an actual "funeral." There was no procession to the cemetery or the traditional lowering of the casket into the ground.

Thank fuck.

My heart was already battered and bleeding. Watching what was left of my father being placed into the ground was probably more than I could bear.

Instead, we were having this service in remembrance of him and then a short reception afterward. I dreaded this entire day, but at the same time, it would in some ways be a relief to have it over.

The turnout moved my mother to tears, but there was only one person I was interested to see walk through the doors.

As the time drew closer for the memorial to start, I began to wonder if she was coming. Just when I was thinking of calling Alex, the crowd seemed to part, and he stepped through. And with him was Bells.

Seeing her was like a punch in the chest. I knew she'd just been in my arms a few hours ago, but this was here, now. She looked smaller to me. Fragile.

Yes, I'd always viewed Bells as someone I needed to protect. She'd always been half my size, but I'd never really seen her as easily broken.

She looked a tiny fracture away from shattering.

My stomach hollowed out and my mouth ran dry. People glanced at her as Alex led her down the aisle toward the front row. His hand was closed around her waist, and I felt like maybe he was holding her up.

That was my job.

I started toward them, nodding at Alex, and then focused solely on Bellamy. When her eyes latched onto mine, it was all I could do to keep from running the remaining distance between us.

Her eyes were red as if she'd been crying. Her face was pale and her cheekbones a little more pronounced than usual. If we weren't in a crowded room, I would have given Alex hell because I'd entrusted her to him, and he'd done a piss-poor job taking care of her.

We stopped in front of each other. Our eyes crashed over the other again and again like waves on the shoreline.

Alex cleared his throat and stuck out his hand to me. "Liam," he spoke, subdued. "You know how much I loved him. He was like my second father."

It was hard to tear my eyes off Bells, but I did and slid my hand into his. "You were like a son to him. Thanks for being here."

"Nowhere else I'd be."

Bells swayed, just barely perceptively, on her feet. Most people might not have noticed, but I sure as hell did because no one else in this room existed in that moment.

I reached out at the same time Alex started to. I shot him a warning glance, and he backed off. My arms slipped around her waist, and my chest took all her weight. She was definitely smaller.

I pulled her the rest of the way in so if anyone did notice her swaying, they would think she was just coming in for a hug. My arms and body engulfed her, and I inhaled, my eyes shutting just briefly.

"Liam." Her voice was muffled against the black dress shirt and suit jacket I wore.

I shifted only slightly so my lips could brush her ear. "I got you now."

I held her through the little shiver that shook her entire body, then pulled back and anchored her at my side. The three of us moved down the rest of the aisle toward the front row where all our closest family and friends sat.

It was oddly smaller than you would think. Caribou "royalty" must have extensive ranks, right?

Wrong.

When you hold a certain position or celebrity, you must be very careful who you let in.

I was well aware of the watchful eyes of every person in the room, but I ignored them. This day wasn't about them, my relationship status, or even mine and Bellamy's grief. This wasn't juicy gossip.

This was death.

This was respect.

People could back the fuck up.

Bellamy's footsteps stuttered, and I glanced down at her to frown. "You okay, sweetheart?" I murmured only loud enough for her to hear.

Her eyes stared straight ahead with a teary, scared look on her face. I followed her attention and landed on Mom, who was standing at the end of our row, her eyes locked on my girl.

I knew she didn't want to see Bellamy. I also understood this day was probably the most difficult of her life.

But it was mine, too.

And I wanted Bellamy.

I *needed* her.

She had every right to be here. She was family. Dad said so. Hell, even Mom said so once.

Alex assessed the situation with precision and moved ahead of us to gather Mom into a hug and whisper condolences in her ear. She pulled back, dabbing at her eyes, and smiled weakly at him, then gestured for him to go past her down the row to where his parents and sister sat.

Renewing the firm grip I had around Bellamy's waist, I nudged her forward, practically supporting all her weight. Mom measured my girl as we drew close, taking in her appearance and the way she moved. To my surprise, some of the resentment seemed to drain right out of her.

"Thank you for being here," Mom said to Bellamy as I paused at her side.

"I'm so terribly sorry for your loss." Bells said, her voice sounding like it had been dragged over blistering coals.

I nudged her, and she moved to sit beside Alex while I took up position on her other side. Mom sat on the end beside me.

I could wax poetic about the service, the readings, and the hope that suffused the room about how a man really isn't gone but still living in everything he created around us.

I won't. Truth was I was bitter and pissed off he was dead, and if it weren't for the delicate hand clinging to mine, I would have excused myself to the bathroom and swallowed the pills burning a hole in my pocket.

Oh yes, I still had them with me.

I didn't have any intention to take them, but just knowing they were there offered something. Escape maybe? Or maybe I was hoping in them I would find some sort of clarity, some answers as to why life had to be so goddamn hard.

Or maybe I was just looking for an excuse to have pills in my pocket. An excuse to take them.

Partway through the service, Bellamy laid her head on my shoulder, and all thoughts of the pills blew away. I still barely listened to the preaching. Instead, I leaned my cheek against the top of her head and thought about the times when the snow would melt on the mountain and grass would reach up toward the sun.

I was always sour because there wasn't enough snow to board. I was bored, I'd claim.

Dad taught me to play baseball out there under the sun. Said there was more to do outdoors than just board. We both knew my first and only love would be snowboarding but sitting here now as a man I didn't really know delivered words about hope and loss, I appreciated those days under the rays of the sun with green beneath my feet.

I remembered what it was like to hear the crack of the bat against the ball and the sound of his voice telling me to run.

These were the types of things I would remember about Renshaw Mattison. These were the types of memories that would live on.

I was partly startled when Bellamy slipped her hand out of mine and gave my thigh a light squeeze. I sat back and gazed down at her. "It's over," she murmured.

I leaned down and touched our lips together. The sound of my deep exhale through my nose as I held our lips together sounded kinda like a prayer. When I pulled back, her eyes were still closed, so I dropped a whisper-like kiss on the tip of her nose.

Her eyes reopened when I pulled back, and it struck me then that the normally bright blue of her irises wasn't.

The color was more a deep bruise, as if all the pain she'd been experiencing had tainted her stare.

"Can we talk?" she asked, quiet.

I started to answer, but Mom appeared just behind my shoulder. "Liam. We need to move to the reception area. People will want to greet us."

Yes, by all means, let me put other people at ease by taking on their grief and adding it to my own.

I didn't say that. Instead, I stood and gestured for Mom to lead the way. Before trailing after her, I took both Bells's hands and tugged her to her feet. "C'mon."

We got stopped a half dozen times on the way, but it seemed easier to nod and smile when Bellamy's hand was entwined with mine.

In the reception room, Mom took in our joined hands, and a concealed look of disapproval passed behind her eyes. "Liam, maybe Bellamy would be more comfortable at the table. She looks about ready to drop."

"Yes," I murmured, glib. "Stress will do that to you."

Mom let the remark pass and reached out for our first greeter.

I turned to escort Bells to the table, but she let go of my hand and stepped back. "I'll go sit with Alex."

My teeth gnashed together because she shouldn't be going to Alex. She should be staying at my side.

I let her go. Mom might have been trying to be bitchy, but the truth was Bellamy did look about ready to fall over.

This was clearly getting to her. It was beyond transparent to me that shielding her from afar was not an option anymore.

I spoke to an ungodly amount of people, all the while wondering why this was some kind of tradition.

Why should the beleaguered be responsible for making those less beleaguered feel better?

Eventually, the bitterness splashing over my tongue was too much to swallow. I wanted to go sit with my girl and my best friend. Resting a palm on the small of Mom's back, I leaned down toward her ear. "I think we should go in and sit. People won't eat until we do."

Mom gasped slightly. "You're right." She grimaced. "I have no desire to eat."

"Me either. Maybe just make a small announcement to tell everyone to enjoy the refreshments."

She nodded, and I moved to guide her along. She didn't move as fast as I wanted. Instead, she patted on my waist.

Glancing down, I said, "What's the matter?"

"I think someone is here to see you," she said, lifting a hand to someone who just appeared in the door.

I looked up. Surprise burst inside me, and before I could react, a woman launched forward into my arms.

9

Bellamy

I guess Alex was right.

Holly Mattison was too classy to cause a scene at the memorial. Though, really, she didn't need to.

Now I knew where Liam got it. Where the snow in his veins came from.

His mother was the queen of frost.

If I hadn't fully comprehended how much she blamed me before, I sure as hell did now. But that's okay. I'd withstood an avalanche, just come through a blizzard. What's a little frostbite?

Having Liam beside me today was enough to help me endure anything. He held my hand, kissed my lips… That little spark I'd felt before came to life again.

Until, of course, he sent me away to sit with Alex. Until his mother gazed upon me with ice in her eyes. I started to doubt then. I started to wonder if perhaps his displays of tender affection had been for all the watchful eyes.

Perhaps Liam had been playing a part. Keeping up appearances for the FBI. Maybe once today was over, we'd go back to no contact except for a relapse in the night.

I told myself I was being a paranoid ninny. The way his eyes would drift to where I was every few minutes was not him pretending to care.

Watching him steer Holly toward us, I began to relax.

Then everything blew apart.

Again.

It took a moment to register what I saw happening, that the woman who launched herself at Liam was not some acquaintance of his father overcome by grief.

Oh no.

This was no ordinary woman. Hell, she probably wasn't even grieving.

This was a vulture, the kind that hovered over the body until it picked every last piece of meat from bone.

Kelsey. Kelsey the manipulator. Kelsey the jealous. Kelsey the girl who kisses other girl's men so you rush off heartbroken and sulk for eight years.

Fine. I was dramatic.

I earned it.

And Kelsey was still all of those things.

I watched in horror and a little bit of awe as the tall, slender blonde pulled back and gave Liam one of those sad smiles while her eyes practically ate his face.

The sting of jealousy was intense and quick. All the sorrow and pain I felt was stomped on by an intense need to tell that little tart he wasn't hers.

His body rotated so he was facing her, his back to me. I couldn't really tell anything from his body language, but she sure acted as if it were a high school reunion and not a funeral.

Bitch.

I watched through narrowed eyes as she reached out and cupped Liam's face, rubbing her palms over his unshaven jaw. Blindly, I reached out and grasped Alex's hand, squeezing.

"Ow, woman—" His exclamation fell short when he no doubt saw what I did. "Oh, shit."

"I thought she didn't live around here anymore," I said, quiet.

"She doesn't. Her parents do. They must have told her about the accident."

I made a rude sound as she flipped some of her luxuriously thick hair behind her shoulders and smiled up at Liam.

Alex leaned close to my ear. "Don't worry about her, girl who got away. He's not interested."

"She is," I intoned.

"Zebras can't change their stripes," Alex quipped.

As if that even helped.

She was as gorgeous as I remembered. Age had only made her more beautiful. Her body was curvy and warranted a second look. Her skin glowed and her hair shined. She definitely didn't look like she'd spent the morning crying and then throwing up everything she'd forced herself to eat for breakfast.

She was easy. No one was trying to kill her. She didn't kill Liam's father.

His mother stood there smiling at her, clearly not hating her one bit.

As if she had some sort of sonic radar for my insecurities, chipping away at what was left of me, she looked up. From across the crowded room, our eyes met.

A little surprise filtered through hers, but then her perfectly painted lips pulled into a knowing smile.

This was the part where I gracefully stood, excused myself from the table, and walked calmly toward the woman eyeing my man like he was a perfectly cooked steak. This was the part where I lifted the crystal goblet of water I was drinking and poured it all over her blowout.

This was the part where I skipped all that badassery.

Well, I did stand and excuse myself from the table. But instead of heading toward them, I headed away, making a beeline for the closest restroom.

I barely was able to make sure the room was empty before surging into an open stall and throwing up what little was left of my breakfast.

I was beginning to think this baby had an aversion to all food.

I heaved and gagged until I couldn't anymore. Before I could sink back, familiar arms slipped around me and lifted, bringing me up against a solid, wide chest.

"This is the ladies' room." I reminded him.

"I locked the door."

"I hope no one else has to pee."

Liam made a rude sound and sat me on the long counter between the sinks. I wrinkled my nose and tried to hop down, but he blocked me with his body and pinned me in place.

"You saw that."

I rolled my eyes. "The entire room saw it."

"I haven't seen her since that morning, Bells."

"Oh, you mean the morning she orchestrated a scene to make it look like you were cheating on me?"

He brushed the backs of his knuckles over my cheek. "Don't be like that, sweetheart."

I scoffed. "Like what? Honest."

"Like you're jealous."

"Maybe I am," I said before I could think better of it.

Liam cupped my cheeks and sank lower in his stance so he was closer to eye level. "Now what on earth could you possibly be jealous of?"

Tears flooded my vision, making the sight of him wavy and unclear. "She isn't the reason your father is dead."

"Ah, baby." He kissed one cheek. "You aren't either." Then kissed the other.

I squeezed my eyes shut so hard a tear leaked out. Liam kissed it away.

"Why are you doing this?"

"Doing what?"

"Acting like you still love me. We're alone in here. No one can see."

He stilled. The frostbite I'd felt before was incomparable to this. I shivered, and he pulled back enough to look down at me, his eyes glistening, icy slits. "What did you just say?"

I swear his breath was visible because his tone was so cold.

I felt my shoulders slump. "Everything between us is different."

"Look at me."

When I didn't immediately listen, he shook me gently and forced my face up.

Our eyes met.

"I love you." He vowed, his voice shaking. "I love you so hard it's caused me physical pain to be away from you these last few days."

"Then why?"

He groaned and put his forehead against mine. I heard him swallow and then inhale.

Sudden knocking on the door interrupted whatever he was going to say. "Liam?" Holly's muffled voice came through.

He groaned softly.

More knocking. "Honey, are you okay in there?"

Her voice became more muffled, and then another round of knocking burst into the room.

"Yo, man. Moms is worried out here, and I have to tell ya you're in the wrong stall."

"It's okay," I told him, reaching out to touch his hand. "We can talk later."

His eyes flashed up to mine, but then he carefully lifted me off the sink to place me on my feet. After adjusting the black blouse I was wearing, I washed my hands and motioned for him to go.

Instead of going out ahead of me, he linked our hands, unlocked the door, and pulled it open.

Holly was in the doorway, Alex just behind her.

"Are you all right?" Holly asked her son. Then her eyes slid to me.

"I'm fine, Mom. But Bellamy isn't feeling too well. She needs to lie down. I'm going to drive her back to Alex's."

Alex glanced at me and then at Liam. They did that silent conversation thing they always did.

"But the reception..." Holly protested.

It was hard, but I tugged my hand free of Liam's and straightened away from him. "She's right, Liam. This is important, and you should stay. I can get myself back to Alex's."

"It's probably best," Holly remarked.

Liam stiffened. "Don't you think it's a little cruel to continue to ask me to choose between you and Bellamy, Mom?"

Holly's eyes widened. "I haven't—"

"You have. And I've allowed it because I love you and because you're hurting, and I know you need me."

Holly put a hand to her throat, stricken.

"She needs me, too." Liam looked at me, his eyes piercing mine with honest sincerity when he spoke. "And I love her. I won't keep hurting her this way."

Behind Holly, Alex nodded with approval.

My heart wanted to sing because Liam loved me. But how could I be happy when the man I loved felt he had to make a choice?

"This is the last thing I wanted," I said. "I came to pay my respects and support Liam, which I did. I'll go now." I looked at him. "You can find me afterward, and we can talk."

A short distance away, I saw someone hovering in the doorway to the hallway. It was Kelsey, waiting to pounce. Probably loving all the stressed-out vibes we were all surely wafting her way.

Without another word, I started down the hall toward the exit, holding my head high and ignoring her completely.

The familiar timbre of Liam's voice drifted behind me, but I kept going. Just before I passed Kelsey, Liam appeared beside me, slipping an arm around my waist. "You're not walking out of here without me."

Butterflies went crazy in my stomach, giving me a slightly nauseous feeling, but this one I didn't mind. Still, I didn't want to pull him away from this.

He must have seen it in my eyes because he shook his head before I could even speak.

"I've given enough of my time to everyone else. It's your turn."

The second we stepped outside in the cold winter air, Liam scooped me up and carried me across the lot to his big orange truck.

10

Liam

Running scared was what cowards did.

I was no coward.

Partially broken, flooding with darkness, and drowning with guilt?

Yes. But a coward, no.

It wasn't hard to walk out of the reception with Mom, Alex, and even Kelsey drilling holes in the back of my head as I went. In fact, it was the opposite of hard.

I felt as if a weight had been lifted off my shoulders.

Dealing with death was hard. Finite. Dealing with the living was arguably worse. There was something a lot less finite about life. Its ability to change by the second was truly scary.

I'd been walking around, a jumble of confusion, feeling like a rope that was cut and frayed at both ends. I wanted to be there for everyone, but it seemed no matter what, I would let someone down.

If I got anything out of my father's death, it was that I had to live. No matter how hard.

Reaching across the seats, I rested my hand palm up toward Bellamy. Without hesitation, her palm flattened against mine.

We were in a weird place. An awkward place. A place we'd never been together before. Usually, everything between us was easy, even when life was complete and utter chaos. Usually, when I looked at her, my heart beat a little faster and I knew exactly where I belonged.

I still felt like that. Chemistry still crackled in the space around us. The invisible tether between our bodies still tugged.

But there was a new dynamic, too.

Almost as if we were fighting against everything that always held us together.

This was my fault, too.

I was going to fix it.

We walked into Alex's place, the silence disrupted by the giant drooling dog. He rushed me, and I chuckled, glad to see him. I'd missed him too the past few days. Almost as soon as he got a couple pats from me, he went to Bellamy, treating her far different than the way he'd bulldozed me. Instead, he sat at her feet, his tail beating against the floor impatiently, and gave a low woof.

She laughed and sank to her knees, which remarkably made the dog look slightly taller than her. She scratched his belly and chest and avoided his giant tongue. When she was about to pull away, he put out a massive paw and rested it on her arm.

"I missed you, too, buddy," she murmured, smiling. "C'mon." He leapt up and danced into the kitchen ahead of her because he knew exactly what she was doing.

Bellamy had to lean over the dog to reach the treat-filled container on the counter. I braced myself, thinking I might have to intercept him from taking off her hand as she pulled out the snack.

"Use your manners," she told him, holding it out.

He gently took it from her fingers. Far gentler than he'd ever been with me.

Beneath my ribs, my heart did a somersault. Watching them together made me relive all the moments I'd spent without them over the past several days.

Charlie trotted off, and Bells smiled after him before returning the container to the counter. She seemed comfortable here. Like she'd settled into Alex's place with no trouble at all.

Without me.

That awkward feeling settled back between us, and she turned around, leaning against the counter, and looked at me.

"He's definitely your dog now," I said, trying to smile but unable because I felt like I was losing her. She was slipping away.

"One more thing I've taken from you," she whispered.

I jolted. "I didn't mean—"

She shrugged, not unkindly. "It's still true."

I went across the room, urgency propelling my feet faster. "That is *not* true," I stated vehemently. "You haven't taken shit from me."

"Except your father, your career..." Her eyes strayed to Charlie. "And your dog."

"Bellamy!" I rasped, surging forward and grasping her by the shoulders. She felt thin and small beneath my hands, and I gentled my grip a little.

She glanced down at where I held her, a small sound erupting. Her eyes lifted, wide. "You touched me."

I frowned. "I always touch you."

She shook her head sadly. "Not lately. Lately, it seems like you try not to."

My stomach clenched and so did my jaw. "I touched you last night." I defended without heat.

"You didn't speak to me. You left before the sun came up."

"I kissed you at the service just a little bit ago."

"Keeping up appearances."

I sucked in a breath. This was worse than I thought. So much worse.

I pushed away from her to pace. "You actually think the only reason I touched you today was because I was worried what the people in this town would say if I didn't?"

"No one knows what really happened."

I crossed my arms over my chest and regarded her. "Apparently, Alex told you what the official story is."

"Well, someone had to," she snapped. Immediately, she turned contrite. "I'm sorry. I shouldn't have said that. You've been through so—"

"I was wondering when you were gonna show up." I half smiled.

Her eyes widened. "Excuse me?"

"Defeated isn't usually a word I would use to describe you."

"You think this is funny?" she asked, straightening off the counter.

I scrubbed a hand over my face. This was not going well. "Of course not, sweetheart. Nothing about any of the past few days is funny."

"You act like you want me to be mad," she muttered.

"Maybe I do."

Her eyes snapped up to me. "Why?" she whispered.

"Because it would be a hell of a lot better than this!" I exclaimed, gesturing between us. "This sorrowful acceptance of…" I couldn't even bring myself to say it.

"The end?" She finished.

I made an angry sound and lunged toward her. "This is not the *end*," I spat. "I've had enough endings to last my entire lifetime."

Charlie didn't like my sudden movements or the aggressive way I spoke. With a low warning growl, he inserted himself between us.

I glanced down at the dog, then back to Bellamy. "Bells. I would never hurt you."

She smiled sadly. "I know. He's been a little on edge since that night."

"How did he get to the hotel?" I asked, curious.

"He attacked the man in the house, not Spidey, the first guy. He was just trying to protect me. When the man recovered, he was going to shoot him." Her lower lip wobbled, and my heart sank. I still didn't know the full events of that night. There hadn't been any time to really talk to her. "So I shoved him out the back door and told him to run. He must have been so confused."

I made a soft sound and reached for her, wrapping my arms around her upper body while the dog stood between us. Charlie didn't object to the hug, maybe because he was part of it.

"It's okay now," I murmured, stroking the back of her head. "You saved his life. You saved mine that night. And yours."

"Not Ren's." She sobbed, her shoulders shaking as I held her.

I tried to pull her even closer, but the dog was in the way. "I'm sorry I haven't been here, sweetheart. I truly wanted to be."

"Your mom needed you more." After a small hiccup against my neck, she said, "She blames me."

My stomach dipped. "She's irrational right now."

"You smell good." She blubbered and pushed a little tighter into my neck.

I half smiled at the random comment. I liked it. No. I loved it. Bellamy didn't really believe this was the end of us. Just as I couldn't either.

"What do I smell like?" I asked, shifting closer. I loved my dog, but he was pissing me off. He was keeping me from full-on contact with my girl.

"Snow," she murmured. "Like home."

I pulled back and picked her up, lifting her over the dog and bringing her against me. Her legs wound around my midsection and her arms wrapped around my neck. Her body melted against mine, draping over my upper body, melding to me in all the right places.

I started to carry her to the sofa where I could sit with her in my arms and fix all the damage our separation had caused.

Charlie barked. Then barked again.

Bellamy sat up, blinking her red-rimmed eyes. "He needs to go outside."

I groaned. Bells patted my shoulder, and I let her slide down my front, totally enjoying the immediate lick of flames that tightened my balls and caused a quick intake of breath.

She went to the table where her coat was, picked it up, and pushed her arms through.

"What are you doing?"

"Taking out the dog," she said as if it were obvious.

"It's ten degrees outside. I'll take him."

The stubborn glint I was used to flashed in her eyes, and it actually made me feel better. I liked her spunk. I liked her fire. It was good to see it wasn't gone.

Still. She wasn't taking out the dog.

"Bellamy," I grumbled. "Keep your tiny ass in this house."

"My ass is not tiny." She sniffed, lifting her nose.

I pointed toward her lower half. "That ass was up against me all night last night. It's tiny."

Charlie barked again and pawed at the back door.

"You tell him, Charlie." Bellamy nodded.

I rolled my eyes.

As I was closing the door behind us, Bellamy called out my name. "Liam?"

I glanced around. She was standing there watching me go with this look of… anxiety in her eyes.

"What, sweetheart?"

She worried her lower lip, then released it. "You're coming back, right?"

I did this to her.

Me.

"I swear."

She nodded, and I pulled the door around to close.

We didn't stay out long. After that question and look in her eyes, I wanted to get back to her as fast as possible. Thankfully, Charlie cooperated and did his business, then ran back to the porch. He loved the cold, but it was bitter outside right now, not even fun for him.

When I stepped back in the house, I expected to see some sort of happiness in her eyes or even just some minor relief.

I saw neither.

Bellamy was standing with her back to me, facing the counter where a fresh pot of coffee was brewing. Her posture was rigid and her head was focused down. It seemed that whatever headway I'd made with her before I stepped outside was somehow gone.

"Bells?" I said, cautious, as I pulled off my coat and boots.

She still had her coat on from when she'd started to get dressed for outside. Why was she still wearing her coat?

She didn't answer when I called out to her, so I tossed my shit aside and walked to where she stood. I reached for her arm to gently pull her around, but she flinched and jerked back.

All at once, she whirled, tears on her cheeks. "Is this why?" she asked, shaking something clutched in her hand.

"Why what?" I said, glancing down.

It was a white piece of paper that looked as if it had been balled up but someone tried to smooth back out. My veins frosted over.

"Is this why you've barely spoken to me in three days?"

"Where did you get that?" I intoned, low.

She made a sound and glanced down at it, the paper wrinkling more under her intense grip. She read, *"It's rather poetic that you will have to live knowing you sacrificed your father for a woman. And she will have to live with knowing you will blame her for that for the rest of her days."*

I reached for it, but she snatched it back.

"Bellamy,"

"You've read this?"

"Yes," I replied, terse.

"When?"

"It doesn't matter."

"When!" she cried, hoarse.

"That night." My words were subdued. "Right before I brought you here."

The paper floated to the floor like a feather when she let go, allowing her arm to drop back to her side. "When you said you didn't blame me, who were you lying to, Liam, me or you?"

"I wasn't lying."

She looked up, her eyes meeting mine. "Then why did you keep this from me? Why didn't you tell me?"

I opened my mouth.

She cut me off with quiet, heavy words. "Because part of you… even just a small part, believes it."

I started to shake my head, the denial swift.

She grabbed the black tie around my neck, wrapping her hand around it to tug. "The truth, Liam."

I met her eyes and spoke. "Yes."

11

Bellamy

We had a lot of talking to do, a lot of figuring things out.

He was here. That was all that mattered.

He was here, and he promised he wasn't leaving.

I went to make some coffee. Liam liked coffee. As the rich brew began percolating, I realized I was still wearing my coat. Grabbing the sleeve to yank it off, I heard the crumple of paper in the pocket and remembered what I'd found at the house yesterday.

~~It was just paper.~~

What I read on that paper blew up my world. Liam got a letter from Perry Crone and never told me about it.

Worse: Liam got a letter that claimed my debt was paid in full.

The price?

The death of his father and the fact that it would ultimately tear us apart.

In the end, Crone was getting exactly what he wanted, wasn't he? This was far worse than my death could ever be, because instead of dying all at once, I would die a little every single day.

Thousands of tiny deaths that would chip away at me and Liam day after day, month after month. To spare us both a lifetime of pain, I should leave.

I couldn't.

I'd cost Liam enough already. I couldn't take his child, too.

Now here we were in the kitchen, standing so close, sharing the same air. I was suffocating, and based on the look in his eyes, so was he.

All we had now was the truth. Cold, hard reality.

"Yes?" I whispered.

His eyes fell from mine, but not before they flashed with guilt. "Yes," he repeated, husky. "I blamed you."

The frost within Liam I sometimes felt reached out and bit me.

Slipping from between the counter and his body, I moved to put some distance between us. I knew he blamed me. Deep down, I knew this. Why was it ten times harder to hear when he admitted it out loud?

Liam's hand wrapped around my wrist, holding gently, just enough to keep me from getting too far.

"When I was kneeling over my father…" He began, and the crackle in his voice made me think of ice on the verge of shattering. "As he was gasping and bleeding out all over our kitchen floor and I pleaded with him not to die—"

His pain was so thick, so stagnant that it became mine, too. It didn't even matter he blamed me or that I had no clue how we moved on from here. All that mattered was he was standing in front of me, breaking into a million pieces.

I moved into him, wrapped my arms around his waist, and squeezed, pressing my head against his chest.

He didn't push me away, but he didn't embrace me either.

It was okay. I didn't need comfort right now. He did.

"I did blame you. Beneath the panic and fear, even beneath the bargains I tried to strike up with God, all I could think was that if you hadn't come home alone that day... If you hadn't been so careless... If you had just answered the phone when I called you..."

I looked up. A tear trailed down his cheek, leaving a glistening path from his frigid, silvery eye. He felt my stare, and his snapped to mine, stricken.

"It's okay." I comforted him, snuggling a little closer.

"It's not," he murmured. "It's not okay. But in those moments, when his hot, sticky blood stuck to my fingers as I tried to push it back into his body and his unfocused eyes ate up my face as if he were trying to remember it one last time..." He paused, swallowing thickly. "I did blame you. I was so goddamn angry at everything and everyone. But mostly you."

"I never should have come to BearPaw," I said. Living alone in hiding for the rest of my life would have been better than causing him this pain.

Liam made a sound and wrenched me away from him, holding me out just at arm's length. His eyes burned into mine. "No."

I tried to turn away, but he wouldn't let me. Instead, he lifted me up so my feet dangled over the floor and we were eye level.

"Then Dad said your name. It snapped me out of that weird place I was spiraling into. I heard a gun go off... so many fucking shots. All the blame I felt in the previous thirty seconds? It evaporated. It vanished like it had never been there. All I could think was that you could be taken from me, too."

I hung on his words, and not because I was literally dangling over the floor. Because he spoke with such emotion that I would have bought tickets just to listen to him speak.

"When I saw you standing over Spidey, when I saw you were the one doing the shooting"—his lips curled up a little devilishly—"I was so fucking proud of you."

I gasped.

He nodded, sage. "Relieved, too. So goddamn relieved."

My feet touched the floor again, but my legs were wobbly and weak.

Liam wrapped an arm around my waist and pulled me into his body. "There's no way in hell I could live in a world without you. I would never survive. Even though I've stayed away these past few days, you've been the only thing keeping me sane. So yes." He gentled his voice, stroking a thumb across my cheekbone. "I blamed you for a fraction of a minute in the heat of a moment when my father was dying and I had a bullet hole in my shoulder. But then it was over. I haven't blamed you since."

"Really?" I asked. It was pathetic. He just poured out his heart, and I was standing there bumbling so badly, wanting to believe.

"I swear to Christ."

"Please don't." I grimaced. He had a filthy mouth.

His low chuckle eased so much tension I didn't even know I'd been holding. "I don't blame you for my father's death, Bellamy. He stepped farther into me, his eyes boring into mine. "This was *not* your fault. I want you here, so don't ever, *ever* say you never should have come here. I'll wash your mouth out with soap."

Tears of relief, joy, and pain slid over my cheeks.

Liam swiped them away. "I don't blame you," he whispered.

I dissolved against his chest, my whole body quaking with relief and sadness. He held me tight, in only the way he could, and in all honesty, it was his touch that convinced me more than all those beautiful, perfect words.

Touch didn't lie.

After I pretty much drenched his shirt with tears, I pulled back, dabbing my eyes with his satin tie.

"Help yourself," he muttered, amused.

"Liam?"

"Sweetheart?"

"If you haven't blamed me these past three days, then why? Why haven't you been here? Why didn't you tell me about that letter? Why have you been avoiding me?"

His body stiffened a little, but he didn't pull away completely until he was sure I was steady on my feet. Then he paced over to the small window above the kitchen sink.

With his back to me, he answered, another admission that rocked my world. "I might not blame you, but I sure as hell blame me."

I gasped. "What?"

He didn't say anything or react to my shock. He just stayed at the window, staring out.

I raced over, grabbed him by the arm, and tugged until he glanced down at me.

"You deserve better than me, Bellamy."

12

Liam

There. I said it. Out loud. In the flesh.

When she said nothing at all, I glanced down at her. She appeared stunned, eyes almost glazed over with surprise.

I made a rude sound. "Why do you have that look on your face?"

She blinked. "I think I misheard you."

"I said you deserve better than me."

She laughed.

Straight up laughed.

I scowled. "What the fuck are you laughing for?"

She put a hand over her mouth, stifling it. Apology in her eyes. Lowering her hand, she said, "That's insane."

I turned away from the window, fully facing her, leaning a hip on the side of the sink. "I'm a lot of things, sweetheart, but insane ain't one of them."

Something passed behind her eyes. Something I didn't understand. "Of course you aren't." She reached out and circled her fingers around my wrist. Her hand was so small her fingers couldn't reach all the way around.

Or maybe it was just because I was that much larger than her.

"Liam, you really think that?"

Gruffly, I replied, "I don't think it. I know." Agitated, I moved out of the kitchen and into the sunken living room. Charlie beat his tail against the couch. The damn dog took up almost all of it.

I scratched behind his ear anyway, then flung into a large leather club chair.

A moment later, Bellamy came into the room, carrying a mug of steaming coffee. She held it out to me, so I took it, not willing to rebuff anything she did for me.

"Where's yours?" I asked, taking a sip. She'd made it exactly how I liked it.

She wrinkled her cute nose. "I don't want any."

"I'll make you some hot chocolate," I said, moving to stand.

She gestured me back. "No. I'm fine."

It was an odd day when she turned down cocoa. I took in her face, the pallor of her skin, the dark circles beneath her eyes, and how her clothes seemed a little loose on her frame.

With a sigh, I set the coffee beside the chair and reached for her. She came without hesitation, and my battered heart sang because that awkward feeling we'd been suffocating under was nowhere to be found.

"God, I missed you," she confessed quietly.

"I tried to stay away, Bells. I just can't… I take one look at you and fucking break."

She palmed my face, rubbing over the longer beard I was sporting. "I don't want you to stay away."

"I let you down," I said, the words ripping right out of me. The darkness swirling inside me began to rise to try and snatch them back, as if keeping them tucked away inside me wouldn't only allow the darkness to fester.

"I don't even think it's possible,"

I shook my head, cutting her off. "I wasn't there to protect you. I got too caught up with the resort, my dad… my own demons, and it almost got you killed."

There was that look again. The one I didn't understand. The second I mentioned my demons, it dropped over her baby blues like a veil.

"I've been blaming myself, and you've been blaming yourself," she said, tucking herself against me, her cheek on my shoulder.

Having her in my lap this way was indescribable.

"It's my job to protect this family."

"You take on too much for one man, Liam." Her hand smoothed over my chest and curled around the side of my neck. "You carry the weight of everyone and everything you love like its solely yours to bear. It's isn't." Bellamy lifted her head. "The fact that you've been punishing yourself for something you had absolutely no control over hurts me."

"I don't want to hurt you," I murmured, leaning my head back against the leather. I couldn't help it. The soothing sound of her voice made me feel heavy.

"You haven't failed anyone. And you most definitely are good enough for me. Hell, if anything, you're *too* good for me."

I opened my eyes. "Don't ever say that."

She crossed her arms over her chest, a mutinous expression on her face. "Well, that's exactly how I feel when *you* say it."

My hand settled on her thigh. "I can't even imagine what you went through that night." The sudden lump of emotion in my throat threatened to choke me. "I wasn't there. I'm so fucking sorry I wasn't there."

Bellamy moved, straddling my lap and pushing close. "You were there. In all the ways that matter. If you hadn't barreled in when you did, he might have shot me. You surprised us both, you know." Her voice turned rueful. "How did you even know what was happening?"

"Charlie," I said. The dog lifted his head off the sofa and looked at us. "He walked right into the hotel and wouldn't stop barking at the staff. They called me, and I figured something was wrong."

"And Ren was with you?" she asked, trying to piece it together.

"No," I answered regrettably. "I think he was in Mom's office down the hall. He heard me yelling at my assistant to get the police over to the house as I was racing out."

"He followed…" she whispered.

"Yeah."

"Any parent would do the same." Bellamy's hand fluttered to her midsection.

My eyes dropped to her fingers on her stomach. "Bellamy," I intoned, a funny feeling worming around inside my chest.

Her hand fell away, her eyes timidly meeting mine. "You said you wished I hadn't gone home alone. That I was being careless."

I surged up so my back wasn't touching the seat anymore. Wrapping a hand around the back of her neck, I said, "I told you it was a brief moment."

"But you're right." She insisted. "If I hadn't gone home early, it might not have happened."

I sank back. "Honestly, sweetheart, I think we all knew this was coming. If not then, another time. I just hadn't expected it would be Dad…"

She nodded, staring down at my middle, seemingly lost in her own mind.

"Bells," I murmured, reaching for her hand, linking ours together.

"I had a reason for being home early, Liam. I wasn't being careless, at least not intentionally. I was…"

I felt my lips turn down. Watching her struggle was something I would never like. "You were what?"

"I, ah… I'd had a doctor's appointment earlier in the day, and I was at home, waiting for some test results."

My heart stopped.

My lungs stopped.

Everything inside me stopped.

"Liam," Bellamy said. I saw her name on my lips, but didn't hear her voice. "Breathe!"

I couldn't. I was stuck, panic in control now.

Not her, too. Sweet mercy, please not Bellamy. I've already lost my father.

Plush lips pillowed against mine, gliding over my mouth and snapping me back to the present. I pulled in a deep breath, but she stayed, her tongue skating over mine with a graceful caress.

I moaned and sat up, gripping the back of her head and taking control of our kiss. Slashing my lips over hers again and again. I wasn't gentle, and neither was she. I kissed her with fierceness, anger, and longing. I kissed her the way I'd wanted to since I'd pulled that gun out of her hand and ushered her into the back of an ambulance. I made love to her mouth because, in the end, words were only words, but action left behind memory.

I only pulled back when my lungs screamed and I knew she needed air.

Her lips were swollen and her eyes were wide as she stared at me, our chests heaving.

I grabbed her face, pleading with her stare.

"It wasn't those kinds of tests, Liam. I'm fine. I'm healthy."

I fell back, dizzy with relief. "Next time, lead with that, huh?"

"I'm sorry." She chewed on her lower lip, and I noted the way her fingers trembled, tucked into her lap.

I took them in mine, lifting one to kiss the back of her hand. "There's something."

She nodded, avoiding eye contact. "There's something."

"Tell me."

"I'm pregnant."

13

Bellamy

There. I said it. Out loud. In the flesh.

"Pregnant," he repeated, and I nodded, nervous.

My goodness, I was nervous. This was probably the worst timing ever. The love between us was there, *so* there, but we were still trying to figure out everything else.

His eyes fell to my midsection, which was still flat. I'd actually lost a few pounds because all I did was throw up.

Suddenly, Liam's hand shot out, almost startling me because up until that point, he'd been so still. Hovering his giant palm over me, not touching, he whispered, "There's a baby in there?"

"Your baby."

Silver eyes flashed up to mine, going wide and bright. Possession unlike anything I'd seen before stole his features. I shivered slightly because it was quite intimidating.

"Why didn't you tell me?" he partly growled, standing up quickly and lifting me with him. Despite the heat in his eyes and tension in his tone, he sat me down quite gingerly, taking a moment to make sure I was firmly on my feet before pacing away.

"We've barely had a moment alone," I said. "This hardly seemed like a thing to blurt out while your father was dying or at his funeral."

"How long have you known?"

"I was waiting for the blood test results when I was attacked. Then your father… and we haven't really been speaking."

Liam spun. "So you never got the results?"

"Not for the blood test," I said, "But I don't need it."

"Bellamy!" he bellowed. "Explain!"

"Don't you yell at me!" I snapped, then turned away. I tried to hold on to that indignant feeling. That stubborn feeling I got when he tried to boss me.

It was pretty fleeting.

Instead, I was filled with emotion, the kind I was getting pretty freaking tired of. My God, would I ever stop crying?

From behind, Liam made a choked sound. The brush of his hands was like a caress when he laid them on my arms to pull me around. "I didn't mean to yell, sweetheart, but please. Are you pregnant or not?"

Blinking back the tears, I sucked in a breath and tried to get ahold of myself. "I'm most definitely pregnant," I said. Pulling away, I went to the kitchen where my bag was sitting where I'd dropped it after we arrived from the reception. I reached in, closing my hand around what I wanted, and then walked back to Liam.

His eyes practically burned through me, his stare so intense. He had always been intense, but this… It scorched me.

Stepping in front of him, I held out the small black-and-white picture, one of the corners curled up a little from being carried around in my bag for several days.

Liam glanced between me and the image, then took it and held it up to study.

He glanced over the edge of it for a brief moment before staring back. "This is a sonogram?"

I nodded and pointed to the little blob that didn't really look like anything. "That's the baby right there."

A soft sound ripped from his lips. He stared in awe for long moments, then lowered the picture to glare. "You had an ultrasound without me!"

"Not on purpose," I replied. "It was that night at the hospital. You were getting stitches. The nurse came at me with some kind of drug, and I exclaimed I was pregnant."

"They tried to drug you!" he roared and started away.

I grabbed his wrist. "They did not try to drug me. Geez."

He glared.

"It was probably something for the shock they said I was in."

His eyes softened. "You've been through too much."

"Anyway, they did the ultrasound because they wanted to verify what I said. They, ah, wanted to make sure that after everything that happened, I was still pregnant."

"You could have lost the baby." His voice was husky.

My throat constricted at the emotion in his tone. At the emotion his words conjured up in me. I knew this baby was a surprise, but the thought of losing him was crippling. "He was okay. They gave me that picture. I heard his heartbeat, too."

"His?" Liam questioned.

I shrugged lightly. "It's too soon to tell, but when I think of the baby, it's a boy I see."

"All that equipment in your room…" He recalled, glancing at me.

I nodded, guilty. "It was for me."

"Why the fuck didn't you have someone come get me?"

"I didn't even know for sure until they did it. You were already dealing with enough. You were shot, for God's sake. We thought your dad was in surgery. Your mom… It wasn't the time for you to worry about anyone else."

"That's my kid!" he exclaimed, glancing back at the sonogram he was still clutching. "It's my job to worry about him."

"I'm sorry," I whispered. I was sorry. For so many things.

I moved away, offering him some space. Not telling him right away might not have been the best decision, but it was the only one I could make at the time. It still felt too soon to drop something like this on him, but I couldn't wait anymore.

I couldn't demand full truth from him if I wasn't willing to give it.

"I know this is a shock… Believe me. When I realized how late I was and the reason I'd been throwing up like crazy—"

"You've been sick?" he asked, instantly concerned.

I nodded. "At first I thought it was stress. But then it kinda became obvious it wasn't. I thought women only had *morning* sickness, so I was confused because mine is mostly at night. 'Course, now I seem to throw up all the time." I grimaced. "This baby doesn't like food."

Liam stalked across the room, pulling me to him. "I should have been here. You've been doing this alone."

"It's only been three days," I murmured against him.

He made a sound, and I felt his lips in my hair. "That's three days too long."

I couldn't help it. I smiled against his chest. I'd missed him. Him and his overbearing ways.

He pulled back, still holding on to me, and searched my face. "How far along are you?" He lifted the picture and squinted at it like he was going to be able to tell by staring.

Suppressing a smile, I replied, "About eight weeks. Well, maybe closer to nine now."

His eyes flared. "You've seen a doctor?"

"Not yet. I got the name of one and a prescription for some vitamins, but I just haven't had the chance to pick them up or make an appointment."

"Unacceptable," he announced, pushing the picture of the baby into his pocket.

I lifted my eyebrow. "What are you doing with that?"

"I'm keeping it."

"That's the only picture I have!" I gasped.

"You can look at it whenever you want."

Oh my God! He was a thief!

The incredulous look on my face seemed to amuse him. He strolled over to me. "Now, sweetheart." He cajoled. "You get to carry that baby around twenty-four-seven. The least you can do is let me have this picture."

"This baby makes me puke my guts up!" I accused.

Liam wrapped his arms around me. Jerk face or not, being in his arms felt incredibly good. "I'll have a talk with him," he said as though that would fix everything.

I scoffed. He was ridiculous.

After soaking up a little bit of love, I pulled back, nerves coiling in my stomach. "You're not upset?"

"I'm pretty spicy," he said, eyes narrowing.

My body tightened, and I stepped back. "I know," I heard myself say. "It's a lot to take in. And the timing couldn't be worse. Here I am running from the mob, and the reason you lost your father... and now—"

"You are not the reason I lost my father," Liam rebuked harshly. "That bastard Crone is."

Rationally, I knew Liam was right. I mean, I hadn't wanted Ren to die. But irrationally? It was going to take a while for me to let myself believe it.

Glancing down at the floor, I took a breath. "I'm sorry, Liam. I know this is a shock, and I know it's not what you need right now... I want you to know I didn't do this on purpose. It was an accident."

Liam's nose flared and his eyes widened. "No, Bells," he declared. "This baby was no accident."

14

Liam

"You think I got pregnant on purpose?" she asked, her cheeks paling.

I chuckled. "I'm pretty sure you didn't make that baby all by yourself."

She put a hand to her stomach, and my chest literally caved in. She was a sight for sore eyes. The best damn thing I'd ever laid eyes on. No amount of medals or trophies, no paycheck or snow drift could ever compare. This was even better than a brand-new custom-made snowboard.

My entire life was standing right in front of me.

"I don't understand." She frowned.

I swept forward and lifted her off her feet. "Sweetheart, you told me you wanted everything, and that's exactly what I gave you."

Her eyes widened, and she sucked in a breath. "You wanted this to happen?"

"I didn't necessarily plan it," I said nonchalantly, setting her down. "After that first time I was bare inside you, the idea of you having my baby was almost primal.

I've thought about it more than once. This definitely isn't something I'm surprised to learn."

"Well, it surprised the hell out of me."

I laughed. But then I sobered up. I realized she hadn't exactly acted happy… just cautious. Taking her face in my hands, I studied her. "Are you unhappy about this?"

"I thought you would be!" she wailed, her eyes filling with moisture.

I'd seen enough of her tears to last an entire lifetime. "Don't cry," I murmured. "You really thought I would be upset about this?"

She nodded. "Our life is a mess. You've been living with your mother, and I've been living with your best friend!"

Jealousy was like an electric current. "Does Alex know?"

She looked offended. "I would never tell anyone without telling you first."

"You should have told me right away."

"I didn't want you to feel trapped with me," she said sadly.

"Sweetheart, I could be physically stuck to you with permanent glue, and I still wouldn't feel trapped."

"I was so afraid you'd be upset," Bellamy confided.

I tipped up her chin so I could stare into her eyes. "I could never." Both my hands hovered around her midsection, still not reaching out to touch. "There's really a baby in there," I said, awed. "A piece of you and me."

"I'd show you a picture, but I don't have one," she muttered.

I chuckled, the warm feeling of joy choking me up a little. "Can I?" I asked, gesturing toward her.

"You don't even have to ask."

My palms covered her waist, overlapping and spanning it entirely. Rubbing gently, I smiled. "Hey there, little guy."

She sniffled, the sound forcing my eyes away from her belly. "You're happy," she noted, eyes glistening.

"Oh, sweetheart. I am *so* happy. Don't doubt that for another second. I am thrilled as shit about this."

Sobs broke from her throat, the kind that shook her body and made her a snotty mess. I lifted her and sat in the chair, tucking her into my lap. I stroked her hair while she cried and hated myself for not being here the past three days.

I never should have allowed grief and duty to pull me away.

"Hey," I murmured when her crying quieted. "What about you? Are you happy?"

She looked up, eyes puffy and tired, but underneath, there was a spark in the blue. A glow. "I love him so much already," she confided. A small smile played on her lips. "I know the timing is all wrong, but I don't care."

"Fuck the timing." I smirked. "We'll make it work."

"I don't know how." She fretted.

I gave her a stern look. "You gotta stop stressing, sweetheart. That's not good for you or the baby."

Bellamy laid her head back against my shoulder and sighed.

A baby. A genuine smile graced my face. Too soon, it faded. "I wish Dad was still here to tell."

Bellamy sat up. "He knew. I guess I did tell someone else before you."

My gaze sharpened. "Dad knew about the baby?" I asked, covering her stomach with my hand.

She nodded. "Remember, I got to the room before you and Holly. He was awake, and it was right after my ultrasound. I told him. I wanted him to know that it wasn't me he saved that night. It was his grandchild."

Realization dawned. That night and my father's sacrifice took on a whole new meaning. Because of him, my child would get to live.

"He was happy," Bellamy disclosed, both hands covering mine where I held her. "He touched my stomach, too."

Overcome with emotion, I couldn't speak. It meant more to me than she could ever know that my father knew about this baby. That he knew he was a grandfather.

Here I thought I'd lost that father-son relationship when he passed, but in a way, his death allowed it to live on.

I pulled Bellamy close, rested my forehead against hers, and struggled to breathe normally.

Life had been so defined by death.

Not anymore.

Now it was defined by life.

My son or daughter wasn't just a piece of me and Bells, but a piece of my father, too.

I gasped, remembering some of his last words. *Take care of them… of him.*

"What is it?" Bellamy worried, pulling back.

"He knew," I murmured. "Dad called him a him," I said, reaching again for her stomach.

She smiled. "I think it's only fitting that this little guy is named after him. After all, Ren is the reason this baby is still here."

My eyes clung to hers, asking if she really meant it.

She smiled softly. "I know it's early, but Renshaw William Mattison has a very nice ring to it."

"William?" I croaked.

My God, this woman was slaying me.

"Oh yes." She stroked my face. "I couldn't possibly have a son and not give him the name of my most favorite man alive."

"How did you do that?" I rasped, clutching her.

"Do what?"

"Take one of the worst days of my life and make it one of the best."

"Oh, that wasn't me." She smiled, glancing down. "That was little Shaw."

"Shaw," I echoed.

"Your dad will always be Ren. So this little one will have to be Shaw."

I kissed her. There were no words that could even portray how I felt in that moment. How absolutely in love with her I was. As my tongue slid over hers and languidly explored her mouth, I wondered how the fuck I'd stayed away for three days, why I even tried. I was ashamed I'd blamed her for what happened for even a minute, ashamed I made her scared to tell me about the baby.

Ripping my mouth from hers, I sucked in a breath. "This won't happen again," I declared. "The next time you get pregnant, I want to know the second you do."

"The next time?"

"Oh, sweetheart…" I smirked. "You didn't think this was the only time I'd be getting you pregnant, did you?"

My lips devoured hers before she could even reply. Hunger opened inside me that felt close to desperation. I knew we had so much more to deal with. Life wasn't really any less complicated than it had been before we'd walked into this house.

In fact, it was more complex than before.

But I was happy about it, which was more than I could have said that morning.

It felt as if I had a piece of me back. A huge chunk that had been ripped raggedly away was now healed like it hadn't been broken at all. The awkwardness between us was shattered, with perhaps only a few shards left behind.

I could work with that.

I could do anything if Bellamy stayed in my arms.

A renewed sense of strength fortified me because I realized I hadn't lost absolutely everything. I still had a lot left to protect. My father died making sure of it.

I wouldn't let his sacrifice go to waste.

15

Bellamy

"I really don't think I should be here," I said as Liam held tighter to my hand and towed me along behind him.

I might well as have roller skates on my feet because he had no problem at all pulling me along.

"I'm not doing this anymore, Bells." Liam insisted, steel in his tone. "Please don't ask me to."

"I'm not!" I burst out, ripping my hand out of his and digging in my feet. "I wanted to stay at Alex's while you came to check on Holly. I completely understand that you need to be here for her. She lost the most important person in her life."

"And you're mine!" he snapped.

My shoulders fell. Why were we arguing?

Liam cursed, backtracking to where I stood. "I didn't mean to make it seem like you were the one forcing me to choose. I know you aren't."

"She's just upset," I said, motioning toward the house. We were standing in the garage at his parents'.

Alex had come home and interrupted the steamy make-out session we were engaged in, which made Liam surly.

Of course, when Alex said he'd driven Holly home from the reception, Liam switched to concern. And so there we were. I shouldn't have been there, though. His mom didn't want to see me.

"We're all upset," Liam said patiently. "But I can't," he said, and this look passed behind his eyes, a storm cloud concealing the sun. I shivered, and a feeling of frost nipped at my heart.

Liam grasped my shoulders, and I was partially shocked his touch was warm. "I can't be apart from you anymore. It's too hard."

His hand reached down and caressed my stomach. Butterflies fluttered up beneath my ribcage. I had a feeling he was going to be doing that a lot for the next seven or so months.

Putting my hand over his, I stared into his eyes. "I know you're struggling."

A shuttered look dropped over his features, and my hand tightened around his.

I was afraid to push, afraid not to.

This time, I chose not to, instead lifting on tiptoes to brush a kiss against his lower lip. Barely pulling back, I spoke. "If you want me at your side, then that's exactly where I'll be."

I'd take the frost from his mother, the accusing stares, and even the veiled comments. I'd take all that and more if my presence gave Liam any kind of peace. He'd done far more for me.

Dropping his face just a fraction, he kissed me. I opened instantly, still teetering on my toes.

The door leading into the house opened, and Liam's mother's voice called out. "Liam? Is that you?"

Liam lifted his head but curled his hand around my waist, keeping me close. Maybe he was afraid I'd bolt. Maybe he was afraid he would.

I couldn't imagine what it had been like for him, dealing with his father's death and trying to shoulder his mother's pain as well. I felt sorely embarrassed just then. Embarrassed of my own behavior. I'd basically hidden for days, too afraid to face the fallout from everything I'd caused. Too afraid to look Liam in the eye. We'd been hiding from each other, from what we thought was the end.

It hadn't been the end, though, and we'd needed each other.

"Yeah, Mom. It's me." He turned. "And Bellamy."

She was silent, and I peeked around him as she came out into the garage. "You brought Bellamy here?"

The offer to leave was ripe on the tip of my tongue. I held it in, though, because Liam's wishes came before Holly's.

Instead of saying anything else, Liam tugged me to his side, linking our hands.

Holly glanced down to them and then up to me. "Well, come inside. It's freezing out here."

Liam didn't outwardly react, but I couldn't help but gape. This was not at all the answer I expected to hear.

The three of us went quietly inside, Liam keeping hold of my hand the entire way upstairs. My eyes were drawn to the magnificent view as they always were every time I came here.

"People asked about you at the reception," Holly told him. "They understood when I told them Bellamy was ill."

"You shouldn't have put it on Bellamy," Liam said.

Holly glanced over her shoulder.

"It's fine," I answered. "It's the truth."

Liam frowned and looked at me. I lifted my chin and nodded. I'd been weak these past few days. It was time for me to get it together and be strong. Liam shouldn't shoulder all of this alone.

Holly stopped walking and turned. Her eyes settled on me, and they were heavy with grief. I braced myself for whatever she would say. I actually hoped she hurled it all at me. Maybe then she would weigh a little less.

"I owe you an apology."

I drew back. That was unexpected. "I'm sorry, what?"

A faint smile tugged at her drawn face. She turned toward Liam. "What you said to me at the reception…"

"I shouldn't have," Liam said. "I was upset."

"Rightfully so." Holly agreed. "I have forced you to choose between me and Bellamy, something I never expected myself to do." Emotion started seeping into her voice, and her shoulders began to sink. "We are all in pain, and it was so hurtful of me to deny you any kind of comfort. Especially after all the comfort you have been to me."

"I've been here because I've wanted to be," Liam told her.

"You wanted Bellamy here, too."

I cleared my throat. "I want you to know I take full responsibility for this, for your loss."

Liam stiffened immediately and turned to me. "We talked about this, Bells."

"Let's sit." Holly gestured toward the fireplace.

Liam tugged me down beside him on the sofa, and Holly took a seat on the other side of the coffee table.

"This isn't your fault," his mother said, settling the full weight of her eyes on me. I think it was the first time she really looked at me since Ren passed.

"If I hadn't come—"

Liam made a sound of protest and pulled my hand into his lap. I couldn't help it. I smiled a little because he was acting like a spoiled child with his favorite toy.

I had to admit I liked being Liam's favorite toy.

"If I hadn't accepted you after you told us what you were involved in—"

Liam's voice was sharp and finite. "Mom."

She held up her hand, not even in the least intimidated. "Ren accepted you as well. He loved you."

Liam's fingers vibrated against mine. Her admission blew me back into the cushions of the couch. Automatically, Liam rotated so we were closer, so he was angled slightly toward me as if he were prepared to shield me.

"I loved him," I whispered. I wholeheartedly meant it. Renshaw Mattison was a rare breed of man. Driven, successful, royalty in his own right, but unbelievably humble. Even through all his success, he seemed to always know the true meaning of life.

Holly nodded, sorrow written on every visible part of her. "Point is if I continue placing blame on the what-ifs of what happened, then Ren would be responsible for his murder. I would be."

"Perry Crone and his hired killer are responsible for Dad's murder and no one else," Liam intoned.

Both his mother and I paused to glance at him. Rage as cold as ice permeated the room. It was chilling because this wasn't the kind of anger that lit up a room and bubbled over with aggression.

No. This was frost, pure and simple. The kind that could drive a man to do things he might regret.

Premeditated things.

"Yes." Holly agreed but then continued. "Beyond those men, there was a series of choices. A series of circumstances that all led up to this. While it's easier to blame a single person"—she lifted her eyes to me—"easier to focus all the anger and pain at one thing in particular, it isn't fair."

"I understand," I told her. I truly did.

"Which makes it all the more hideous," Holly murmured. "Renshaw and I both accepted you and all the… problems your relationship with Liam presented. I can't regret those choices because you haven't just brought sadness into our lives, but love, too."

"I'm pregnant," I blurted out. Holly gasped, and I winced up at Liam. "It just came out."

He chuckled and kissed my temple. "Minor."

I wrinkled my nose. What did that mean?

"You're pregnant?" Holly asked, sitting so close to the edge of her seat that she was teetering.

"Yes." I smiled timidly. "It was a surprise."

Liam squeezed my hand and picked up where I left off. "A happy one for once."

I shouldn't have just blurted it out like that. I got caught up in the moment, in the way she was trying to make amends. I probably should have waited, but admittedly, I wanted to make her happy. I wanted her to look at me and see something other than everything I'd cost.

It might be selfish, but it was honest.

I mean, who wouldn't want the grandmother of her child to like her?

I looked at Liam, silently asking him permission. He nodded.

"Ren knew," I said gently.

Her eyes went wide, and the tears swimming in them splashed over. "He did?"

I nodded. "I told him just before…" I cleared my throat. "Before he passed."

"Oh, he would have loved a grandchild." Holly sobbed.

"He was happy." I would never forget the moment I told him. It was utterly bittersweet.

Holly leapt up and hugged Liam over the coffee table and then hugged me. I hugged her back, partially surprised.

She pulled back, concern darkening her face. "After everything you've been through, you're healthy? The baby is safe?"

Liam stood up, keeping hold of my hand, and fished the stolen picture out of his pocket. He handed it over, and he made a small sound. "You can't keep that."

I rolled my eyes.

He shrugged. "That's my kid." His eyes returned to Holly, who was eating up every inch of the sonogram. "The baby is safe and that's the way it's going to stay."

The hairs on the back of my neck rose. I slid a look toward him.

"This is wonderful news," Holly finally said, looking up from the picture. "Something to look forward to."

Liam leaned forward and took the picture, clutching it.

I stifled a laugh.

It made my heart sing the way he was absolutely in love with his child from the second he knew about him. If he was this besotted now after one blobby picture, I could only imagine how he would be when he held the baby in his arms.

Just the thought of seeing him with our baby in his arms made my insides turn to mush. I melted into his side with a sigh.

"I'm sorry for the way I've treated you," Holly said.

"You have nothing to apologize for."

"I do." She turned to Liam. "I'm sorry for putting so much on you as well. I'm the parent, not you."

"I'm a grown man, Mom. I can handle it."

But can he? Really?

"You're going to be a father. You have more important things to worry about than your mother." She said it cheerfully, but I knew better. I couldn't even imagine what it was like to stare at the woman you blamed (if only partially) for the murder of your husband, try to accept her, and then learn she was carrying your grandchild.

Holly was concerned, and if she wasn't, she wouldn't be the woman I knew she was.

"I'll always have time for you, Mom. And this baby is going to need you."

"You're the only grandma he's going to know," I said, the realization smacking me in the center of my chest and robbing me of breath. I reached up and rubbed the spot, trying to make it burn less.

"Bells," Liam murmured, glancing at me.

"I'm okay." I smiled, then laid my head on his shoulder.

My God. My child won't know my mother or my father.

"It's been a long day," Holly said, standing. "Liam, would you like a drink? I think I'll pour a glass of wine." On her way toward the kitchen, she stopped. "Tea, Bellamy?"

My stomach churned. "No, thank you," I said. "But you and Liam go ahead."

She frowned, and I knew she thought I was rejecting the offer because I was upset.

"Tea would be lovely, but only if you let me help you."

She gestured toward the kitchen, and I left Liam. He followed along, and I handed him a longneck out of the fridge. Holly poured wine as the kettle heated water.

"Honey, right?" she said, recalling what I preferred. I glanced over to her holding up the container of amber-colored liquid.

My stomach revolted. My body spasmed from the center of my diaphragm, and I took off running down the hall toward the bathroom.

I made it to the toilet in time and emptied my stomach in a few painful heaves. When I was finished, Liam picked me up from behind, slowly bringing me to my feet.

"You have to stop coming in the bathroom while I'm puking."

"No."

"This is all your fault!" I said for lack of any other retort.

"I know."

I was offended. "Why do you sound so proud of yourself?" I croaked.

He sat me on the counter. "Now, sweetheart. I could never be proud of making you so sick."

I harrumphed because he was lying.

His warm chuckle actually smoothed out some of the turbulence in my belly, and I swayed toward him with a sigh.

We stood there for long, quiet moments, him stroking the length of my hair and me inhaling his scent like I was some sort of weird addict.

I yawned against him, and he pulled back. "You're exhausted. I'll get us a room over at the resort until we figure out where the hell we're going to live."

That made me remember. "You had the cabin cleaned up."

"You weren't cleaning up after those assholes."

"I liked it there," I said sadly.

"Me, too." He kissed my forehead. "We're gonna like the next place, too. We need something bigger anyway."

I felt suddenly overwhelmed. For as slow as time dragged the past few days and as uncertain as it all seemed, things were now moving at a breakneck pace.

The funeral, his mom, the baby, a new house… hell, even the appearance of his ex. All in the matter of a single day. And it wasn't even all of it.

"Whoa." He rubbed his hands along my arms. "I can hear the wheels in your head turning."

I glanced up, guilty. This was what I wanted, but it was still a lot.

"How about we just get a room tonight, and maybe see if you can hold some food down?"

"I want cereal," I announced.

He lifted an eyebrow. "You want cereal."

"Raisin Bran."

"What the fuck…?" he muttered.

I pointed to my stomach. "You gonna argue with this baby?"

He shrugged. "Kid knows what he wants. I can respect that."

Liam lifted me off the counter so I could wash my hands and rinse out my mouth. When I glanced in the mirror, he was frowning.

"What?"

"We need to get you in with the doctor."

Nerves coiled inside me, and my hand went to my waist. "You think something's wrong?"

"No." He shook his head, wrapping around me from behind. "But you look like hell and you've lost weight. I'm pretty sure you should be gaining."

"I've had a rough few days." I defended.

His face darkened.

"I love you," I whispered because I was worried he'd blame himself.

Everything about him softened. "I love you, too, baby. C'mon." He linked my hand with his. "Let's go find you some nasty Raisin Bran."

"It's not nasty!" I protested.

"I've never seen you eat it, ever," he pointed out.

I grimaced. He was right.

He chuckled and turned back. "It's okay, sweetheart. I'll get you all the boxes at the store."

"Bellamy," Holly said as soon as I appeared in the kitchen. "Are you feeling okay?"

I nodded. "My morning sickness is more of an all-day thing."

"You've been like this a while?"

I nodded, not wanting to say how long.

"I kept you away," she said to Liam.

"I called and checked up on her a lot, Mom," Liam replied.

"He didn't know about the baby," I explained.

"You didn't tell him?" she said, near accusatory.

"Uh…" I stuttered. "Um, I just found out." All the progress I felt I'd made with Holly today seemed to blow away with a soft breeze. I knew things weren't perfect between us, but I really did think things would be okay. As fast as she jumped on me just now, I realized it was going to take a while.

In the back of her mind, would Holly always assume the worst of me?

I remembered that first night I made everyone dinner. How happy we all were, how overcome with emotion I was when she called me her daughter.

I missed that now.

I missed my own mom.

Liam shifted, casually stepping in front of me even though I knew there was nothing casual about his movement. "Bellamy told me as soon as she could."

"Of course." Holly agreed. "Bellamy, you should try some ginger. Put some into hot water, or maybe even get some ginger candies. It will help with your nausea. I would have made you some, but I don't have any ginger root here."

The thoughtfulness of that comment made me wonder if I was overreacting. "Thank you for the suggestion. I will definitely try it."

On impulse, I reached out and fisted my hand in the back of Liam's dress shirt. It was hard because it was tucked in, so I settled for just laying my palm against the small of his back. Reaching around, he tugged me forward, anchoring me into his side and tucking an arm around me.

"I'm getting us a room at the resort for the time being." Liam started. "Before we go, is there anything I can do for you?"

"The resort?" Her forehead bunched, then cleared. "The cabin."

"We won't be living there anymore." Liam's voice was terse.

"Of course not." She confirmed. "Why don't you both stay here? You're already settled in your room, Liam."

"We've all been through a lot. Us moving in here is a lot different than me bunking in my old room." He smiled.

I didn't want to be relieved he hadn't agreed, but I was. I wasn't sure staying here would help diffuse any tension Holly still felt around me. But at the same time, I knew they needed each other.

"I would love to have you. This house is just too big for just one person. Besides, I think Bellamy would get more rest here than at the hotel," Holly implored.

Before Liam could say anything, I spoke up. "That's really generous." In the end, me being slightly uncomfortable here was not much of a sacrifice. "As beautiful as the hotel is, this house definitely has it beat. Charlie sure will appreciate the extra space."

"So it's settled?" Holly asked, hopeful.

I felt Liam's muscles tense. Lightly, I rubbed my palm over his back. He glanced down at me, question in his gaze. I smiled softly, hoping he understood that I appreciated what he was willing to do, but I wanted to stay here.

Liam relaxed and smiled at his mom. "Thanks, Mom. I promise we won't take too long finding a new place."

"Take as long as you need." She offered, beaming. She seemed so relieved to not be here alone that I felt guilty for not wanting to stay here at first. "I'm going to go set up the guest room downstairs. You'll both be more comfortable down there than in Liam's old teenager room."

"Now she offers me a bigger bed," he exclaimed.

"I want my future grandchild to be comfortable." She glanced at me and winked.

"Second best already." Liam pretended to be hurt.

Her light laugh floated behind her as she hurried off to set up our room.

When we were alone, Liam turned to face me. "You didn't have to do that."

"But look how happy it made her."

"Your happiness means just as much to me," he declared, playing with the impossibly long strands of my hair. I'd barely combed it in days. A low, subdued ponytail was all I could manage for the service.

"I'll be happy as long as I'm wherever you are."

"If at any time it gets to be too much, just say the word."

I nodded.

"Bells…" He warned.

I sighed. "I promise."

I could see in his eyes he wasn't sure if he should believe me or not, so I leaned close, slipped my arms around his waist, and hugged.

"Thank you," he said against my ear.

The genuine relief and gratitude in his voice was all I needed to strengthen my resolve. It didn't matter how awkward or uncomfortable I might get around Holly. I was going to make this work.

16

Liam

I woke up to the sounds of her puking.

She shut the bathroom door, as if she thought it would mute the sound.

Or keep me out.

The second she sat back from the toilet, I was there, scooping her up. But I startled her, and she jolted forward, heaving again.

I didn't like this.

Not one fucking bit.

The fact that she had my baby growing inside her was epically awesome. However, knowing it made her like this, not so much.

As I sat there listening to her heaving, guilt ate me up. I hadn't been there. She was pregnant and sick, probably thinking I abandoned her.

Sure, she said she understood.

I had no excuse.

This time when she sat back, I slipped around her slowly, not wanting to jar her. "You all done?" I murmured.

"God, I hope so," she croaked.

I lifted her off the floor to carry her back to bed. She shook her head adamantly and pointed to the sink. Begrudgingly, I set her down and let her get cleaned up.

The second she turned from the counter, I lifted her again and sat in bed with her in my lap. "You still have that doctor's number?"

"It's in my bag," she answered, cuddling close.

I smiled faintly into her hair because, goddamn, I missed this. The feel of her. The scent of her. After a moment of wallowing in her presence, I stood. She squeaked and gripped onto me as if I would drop her.

I'd eat my own gangrened foot before I dropped her or my kid.

With a chuckle, I tucked her into the center of the bed, then grabbed her bag and handed it to her, along with my cell. "Call and make an appointment. For today."

She made a face. "They aren't going to have any openings today."

"Why the hell not?" I demanded.

"That's not how doctor offices work."

"You have a baby in you!"

She gasped. "Thank God you told me!"

I raised both brows. "Don't you sass me, woman."

She made a dramatic noise and an equally dramatic facial expression. "I know this may come as a shock, but I'm not the only pregnant woman on this planet."

Planting my palms on either side of her, I leaned close. "Well, you're the only woman on this planet who's pregnant with *my* baby."

A little purring sound erupted from her as she looped her arms around my neck. "Are you trying to turn me on? Because *that* is sexy."

Desire sizzled through my veins, and my eyes bounced between hers. "You like that, do you?"

Her teeth sank into her lower lip. "Very. Much."

Against the mattress, my fingers flexed into the sheets. Oh God, it would be so fucking easy to grab her, to move over her body and claim her. The way she was looking at me right now made my dick stand at attention.

With a groan, I pulled back. Denying myself. Denying her.

"Liam." She pouted.

I chuckled. "You want a piece of this?" I gestured to my half-naked frame. "Make the appointment."

"So it's really like that, huh?"

I flashed my teeth. "It's really like that."

Her voice wobbled, and her face became unsure. "Are you sure it's not something else?"

I frowned. "What else would it be?"

"Are you sure you aren't upset with me?"

A rough noise ripped out of me as I moved over her on the bed. "I am not mad at you. I am not anything but deeply, insanely in love with you and my baby."

"Usually you can't keep your hands off me."

"I held you all night, sweetheart," I pointed out, keeping my voice gentle. Having her beneath me, looking up with vulnerability in her eyes, was testing my patience.

So was the fact that she seemed hurt that we had yet to have sex.

I kissed her nose, her eyelid, and then moved to kiss the other. My arms were starting to shake from holding my body weight off her, but I didn't move.

"You know what I mean," she murmured, lifting her chin so I would also kiss her lips.

"I told you," I said. "I need to make sure you and the baby are okay before I go making love to you."

"Again, I tell you I am not the only woman on this planet to be pregnant. Pregnant women have sex all the time. It's how they get pregnant." She was stubborn and petulant.

I found it charming and irresistible, so I laughed.

Bellamy scowled.

Suppressing my grin, I replied, "And I told you I only give a shit about one pregnant woman."

I kissed her again, lingering on her mouth just a little longer. She was sweet, sweet torture.

With a groan, I pushed back, gesturing to the phone again. "Make that call. I'll get you some ginger tea."

"Hey," she said, grasping my wrist.

I turned back.

"I like being pregnant with your baby. Even if it does make me sick as a dog."

Warmth suffused my chest. I kissed her forehead and then went to make the tea that seemed to settle her stomach.

Or maybe that had been the Raisin Bran.

She'd eaten two bowls and didn't even blink. They weren't small bowls either.

I made the tea as quietly as I could, then carried it back to the bedroom.

Bells looked up when I walked in, phone still pressed to her ear. "You're sure you don't have anything open for two weeks?" she asked into the line.

Well, that was unacceptable.

I tossed Charlie a snack, which he seized right out of the air, and snatched the phone out of Bell's hand. I put it to my ear while handing her the mug.

She took it but glared. I thought it was cute.

"Hi, who is this?" I spoke into the line.

The woman paused. "This is Eileen at Dr. Crawford's office."

"Hey, Eileen, nice to meet you. This is Liam Mattison."

"Liam Mattison," she repeated. "Of BearPaw Resort, the Olympic medalist?"

"One in the same."

"Oh, hi." She giggled. "I mean… How can I help you today?"

"That woman you were speaking with just a moment ago, the cranky one?"

Bellamy gasped. "Liam!"

"Yes?" the woman answered cautiously.

"That's my, ah…" I glanced at her and frowned. "My girlfriend." That just wasn't a good enough title for Bellamy. It sounded cheap.

I hated it.

"She's pregnant. We just found out."

"Oh! Congratulations!" Eileen exclaimed. "How exciting!"

"Thank you." I smiled into the line. Bellamy muttered something about people kissing royalty ass. I stifled a snicker. "I'm excited. Can't wait to get the little guy on a board."

Eileen sighed into the line.

"Anyway, Bells hasn't been seen by a doctor, and I'm pretty concerned. She hasn't been able to keep much down."

"Oh, that's totally normal." Eileen assured me.

"Thing is I would feel a hell of a lot better if we could get her seen as soon as possible."

Bellamy snorted. "Two weeks." She reminded me.

"You don't happen to have any cancellations or anything available, do you?" I glanced at Bells. "I'd consider it a personal favor."

She rolled her eyes and dramatically fell back on the bed. Brat almost spilled her tea. I was so entertained by her I almost didn't hear the nurse speak into my ear.

"I have a small window open today, but you'd have to be here in an hour."

A slow, wide smile spread over my face. "We can totally be there in an hour."

Bells's mouth dropped open, and an offended look crossed her features.

I gave the nurse my info and told her I was looking forward to meeting her in person. Then I ended the call and tossed the cell on the mattress.

"You've got to be kidding me." Bellamy scoffed.

"I've got skills." I bragged.

"What you have is Olympic medals and a bunch of muscles."

I snickered. "Sometimes being Caribou royalty comes in handy."

"Whatever," she muttered and tipped the mug to her lips.

I climbed on the bed and gathered her close. "Don't be mad, sweetheart. I just want the best for you and my son."

She sighed. "I'm not mad. I didn't want to wait two weeks either."

"Good, because we have to leave in thirty."

Bellamy jolted up. "I need to take a shower!"

Before she could run off completely, I grabbed the back of my T-shirt she was wearing and tugged her back. "Where do you think you're going?"

"I just told you," she answered.

"Kiss me."

"Just because you can charm whatever you want out of everyone in this entire town doesn't mean you can do the same to me."

Oh, I liked a challenge.

I pulled her so she fell back on the bed, straddling her hips. My shirt was oversized on her, so I hooked my fingers in the neck and pulled it down, exposing her collarbone and shoulder.

Swooping in close, I didn't kiss her. Instead, I let the tip of my nose graze over the sensitive skin along her neck and down across her collarbone. She moved beneath me, and I smirked against her, then nudged against her neck again.

"God, I missed you," I murmured. "When I did finally get an hour or two to sleep, I'd lay in that bed upstairs and long for you. You haunted my dreams while we were apart, Bells. There wasn't a single moment in those three days that I didn't want you."

Her chest rose and fell beneath me.

Lifting my face, our eyes collided. Holding her stare, my lips lowered until they hovered just above hers. I could taste her breath this close, a mix of mint and ginger.

Her lashes fanned down over her cheeks, then fluttered open again.

"Kiss me, sweetheart." I beckoned.

She didn't move, but I did. Our lips brushed once, twice, and on the third time, I didn't lift up. Instead, I kissed her the way I'd wanted to all those nights I lay in bed without her. I kissed her in the most honest way I could, hoping she could taste the truth of just how much I loved her.

Her fingers dragged up my spine, creating ripples of pleasure in their wake.

After another few minutes, the thick fog of want began clouding my mind, and I moaned. Forcing myself back, our lips tugged against the other's as I moved, clinging on for just a second longer.

"Thank Christ your appointment is today." My voice was gravelly.

She smiled and arched up into me like a cat. "I missed you, too, Liam," she confided. Her fingers dragged back down my spine, toward my ass. "I miss you still."

It was a sheer act of willpower that kept me from ripping off every last piece of clothing she wore.

"Go get ready," I said, horny as hell.

I watched her walk into the bathroom, not smug in the least I got her to kiss me because, *damn*, all that kiss had done was leave me wanting more.

Bellamy

It was good to see him smile. To hear him laugh and watch him tease me. I might have taken advantage of those things before. Liam was always quick to smile, but maybe I never quite grasped how much it cost.

Most people knew Liam as a star athlete. As a pillar of strength and determination. Everyone liked him because he was informal and treated everyone like a friend. And sure, his impossibly good looks definitely didn't hurt.

The strength inside him was unmatched by anyone else—except maybe Alex, which probably explained why they remained so tightly bonded as friends. Liam was so strong in character it was almost a flaw, almost a weakness.

It was where his darkness came from.

And though it didn't always show because he was very skilled at keeping it under wraps, it was always there. Always in the room with us, forever lurking.

I hadn't forgotten the pill I'd found in the bed. I kept it with me. A tiny, near-weightless thing that actually was very heavy. It almost vibrated with reminder.

Talk to him. Show him. Get him some help.

That was the hard part about Liam. He appeared perfectly fine. If they didn't really look for it, a person would never know he was struggling.

I was extremely concerned he'd relapsed. That everything that happened was just too much.

Time seemed to work against me. Or maybe we just had so much to work through it was hard to bring up everything during a moment of peace.

This morning had been peace. You know, aside from the barfing and his impossibly annoying way of getting everything he wanted.

Things almost felt like before.

Almost.

Actually, no. The scoffing inside my head was loud and rude. My own brain was telling me how ridiculous I was. Things had never been easy for Liam and me. Had there really ever been a before?

Seemed now things were divided by the death of Renshaw. Before and after. But really, things weren't all hunky dory before Ren passed.

It made me wonder if Liam and I would ever have anything that wasn't tainted.

"What are you worrying about over there?" His voice broke into my thoughts.

I glanced across the interior of the Extreme and felt a piece of me loosen.

It doesn't matter. It didn't matter if everything around Liam and me was easy and simple, because the way I felt about him—how much I loved him—was. I knew at least that would never change.

"I'm just thinking about how much I love you," I answered, honest.

Liam made a sound, stole my hand, and lifted it to his mouth. The kiss was long, not really a kiss, more of a prayer of his lips pressing close against the back of my hand.

After this appointment, I vowed. I would talk to him after we knew the baby was okay.

The doctor's office was located near the hospital, and as we drove by, my stomach lurched a little as memories of the last time we were there assaulted me. I barely remembered leaving that place. We were all so numb and riddled with grief that everything else was just background noise.

The sight of the hospital affected Liam, too. His body tensed, and the air inside the truck became edgy and thick.

Liam's hold tightened on my hand, still in his lap. "It's hard," he rasped, eyes focused straight ahead.

"What is?" I cajoled.

"To be happy."

My heart squeezed. "I know, sweetheart," I murmured. "But it's okay to have moments of happiness. Ren would want that. He was happy about the baby, too."

Liam's throat worked, but then he slid me a brief glance before his eyes went back to the road. "Did you just call me sweetheart?"

My lips tugged up. "I guess I did."

The truck slowed and pulled into the parking lot. Without letting go of my hand, Liam deftly steered the giant vehicle into a parking space.

"I don't know how you park this thing," I muttered.

He shut off the engine and turned to me. "What kind of car did you have?"

"In Chicago? I didn't have one. I walked to work."

"Before Chicago?"

"In California, I drove a small two-door. It wasn't a Chevy."

"Traitor."

"I've never driven anything this big before."

He made a sound. "You'll get used to it."

When he came around the outside of the truck and pulled open my door, I squinted at him. "What do you mean?"

"I mean you'll be lucky if I get you anything smaller than a tank to drive around this mountain."

I rolled my eyes. "I don't need a car."

Liam paused as he reached in to get me. "You're getting a car. It's at the top of my list, right after getting us a new place."

I started to argue but stopped when my body slid down the front of his. I didn't even feel the winter wind because I was too caught up in his closeness.

"If you think I'm going to let the mother of my child not have something safe to drive herself and my son around in, then you don't know me at all."

I batted my lashes at him. "I just assumed you would drive me everywhere I wanted to go."

He half smiled. "I will. In a giant SUV with extra airbags."

I mock gasped. "Are you saying the Extreme isn't safe?"

"Shut your mouth, woman." He swatted me on the ass. "Come on. Inside before you turn into a popsicle."

When we stepped into Dr. Crawford's office, an interested hush fell over everyone. Granted, there weren't a ton of people in the waiting room, but it wasn't empty.

All the pregnant women glanced up, eyes going to Liam. Three women behind the desk also came to the window to watch him.

I glanced up at him, accusing. "Stop making everyone look at you," I hissed quietly.

He winked and tugged me along to the front.

"Mr. Mattison," the woman dressed in scrubs purred.

"Eileen?"

She blushed and nodded.

"Thanks for getting us in so fast. You're the bomb."

You're the bomb? Seriously?

The nurse giggled, and I held back a gag. Eileen shifted her gaze to me. It was more calculating than the look she'd given Liam. "Bellamy… Mattison?"

"Lane." I corrected. "Bellamy Lane."

"So you aren't married?" she inquired.

I snorted. "I'm pretty sure you don't need to know that to sign me in." The nerve! Was she seriously trying to figure out if Liam was still ripe for the taking?

His baby was literally inside me.

"See," Liam told Eileen as he signed the clipboard the woman pushed toward us. "I told you on the phone she's cranky."

"I am not cranky," I bit out.

Someone behind us laughed.

I squeezed Liam's hand as hard as I could. I hoped it hurt.

"Fill out these forms and return them to me. The doctor will be with you in just a moment."

I snatched the clipboard and pen from Liam the second we sat down and began filling out the mountain of forms.

"Bells," Liam murmured, leaning close.

"What?" I said without glancing up.

"You're my favorite girl."

I paused. "What?"

He leaned in, practically laying his lips against my ear. "I don't want anyone but you."

I sighed, little shivers racing over my arms. "I know," I whispered, finally looking at him. "But that was ridiculous."

He grinned, slid his large hand over my stomach, and held it there while he kissed my forehead.

The woman across from us sighed.

He didn't remove his hand from my midsection the rest of the time I answered question after question. Finally, a nurse came and escorted us into an exam room.

I expected to wait forever. In my experience, doctors were never quick.

Unless, of course, you had Liam Mattison in the room with you.

"Mr. Mattison," the doctor announced after a swift knock outside the door. "Nice to meet you," Dr. Crawford said, holding out his hand.

"Liam." Liam corrected. "Thanks for fitting us in so fast."

"Of course. It's the least I could do for the founding family of our fine town."

Gag me.

The doctor cleared his throat and shifted. "I'd like to offer my condolences on the loss of you father. He was a remarkable man."

"Thank you," Liam replied, subdued. "He was."

I slipped my hand over the small of his back just so he didn't forget I was there.

After that, the doctor seemed to realize I was there and Liam wasn't the pregnant one. Shocker! I answered a thousand questions. Liam showed him the sonogram, which, yes, he had in his pocket.

Seriously, though, how adorable was that?

Afterward, the doctor did a routine exam. You know, feeling my stomach, etc. Liam stood over me the entire time, watching like a hawk. I thought about apologizing to the doctor, but then I didn't. Let's see if Dr. Crawford was so enamored with Liam after being scrutinized.

"If you'll just unbutton your pants and pull them down a bit," he said, turning to the small counter in the room.

"What the hell for?" Liam bellowed.

"Thought you might want to hear the heartbeat," the doctor said good-naturedly.

"We can do that?" Liam was awed.

"Of course."

Liam moved closer to the table, literally brushing against its side. Doctor Crawford pushed my shirt up and tossed a paper sheet over my lower half. He laid a small instrument beside me and then, using both his hands, tugged the waistband of my jeans so low I had to lift a little so they could slide down. When the doctor reached for the waistband of my lace panties, Liam's hand shot out and covered his.

"What the hell do you think you're doing?" he growled.

"Liam!" I gasped.

"The wand has to go low against her abdomen, much lower than one might realize."

"I'm sorry," I told the doctor, embarrassed.

"Nothing wrong with a man being concerned," he said. "But perhaps I could continue?" He looked down at where Liam was blocking him.

Grudgingly, Liam let go but straightened to his full size and narrowed his eyes.

I gave him the stink eye, but he ignored me.

When the top of my neatly trimmed pubic area came into sight, Liam's back teeth snapped together.

The doctor squirted some very cold, clear gel on my lower belly and pushed the little machine against it to move around.

A few seconds later, the sound of our baby's heartbeat filled the room.

"Is that him?" Liam's voice was hushed.

"That's him," the doctor announced. "That's a strong heartbeat. Sounds good."

It was a miracle the first time I heard the rapid whooshing sound, but this… this was a whole new level. Hearing this sound *and* seeing the emotion play on Liam's face was overwhelming.

Tears spilled down my cheeks as Liam heard his baby for the first time.

He glanced down at me. "It was like this last time?"

I nodded.

"Everything looks and sounds good." Dr. Crawford started to pull back.

"Wait." Liam stopped him. "Just another minute."

The doctor obliged, pushing the wand back against me, moving it a bit. The baby's heartbeat filled the room once more.

Liam's eyes closed briefly, and more tears fell over my cheeks. I loved this baby. So much.

But watching Liam love him?

It was indescribable.

"Does that thing take pictures?"

"This? No. That would be an ultrasound."

Liam nodded. "Let's do one of those."

"We don't normally do one of those until around twenty weeks. Since she already had one a few days ago at the hospital—"

"I wasn't there for that one," Liam deadpanned.

"I see," the doctor replied.

"Liam was getting stitches, and his father was in surgery…" I explained.

"Ah, yes." Dr. Crawford sympathized. "Well, we don't do ultrasounds at every appointment. They are costly and unnecessary. The insurance—"

"I'll pay cash. Today."

"Well, I have other patients waiting…" He began. "But I could have one of the techs do one? Would that be okay?"

Liam smiled. "Perfect, doc."

He chuckled and went about putting aside the instrument and making a few notes on his small laptop. "I'll see you back here in a month. Call if you have any problems or concerns between now and then."

"I will." I promised.

"Remember." Dr. Crawford reminded me. "The goal is to not lose any more weight, but to gain some. You're nearing your second trimester now, so the daily sickness should subside. Make sure you're taking the supplements I prescribed and get plenty of rest." He paused, then said, "I know it's probably been a very stressful time for your family. Keep in mind that stress is not good for you or the baby."

"I'll make sure she relaxes," Liam intoned.

After a few more questions and answers and minor instructions, the doctor excused himself, and a woman in scrubs came in, pulling along the sonogram machine.

"You ready to see your baby?" The technician beamed.

This time Liam was a little more tolerant when the woman put the wand down into my bikini line, but he still towered over us both watching intently.

"I'm sorry," I told the girl when she glanced up warily. "He's like a caveman."

I smacked him in the stomach hoping he would move back, but all he did was catch my hand and link it with his.

"I think it's sweet to see a man so involved." She smiled. A few minutes later, a little blob appeared on the screen. "There's your baby."

Liam made a sound and rotated toward the monitor.

"See that flickering?" The woman pointed to the screen. "That's the heart beating."

"It's so fast," Liam murmured.

I leaned up slightly to try and see around him.

The nurse moved the wand and pressed it a little firmer. "This is the outline." She went on, pointing out a million little things to Liam.

"I want to see, too," I said, smacking him on the hip.

He nudged back a little. "Sorry, sweetheart," he said, still staring.

"What's that?" he asked, pointing to something else.

She answered, and he pointed to something else.

He was absolutely enthralled. His eyes never once left the monitor or our baby. I gave up looking and lay back, watching him instead. My heart swelled.

"He's incredible," Liam murmured.

"It's a little too soon to tell if it's a boy."

"It's a boy," we both said at exactly the same time.

The technician laughed. "You could be right. We'll know for sure next time."

"Where's my pictures?" Liam asked.

After hitting a few buttons on the keyboard, the girl reached around and pulled up a strip of black-and-white photos. She handed them to Liam with a smile.

He beamed, staring down at them as if he hadn't just seen the live thing.

"How many you got there?" I asked, leaning up to see.

"Five," he replied, still staring.

"Five! They only gave me one in the ER!"

Liam chuckled.

A second later, a picture appeared in front of me. I took it and glanced up at the woman. "He isn't very good at sharing, is he?"

"Pretty obvious, huh?" I conspired. "Thank you," I told her, glancing down at the image.

The doctor stepped in, surprising us. "I had a free moment, so I thought I'd just glance over the images here," he said, stepping up to the monitor and getting to work.

I watched him review the screen, checking and rechecking.

"Is something wrong?" Liam asked, impatient.

"Everything looks to be going well. You're nine weeks, and that puts your due date in late October."

"A fall baby," I murmured.

"Thanks, doc," Liam said, pumping the man's hand. "I appreciate everything."

"I'll see you next month," he said and then left the room.

A few moments later, the technician handed me some tissues and slipped out of the room.

I smiled up at Liam. "That's a handsome baby you created."

He looked smug. "Did you expect less?"

Carefully, he folded all five pictures and slid them into his pocket with the first one. Then he plucked up the one the nurse gave me and slid that in his pocket, too!

"Hey!" I protested.

"You don't have any pockets," he said, straight faced.

"I'm wearing jeans," I pointed out.

He just smiled, took the tissues out of my hands, and cleaned all the jelly off my stomach. When he was done, he pulled the paper blanket off my legs and smiled down at my still-exposed belly. His hand was warm after the cold goo, and his palm covered me thoroughly. Stepping close, Liam leaned down and brushed his lips over my navel.

"Looking good in there, pumpkin," he murmured. "How 'bout you give your mom a break and let her eat something other than nasty raisins."

I smiled.

"What's that?" he said, tilting his ear to my stomach. He listened, looking up at me. "He says he loves you."

I was going to cry. Like a big, slobbery, ugly cry fest right here.

Liam turned, pressing a kiss to my stomach, and the tears fell.

Straightening, he moved up my body, wiping them away and then kissing me gently. "I wished I was there that first time, in the hospital."

"This was way better." I assured him.

"I love you."

"Me, too."

He rubbed a hand over my stomach again before straightening. "Come on. Pull your pants up. We gotta go get your prescriptions."

"I'm not taking that anti-nausea medicine." I asserted.

Liam sighed. "Much as I hate seeing you sick, I'm not gonna disagree."

"The less pills, the better," I murmured.

"What?" he asked swiftly. I thought I saw a flash of guilt in his eyes.

"For the baby," I said, muscles tense. "The less pills I take, the better."

"Right." He agreed, helping me off the table.

Neither of us said it, but I think we both knew we weren't just talking about the baby.

18

Liam

For a minute there, I thought she knew. For a moment, I stood there frozen, thinking she somehow found out about the pocket full of pills I was walking around with.

I didn't want her to know—or anyone for that matter. God knew what she would think. The last thing Bellamy needed was the stress of a relapse in her life.

Even knowing that, it wasn't enough to make me empty my pocket. I couldn't quite bring myself to do it. I wasn't sure why. I just knew having them there made me feel a little more in control.

As we walked through the general store to get her vitamins and whatever else she put in the basket, I thought of those pills more and more.

People approached us—every fucking person who looked in our direction.

If I had to listen to another "I'm sorry" or "my condolences," I was going to fucking snap. A couple ballsy people even asked about the "break-in" and the rogue guest-turned-criminal who ultimately killed my father.

This led me to think of Perry Crone and the letter he sent. The way he was almost proud of killing my father.

"Maybe it was too soon to come into town," Bellamy said, her voice subdued. I glanced down immediately, noting her pale cheeks and wide eyes.

I stopped in the center of the aisle and rotated so I was facing her and nothing else. "What's wrong, sweetheart?"

"It's hard on you."

A lot of the tension coiled inside me fell back. My eyes softened on hers as she looked at me with concern. "Nothing a little sugar from my girl can't fix."

She leaned up instantly, teetering on tiptoes to kiss me. I slipped my arms around her and lifted, taking her mouth the way I wanted.

It was probably too hungry of a kiss for the center of a public store, but I didn't give a damn. If people could walk up and ask me about my dad's murder, then I could make them watch me get some sugar.

When I was done, I set her down, and her eyes were wide. Blinking, she asked, "Better?"

I smirked. "For now."

"Hold my hand," she instructed, holding hers out.

"Yes, ma'am." I agreed, linking them together.

When we stepped up in line to pick up the prescription and pay for our items, the pharmacist came out with her white bag of meds. "Liam," he said.

I braced myself for more nosy business. I loved Caribou, but it had a small-town mentality despite the huge number of tourists that came through.

"Hi, Mr. Wagner," Bellamy said, drawing his attention. "Thank you so much for getting that ready."

The pharmacist glanced at my girl and smiled. "It was a pleasure."

"I'm sure you saw what they were for." She goaded.

"A man in my profession never comments on a patient's, uh, condition."

"Of course." She conspired. "But I give you permission this one time."

He smiled widely and held out a hand to me. "Then I guess congratulations are in order."

I admit I relaxed a little when he smiled because that look of sadness was no longer on his face. "Thank you." I grinned.

"If you all need anything, you just let me know."

"Thank you so much," Bellamy said, quickly handing over some cash to the cashier and then picking up the bag.

"I got that," I said, taking it out of her hand.

She gave everyone standing around a wave and tugged me out of the store.

"How'd you know?" I asked outside on the sidewalk. She glanced up. "You know, that everyone was getting to me."

"I could just tell."

"Word's gonna spread like wildfire now." I warned her.

Her mouth formed a little O. "Did you want to keep it to ourselves a little longer?"

I barked a laugh. "I don't give a fuck who knows." To prove my point, I glanced at some stranger walking by and pointed to her stomach. "That's my kid in there."

The man smiled. "Congratulations."

Bellamy smacked me. "Stop it."

"We're gonna have to stop by and tell Alex on the way home. If he hears it from someone else, he's gonna be pissed."

As if just saying his name conjured him up, he stepped out of a shop up the sidewalk.

"Yo!" I called out.

"Yo!" he yelled back before he even turned around to see us.

Putting a hand on the small of Bells's back, I ushered her down the sidewalk to meet Alex halfway. "Visiting your parents?" I asked, gesturing toward The Confectionary.

He nodded. "Figured I'd spend a little extra time with them."

A pang of hurt stabbed me, worse than the pain that seemed to continuously wave through me. The death of my dad sure had a way of reminding people how little time we actually have and how uncertain it all is. "Good call," I said because I didn't trust my voice to say anything else.

Internally, I focused on the weight of the pills in my pocket. It would be easy to slip into the bathroom and toss them back.

"We were just talking about you," Bellamy said, drawing my attention.

"I make a good conversation," Alex cracked.

Bellamy rolled her eyes. "We have something to tell you."

"Charlie finally get the shits after all the food you feed him?" He glanced at me. "Seriously, Liam. You need to put a limit on your girl."

Bellamy gave him a light shove, but when she pulled back, her boot slipped on some ice on the sidewalk. I caught her easily, but not before she took about twenty years off my life.

"Jesus, Bells," I swore.

She grimaced. "Sorry."

I anchored her into my side and kept my arm firmly around her.

Alex stared between us. "So everything cool between you two or what?"

I nodded. "We're straight."

"What's going on, then?" He pressed, all jokes aside.

Putting my free hand on her stomach, I told him, "Bellamy's pregnant."

Alex's icy eyes widened so much we could see the entire blue orbs. "No shit?"

I enjoyed seeing him speechless. It happened so little. I nodded.

"Oh my God!" he burst out. "You dog!" He cackled and leaned in to one-arm hug me. When he pulled back he went for Bellamy, pulling her right out of my hold.

"Is that what all that puking was about?" he asked, lifting her to his eye level.

"You heard that!" She gasped.

"Mm-hmm," he drawled and then hugged her. Bellamy squeaked.

"Be careful!" I snapped.

"Uh-oh," Alex cracked, pulling her back. "Now he's gonna be even grouchier."

She giggled.

I stepped up. "Give me my girl."

Alex passed her to me, her feet just hanging over the ground.

"Put me down." Bellamy insisted.

"I was just going to," Alex said. Then he set her down right in my arms.

"You two are ridiculous," she muttered, trying to squirm away. I held her a little tighter.

"Uncle Alex," he mused. "It has a certain ring to it." He held out his fist between us. "Congrats, man."

"Thanks."

Bellamy made a small sound and glanced down.

"What?"

"Look," she murmured, pointing to the store we just happened to be standing in front of. It was a baby shop, blankets and clothes in the window.

"I had a blanket just like that when I was a baby," she murmured. "Mom had saved it in case I ever had kids." Her eyes averted. "She probably doesn't have it anymore."

I set her down and took her hand. "Come on," I said, tugging her toward the store.

"Really?" she asked. "Isn't it kinda soon?"

I scoffed. "No."

I held the door open for Bells, but she turned before going inside. "Aren't you coming?"

Alex looked like a deer caught in headlights. It was funny as shit. "Me?" he stuttered. "Uh, I don't do babies."

"Why not?" she demanded.

"That ain't my kid!" He pointed. "Baby shopping is where I draw the line." He shook his head and muttered, "Brother husbands."

"It's your nephew." Bellamy insisted.

His eyes flew to me. "It's a boy?"

I nodded.

"Well, shit. We gotta get some shit in blue." He came forward and ushered her inside.

She went ahead, already drawn to all the tiny clothes, but Alex hung back. "Dude," he murmured for my ears. "Is this a happy accident?"

I grabbed him by the shirt. "Don't you call my son an accident again," I growled.

His eyebrows rose. "You planned this?"

I let go of him. "Not exactly."

"So…?" He coaxed.

"I want this baby," I told him. "A lot."

"Yeah, I can see that." He nodded. "I guess I could get used to a baby being around."

I rolled my eyes. "I'm so relieved."

"Put him on a little pair of skis."

"Snowboard." I corrected.

"Now why you gotta be like that?"

"'Cause it's my kid," I pointed out.

"Look," Bellamy said, inserting herself right between us as if we weren't just standing there having a debate.

We both looked down at the same time as she held up a white blanket with a yellow duck in the corner.

"They got it in blue?" Alex asked. "I'm gonna go see." Off he went in search of a blue blanket.

Bellamy glanced up, her smile soft as she rubbed her hand over the soft white fabric.

I put my hand on her belly and leaned down, kissing her forehead. "We definitely have to buy it."

"I miss my mom," she said in a quiet rush of emotion.

"I know, sweetheart," I murmured, pulling her close.

"Look at this!" Alex yelled through the store. We both glanced over to him holding up a giant diaper bag with the BearPaw logo on it. "You can carry your diapers around in it, L."

I gave him the finger.

Bellamy yelled at me because we were in a baby store.

"Come on," I said, pulling her along. "Pick out some more stuff."

"Well, I did see a little hat." She sniffled.

I chuckled. "Go get it."

She left my side to find said hat, and seconds later, someone sidled up to my side. Without looking, I put my arm around her and instantly stiffened, knowing it wasn't my girl.

I pulled back, looking beside me.

"Kelsey," I said, surprised.

"Here I thought you were excited to see me," she quipped, smiling.

"I thought you were someone else," I deadpanned and took a step back.

"I'm glad I ran into you," she said. "I was hoping I'd get the chance to see you before I left town again."

"What are you doing in a baby store?" I asked. Was she following us?

She held up a few items in her hand. "A friend of mine is pregnant." Her brow wrinkled. "What are *you* doing in a baby store?"

"We're shopping," Bellamy said, coming out of nowhere. "For *our* baby."

Kelsey slid a cool glance at Bells. Bellamy was already shooting her a flat-out icy look.

Da-yum.

"Bellamy," she said, polite. "I had no idea you were back in town."

"Funny. You looked right at me at the reception yesterday."

"I didn't recognize you. It's been a long time, and you look tired."

Bellamy sucked in a breath.

I stepped forward, angling in front of her. "Jealousy doesn't look good on you, Kelsey."

"I'm not—"

I cut her off. "I think we both know you are."

She sniffed, flicking her long hair over her shoulder. "Well, I'd say it was nice seeing you," she said, glancing at Bellamy.

"It wasn't." Bells finished.

Kelsey turned away from her completely. "Bye, Liam."

I gave her a gesture with my chin, then turned away toward Bellamy and lifted an eyebrow.

"Don't you give me that look," she intoned, then lifted her chin. "And I could have handled that."

"I know." But Kelsey hurt her once before. Years ago. I didn't do anything about it then, and I wasn't going to make the same mistake twice.

Besides, it was my job to protect her. Even from jealous bitches.

"Are we done yet?" Alex whined, appearing out of one of the racks. "I'm starving."

"Tacos," I said.

"Tacooos." Alex agreed.

We both turned to Bellamy. She nodded. "Tacos."

Alex and I high-fived.

Bellamy laughed beneath her breath. "I'll go pay."

I made a sound and plucked the items out of her hands. "I'm paying." Looking down at the blanket and hat, I frowned. "This is all you want?"

She shrugged. "It's still early. Besides, the company in this place leaves a lot to be desired."

I felt bad. What could have been a fun thing was sort of tainted by Kelsey and the fact that all this stuff reminded her of the relationship she was missing with her mother.

I went to pay, pulling Alex along with me. "So, hey, there's something I'm gonna need you to do," I whispered, keeping an eye on Bells.

I told him what I was thinking.

Alex glanced behind him at Bellamy, and a slow smile spread over the lower half of his face. "I got this."

19

Bellamy

For dinner, I made Liam and Holly pan-seared steak with a simple herb butter, roasted vegetables, and a baguette I picked up at a bakery in Caribou before we came home.

I ate Raisin Bran.

I was really hoping Dr. Crawford was accurate in his estimation that my all-day sickness would soon wane and I would actually want to eat something again. Though, I guess it was a win that I had some tacos with Liam and Alex earlier, and they stayed down.

After the cereal, I made some ginger tea because, frankly, I wasn't about to push my luck. The second I returned to the table and set down the mug, Liam dragged my chair so close to his they bumped together.

I glanced at the food on his plate and wrinkled my nose. Liam nudged the tea in front of me, and I lifted it, cradling the warm ceramic in my hands. Tucking my knees against my chest, I laid my head on Liam's shoulder while he and Holly talked about the resort.

"I need to make an appearance at the office," Liam said after a while.

I glanced up. "It's only been a few days."

"In the world of BearPaw, those few days will probably take me weeks to catch up on."

"Our executive team assures me they have everything handled and running smoothly." Holly assured him.

"I'm not about to leave Dad's entire life's work up to a bunch of suits."

"Haven't those people worked with Ren for years? I'm sure they understand his vision," I said, worried.

"I'm his son," Liam retorted, clipped.

"I know." I spoke gently. "Which is why I think you might need more time."

His fork hit the plate. "I'm perfectly capable of handling myself."

The tone he used was icy. He might as well have told me to mind my own damn business.

I wanted to clap back with something, but I didn't. Liam was hurting. This was a hard topic to discuss. Instead, I straightened away from his body and pulled the tea a little closer into my chest.

"*Shit*," Liam swore beneath his breath. His body rotated toward me, his eyes filled with regret. "I'm sorry, Bells. I didn't mean to snap at you."

"It's okay," I said.

His jaw tightened. "No. It's not."

"I know the team very well. I helped your father select them. I can assure you, Liam, they are not doing anything they shouldn't be." Holly spoke up.

Liam's eyes stayed on me for a lingering moment. I could tell he wanted to say more but held back. With an exhale, he turned to his mom. "They need to know that we are still in charge."

"They know." She promised. "But if it would make you feel better, we can stop in at the office tomorrow afternoon."

"Why not in the morning?" Liam quizzed.

"Oh dear. With everything, I forgot to mention it to you."

Liam's shoulders bunched. My eyes couldn't help but stare at his wide frame and the way it shifted beneath his T-shirt. "What?"

"We have an appointment tomorrow with your father's attorney."

"What for?"

I wanted to reach out and massage the knots I knew were in his back and shoulders. Even his neck looked thick with tension, almost as if he were bracing for more bad news. I didn't touch him, though. A small part of me worried he would shrug me off.

"The reading of his will."

Liam seemed surprised. "His will? I thought everything went to you."

"Not everything."

"Like what?" Liam demanded.

"I'll let the lawyer explain tomorrow."

"I don't want any money," he partly growled. "I don't want anything. I'm not going to benefit from the fact that my father was murdered."

"Liam!" Holly gasped.

My feet dropped from my chair onto the floor when I sat up. Tension permeated off him in waves, as did anger.

"That's not what this is!" Holly exclaimed.

"It's what it feels like," he muttered darkly, tossing his napkin down and stalking out of the room onto the freezing-cold deck. I watched his white breath blow around his head as he paced to the railing, looking every bit like a king purveying his land.

Both his hands slid into the pockets of his jeans, and it was almost as if he gripped the front of his thighs inside the material.

"He's so angry," Holly said, glancing at me. "At first I thought—" Guilt flashed in her eyes.

"You thought it was me he was angry with," I said because she clearly wouldn't.

Her lips pressed together, and her head bobbed. "But then I saw him with you… at the reception. He still looks at you like you're his entire world."

I admit the fact that Holly noticed the way Liam looked at me made the way he'd just snapped at me seem a hundred years in the past.

Truth was I wanted to be Liam's world because Liam was mine.

"He's mad at himself," I murmured, glancing through the giant sliding doors. "He blames himself." Tearing my eyes away from him, I met Holly's gaze. "I think he feels like he isn't in control."

Worry flared in her eyes. "You think he's relapsed?"

"I don't know," I replied, a little less than honest. I wasn't about to tell her about the pill I found because I had yet to bring it up to Liam. "But I definitely think he's struggling."

"I never should have kept him from you." Holly despaired.

I started to speak, hesitated, then delved ahead. "No disrespect, but I don't think Liam would do anything he didn't want to do."

"You think he wanted to stay away from you?" She seemed surprised.

She wasn't getting it. I shook my head slightly. "This isn't about you or me. About who Liam chooses to spend his time with. This is about Liam. Only Liam. And how *he* feels."

"Ren was a big part of his life," Holly spoke, grief abundant in her tone.

"And yours, too."

She nodded. "I think that's why I'm having a hard time helping Liam with his grief. Because my own is so overwhelming."

I sat forward and stretched my hand across the table, covering hers. "You don't have to do this alone."

"I'm so very sorry for the way I acted after the hospital…"

I squeezed just slightly. "You don't have to apologize. I can't even imagine being in your position."

"I'm ashamed."

"Don't be."

She slipped her hand from beneath mine, then grasped it. "You're good for him."

I definitely wasn't so sure of that, but I didn't bother saying it out loud. "Maybe we could push the will reading? Just a few days? Give him some time…"

Holly shook her head, adamant. "Liam needs to go. Not because of the money, either. Because of something else."

My eyes asked her what.

She shook her head. "For Liam."

I nodded, cautious. "I'll talk to him."

Her fingers gave mine a squeeze. "Thank you. I want you to come, too. Liam will want you there."

Her words turned my caution into concern. "Look, Holly…" I started. "If this is going to be something to upset him, I can't—"

"It won't."

Debating, I turned and stared through the door at Liam. The wind was blowing, mussing up his already messy hair. He had no coat on, and snow was blowing around.

Looking at him made my heart ache.

"I think I'm just going to head over to the resort," Holly said, getting up from the table. "Check in on the suits, as Liam calls them."

"I thought you said everything was fine there." I worried.

"It is. But it won't hurt to make sure. I can report back to Liam in the morning, maybe put his mind at ease. If only a little."

"Are you sure you're up for that?"

Holly smiled sadly. "I think so. Ren and I spent a lot of time at the offices. I have so many wonderful memories with him there, almost as many as we have here. Being there will help me feel close to him."

"If it's too much, call. We'll come."

Her smile was soft. "Take the alone time with my son. I think he needs it more than me right now."

A few moments later, she headed down toward the garage. The house was eerily silent when she was gone.

The sky was nearly dark, the first stars already out, ready to shine.

Before following Liam out onto the deck, I grabbed a large furry blanket and tucked it into my arms. He didn't turn when I came outside behind him. The only part of him that moved was his hands, which went a little deeper into his jeans.

I tossed the blanket around his shoulders, tugging it so it fell down his back, then moved around to tuck it closer to his chest and beneath his chin. Strands of his hair blew wildly about, as if not even the wind could contain them. The tip of his nose was pink and so were the peaks of cheekbones.

Silver eyes moved from the view down to me, staring at me in a way that left me naked and vulnerable. In the moment, he himself seemed bare, blatantly seeking out answers in my stare, silently asking me why I was still here.

The blanket slid off his shoulder, and I quickly reached to pull it back. My heart physically hurt as he stared at me. My arms felt heavy, my fingers stiff. Winter caressed the ends of my hair and the tops of my ears.

Still staring, still unspeaking, Liam stepped back from the railing, giving just enough space for me to fit against the wood. I slipped between, using the new position to fully pull the blanket around him and pinch it closed at his chest.

My limbs started to quiver, but it wasn't the frigid temperatures. It was the intense, heavy emotion emanating from Liam. He was simmering over with it. I wasn't quite sure how to reach him, how to prick the armor he wore so even just the tiniest amount could leak out.

His eyes stroked over me, hungry, but his arms remained in his pockets. "I'm sorry," he rasped. "I shouldn't have yelled at you."

"You can yell at me some more if it helps." I offered.

His eyes lifted, going back to the sweeping view. "A kingdom with no king," he spoke, almost to the wind.

I turned around to look out over the same view, and as I did, I wondered just how differently it looked through his eyes.

We both knew the throne was his. The keys to the castle already had his name engraved on them. I didn't say it, though, because I knew it wasn't what he wanted to hear.

"A kingdom shouldn't be inherited. A kingdom should be earned," he said behind me.

My cold fingers wrapped around the railing. Snowcapped mountains rose in the distance, blanketed by night.

"You don't think you've earned your place here? Because I think everyone else would disagree."

"Earned?" He scoffed. "I'm damaged goods. I lost my career because my body gave out. I lost my mind because I swallowed too many pills. My father is gone because I let Crone win."

My breath caught at the harshness of his words. Not the way he said them. No, he spoke matter-of-fact, as if he were telling me the weather. The harshness was in the way Liam meant them.

"And now what? Now I'm supposed to claim this place out of default? Because my father had the misfortune of only having me for a son? What happens when I ruin this, too?"

A sound of distress broke from me, and I spun. Threading my hand in the hair at the back of his neck, I forced his head down. "Don't say that! Your father was so proud of you. He loved you."

Liam lifted his eyes, staring over my head.

Grabbing his face, I forced him down again. "You are nothing by default, Liam Mattison. You are the very definition of a king."

The side of his lip curled up so fast I nearly missed it. Then his face went blank again. "What happens when I lose you, too?"

My breath caught. "What?" I croaked.

A million and one scenarios went through my head. At this point, it was a conditioned response. I turned, looking over my shoulder at the yard and the surrounding areas. Paranoia crashed over me like a heavy drape. "I thought he said I was free," I whispered. "I thought this was over."

Liam touched me then. Like a boat at anchor, I stopped floating away and merely bobbed in place. One hand, that's all. One hand curled around my hip. "You are free," he said, earnest. "Even if you weren't, that mother fucker would have to come through me to get to you."

That was a worse thought than Crone still coming at me.

"Then...?"

"I meant... what happens when I screw up and lose you?"

"That's not going to happen."

His hand dropped away from my hip. "Look how much I hurt you in the past four days."

"You have a right to mourn your father."

"Everything just feels so out of control," he murmured. I wondered if he realized he spoke out loud.

"Liam?" I asked, feeling as if I were dipping my toe into the most frigid water on a summer's day.

He didn't seem to hear me. He was lost to his thoughts.

"Liam," I said louder.

His eyes shot to mine.

I swallowed, taking a breath. Then I asked, "Are you using again?"

20

Liam

I watched Bellamy reach into the front pocket of her jeans and withdraw something. Still partially paralyzed by her question, I stared as she opened up her small fist to reveal a pill.

A pill that matched all the others in my pocket.

"Where did you get that?" I asked, my fingers spasming over the ones against my leg.

"You left it in the bed," Bellamy answered, lifting her eyes to me. "That night you came to Alex's and said nothing at all…"

Shame burned through me. "Bells," I whispered.

"Wait!" she said, throwing up her hand. "I need to say something first, before you say anything at all."

I raised my eyebrows.

"I don't care." She gasped, her blue eyes widened. "That came out wrong. I *do* care, so much. That's why I can't keep carrying this pill around in my pocket without saying anything. What I meant was if you are using again, if you are taking pills, it's okay. I'm with you. I'm with you no matter what. Your struggles are my struggles; your pain is mine. I know I'm not an addict like you, and I can't understand completely." Bellamy dragged in a ragged breath and plowed on, barely pausing.

My heart constricted. Then it rolled over.

I stood outside in the freezing wind, feeling numb as fuck and ripe with pain. But watching her in all her bumbling, animated glory, with the sincerest expression and near desperation in her eyes to make me understand just how much she loved me…

I felt the rays of a sun that wasn't even awake.

In that beat of a heart, I was the luckiest bastard on the planet, no matter how much I'd lost. Because I had her.

"I'll make sure you get help. That you have all the resources you need. I love you anyway. No matter what." She drew in another breath, looking up at me with shining eyes.

Waiting for me to answer. To admit or explain.

I had nothing.

No words. Just feelings. Just beats of a heart that lived inside my chest but belonged to her. All the fighting I'd been doing to keep my hands at bay, all the control I inflicted upon myself snapped so violently my insides stung.

The blanket she'd so lovingly draped over my shoulders flew back and drifted to the ground. My arms slipped around her and pulled her tight against my front. Curling my body in, I molded around her small frame, touching as much of her as possible, cocooning her body with mine.

A rough, keening sound ripped from my throat and floated away with the gusty wind as my lips latched onto hers. The second we touched, the spark ignited, a full blaze sweeping through me, making it hard to rationalize what I was doing.

I kissed her as if my life depended on it. Like I was drowning and she was air. Slanting my mouth over hers again and again… and again. My teeth knocked against hers, but I adjusted and just kept kissing.

Her body began to slide down mine, and I made a sound, lifting her off her feet. Bellamy climbed up my body, hooking her ankles at my back. I sucked her lower lip into my mouth, milking it and massaging it, then did the same to her upper lip.

My entire body vibrated with intense want. Need hammered so forcefully inside me it felt as though my veins might rupture, and then all that would be left of me was a sea of red.

Bells ripped her mouth away and sucked in air. I kissed across her jaw and down her neck. Her nails sank into the back of my neck while my hands dragged down to cup her ass.

Turning from the railing, I walked to the doors, pinning her body against the glass and pushing a hand up the front of her shirt. The lacy bra she wore was no match for my fingers. I ripped down the lace cup and availed my palm of her silky flesh. Bellamy arched into me with a low cry, her nipple hardening instantly between my fingertips.

I went back for her mouth, sweeping my tongue inside, trying to taste every last flavor she could be. It wasn't enough. It wasn't nearly enough. Gripping her hips, I pulled her body down as my pelvis surged up. Her core met with my rock-hard dick, and my mouth fell away from hers.

"Fuck," I swore, rotating against her again.

Her small hand found the hem of my shirt, skirted beneath the fabric, and delved just below the waistband of my jeans.

Pulling back, I held her tight and opened the slider. I strode through the house, past the abandoned dinner plates, and toward the stairs. Bellamy's lips latched onto the side of my neck and sucked while one of her hands tangled in my hair. I barely recalled carrying her down the stairs and striding through the place toward our room.

The door slammed when I kicked it behind us, rattling everything hanging on the walls. Bellamy's mouth released my neck, and the cool air brushed against where it had been. I shivered and pushed her head back to the spot.

"You aren't done yet," I growled.

She sucked me back into her mouth, nipping lightly with her teeth. I groaned and pushed her body against the door, reaching between us for the buttons on her jeans.

My hand brushed against her panties. They were already damp with her desire. A hissing sound escaped my lips as my fingers rubbed over her center.

Bells's head fell back against the door, and I lifted my head, still wanting her mouth on me.

"There's a mark," she rasped, her lips swollen and her eyes heavy.

"Good," I rumbled and stroked over her center again. She cried out, but I swallowed the sound as I kissed her, shoving my tongue so deep she made a sound and drew back just slightly.

I stiffened, reality crashing into me, and I realized what the fuck I was doing. Even though I wanted to move fast, I didn't because I was holding her and she needed my support. Slowly, I stepped back enough to slide her down to the floor.

Her legs wobbled when she put weight on them, so I held her gently at the waist.

"I can't—"

She made a short mewing sound. "Yes, you can."

I shook my head, trying to beat back the desperation pumping through me. "No."

"Liam." She reached for me, and I wrenched away.

She stumbled when I let go, falling forward. I cursed and went back, scooping her up and cradling her close.

"I don't trust myself, Bells. Not with you. Not right now."

"What?" she said, looking at me through desire-heavy eyes.

I stared at her lips, slick and swollen. I thought about the cream between her legs and how warm and silky it was.

"I went to the doctor. You saw for yourself. The baby is fine."

Temptation slashed through me, and my lips were on hers again.

"No," I said, ripping them away a moment later. "It's not just the baby. It's you, too." I sat her on the bed and paced away. My dick was so hard it was throbbing and whispering wicked thoughts into my ear, making this even more difficult.

"I'm so desperate right now, Bells. So volatile. It scares me when I touch you. I don't want to hurt you. I'm so afraid I'll get lost inside you and not be able to control myself."

"You won't hurt me." Her voice shook with absolute certainty.

"No. I won't," I replied. "Which is exactly why you're staying over there and I'm over here."

She stood, surprise making her eyes round.

I held up my hand. "I mean it, Bellamy. I've lost so fucking much. I will not lose you, too. I will not do anything to jeopardize you. You're all I have left… You're my last link to fucking sanity."

"You need me," she said, a look coming into her eye.

I moaned. "Yes, I need you. I need you so much I'm willing to deny myself the thing I want most right now until I'm better in control. Until I'm positive I won't be too rough."

"I don't want you to be in control." She stepped forward.

I stepped back.

"Bells, stop," I said, true force in my tone.

She did, hurt flashing over her features.

"Sweetheart…" I began, and anger replaced the fear in her eyes.

"Stop it," she snapped. "Stop fighting for so much control. You don't need it. Not here with me. Not right now."

Bellamy lifted the shirt over her head and tossed it at her feet. My throat worked as I watched her breathing, the heavy rise and fall of her breasts. One was on full display from when I'd yanked down the cup before. The pink nipple was still erect.

"Take what you want, Liam."

"I won't," I said, coming up against the door, still staring at her chest.

She unhooked the bra and let it fall. Her hands covered her breasts and rubbed. A small sound of pleasure cut through the room.

"I want you, Liam. I want to feel you."

"Don't do this to me, Bells. If I hurt you, I would never forgive myself."

"You're hurting me right now. I ache for you. I want to give you the relief I know you need."

I swallowed.

She took a step closer and then another. I don't know how I stayed so still, because beneath my skin was a full-on rave.

"If you won't touch me, I'll just touch you," she murmured, stepping close. Her fingers undid my jeans and slid the zipper down. "Are you going to let me touch you, Liam?"

In response, I took her hand and pressed it against my dick.

She rubbed along it, then slipped all the clothes off my lower body. Her hand slipped beneath the hem of my shirt as she dropped to her knees before me.

Dear God, nothing turned me on more than a woman who looked like she was praying over my dick.

Her nails dragged over my abs as her other hand grabbed my rod and held it out. She scratched my stomach again as her soft lips wrapped around the tip and slid all the way down.

A choked sound left my mouth, and I thrust forward, pushing my cock against the back of her throat. The pleasure-pain combination of her nails and the way her lips gently dragged back up my shaft literally made my knees shake.

I felt her gaze up my body as she took me deep again. Our stares locked as I watched her suck me good.

She sucked until my balls strained against my body, then released, pushing my length up against my stomach to draw my balls into her mouth.

Slowly, she drew back, leaving my slick, throbbing cock pointing straight at her. I glanced down, barely able to see through hazy eyes, and watched her slip her hand down into her crotch, move it around, and then draw it back out.

I shivered when she wiped the slick juices coating her fingers over the sensitive spot on my head.

My eyes rolled back. They reopened when she started kissing up my stomach, pushing the shirt higher as she went. I ripped it off over my head and leaned back against the door.

Bellamy arched against me, her warm chest rubbing mine.

Without any thought, I kissed her. Swirling our tongues together, wrapping my arms completely around her. Gliding my hands down her back, I delved into her jeans, beneath her panties, and cupped her ass. She pushed her cheeks into my hands and dropped her forehead to my chest.

Slowly, my hands crept down into her crack and toward her dripping center. Her legs were shaking when I brushed a finger over her bud while my other hand caressed her ass.

On instinct, I picked her up, pinned her against the wall, and thrust upward. A sound of frustration filled the room when my dick met fabric and not her hot center.

"I trust you, Liam," she whispered.

I drew back. "I love you so fucking much it scares the shit outta me."

Her palm lay against my cheek. "I know."

In one swift move, I had her on her back on the floor. I yanked the remaining clothes off her body and pushed her legs wide with my palms. I sat there on my knees between her legs, holding her thighs wide and staring at her glistening center.

Her legs stayed wide when I moved my hands. I speared her with my dick in one swift push.

Both of us cried out, and yeah, I might have said a little prayer.

Breathing heavy, I pulled back and plunged into her again. And again.

Then once more.

Her body rocked against the carpet as I pushed deep, her teeth sinking into her lower lip.

I pulled back, and she whined a little, reaching for me. "Don't stop."

"Oh, sweetheart," I rumbled, picking her up off the ground. "I'm just getting started."

I took her against the wall, across the dresser, and then I mounted her on the bed. Her sweet ass lifted in the air for me made me want to hammer in her as deep as humanly possible.

I didn't, though, taking it nice and slow because, as I discovered, when it came to Bells, I had control, even when I had none.

My baby was inside her. My heart might as well be.

Here I thought I would have to almost angry fuck her to get some relief, but I was wrong.

So wrong.

Pulling out, I moved her so she was under me. Her hands slipped up my chest, cupping my pecs. Her thumb drew lazy circles on my neck. Bending down, I rubbed my stubbled chin over her lips and cheek. Our lips caught and held when I moved back into her body, going deep and rocking slowly.

Pushing up, I held myself over her, staring down with awe and lust swirling inside me. "I was never going to find it," I rasped, pushing into her and rotating my hips. "By carrying those pills around in my pocket."

She moaned and opened her eyes. "Find what?"

"Control. Peace."

Bellamy reached around and gripped my ass. I quickened my pace, release working its way up from my balls.

"Let go," Bellamy whispered.

I bore down, pumping into her as rough as I dared. She called out my name over and over, until it was literally the only thing I heard.

She came apart beneath me, and I shattered over her.

We both clung to each other, quaking with aftershocks, her inner walls flexing, milking what was left of my erection, stroking it. Teasing it… Challenging it.

A few minutes later, I pushed up and glanced down, thrusting into her again.

Bellamy's eyes went wide. "Again?"

I was partially shocked. Then again, she literally had no idea how badly her body called to me. How badly I'd been starved.

I began backing out, but Bellamy pushed me back in. Her body was warm and soft. Her walls stretched to fit me perfectly.

"Bells," I whispered, wrapping my arms around her body and holding her to me as I thrust with renewed lust.

She gave up complete control, and oddly, it made me gentle.

After I erupted the second time, I fell off to the side, wholly spent. Bellamy rolled with me, draping her body over my chest and snuggling close.

"I know you don't see it," she murmured, her fingertips dancing over my abs. "But you are a king. The king of my body and of my heart."

I chuckled. "Then I guess that makes you a queen."

She propped her chin on my chest. "Do you feel better?" she asked, a little twinkle in her eye.

"I didn't hurt you, did I?"

"No."

"Yes. I feel better."

She laid her cheek against my chest, and I lightly rubbed her back.

"Liam?" she asked after a while.

"Hmm?"

"You haven't taken any of those pills."

"No, I haven't."

"But you've been carrying them around."

"Every day," I said, truthful.

"Why?"

"In case I needed them."

She nodded and snuggled closer. "Kind of like my emergency bag I used to keep in my closet."

I stilled. That fucking bag. I hated it. I hated everything it stood for. I hated she kept it, that it gave her something she needed to feel secure.

She had an emergency duffle, and I had a pocket full of pills.

The only difference was her bag couldn't fuck up her entire life.

"Where is that bag?" I asked, dragging my fingers up her spine.

"I don't need it anymore," she murmured.

My fingers stopped, and she lifted her head.

"Why don't you need it anymore?"

"Because I have you. If I used that bag, it would mean I would have to run away from you. I don't want to go anywhere you aren't."

Holy fucking shit.

Her emergency duffle and my pocket full of pills, while very different, offered the same thing: escape.

Escape Bellamy didn't want.

My chest was tight. So tight it burned. The lump suddenly in my throat choked me, and my fingers visibly trembled when I brushed the long strands of her blond hair away from her face.

"There's something I need to do."

21

Bellamy

"Like right now?" I asked, even as he carefully shimmied out from beneath my naked body.

He laughed. My God, it was such a pure sound that tears sprang to my eyes.

"Right now." He held out his hand, almost as though he were asking me to go on some adventure with him.

I put my hand in his, allowing him to pull me from the bed. I reached for my shirt, and he growled. "You don't need clothes where we're going."

I made a face. "Says the man who is literally picking up his jeans."

White teeth flashed, and my heart skipped a beat. A laugh. A grin. In the span of a few heartbeats.

He was lighter.

Suddenly, Liam seemed a little less frosty and just a little bit warmer.

What can I say? I was really good in bed. *wink*

"I'm not putting them on," he said, draping them over his shoulder and reaching for my hand again. He led me into the bathroom and stopped in front of the toilet. "I need you to help me with something."

"I'm not holding your wang while you take a pee."

Liam's hair flopped when he threw his head back and laughed. Then he laughed some more.

My lips twitched because his amusement was kinda funny, but at the same time… What the hell was he laughing at?

"Baby, no one says wang. And men don't 'take a pee.' We piss."

I wrinkled my nose. "So you can say things like ass taxi, but I can't call your thing a wang?"

His lips twitched. "You can't call it a thing either."

"Well, what should I call him, then? *Your Royal Highness?*"

Liam seemed to consider it. I smacked him in the stomach. "Why are we standing over the toilet, Liam?"

He pulled the jeans down and delved his hand into the pocket, withdrawing a palm full of pills. Sadness washed through me, but I tried to hold it back.

I failed.

"Oh, *Liam.*"

"Don't you feel sorry for me, Bells."

"I don't. I'm sorry you felt you couldn't come to me."

He smirked. "I just did. Twice."

I gestured to the pills in his hand. "This isn't funny."

"I know it's not," he said, serious. "I've been carrying these around, almost tempting myself." His voice dropped an octave. "They aren't even mine. I stole them out of Mom's medicine cabinet. They were Dad's."

"Maybe that's part of it, then." I hypothesized. "Maybe you took them because they were your father's."

His voice was stern, "Don't make excuses for me."

"So why didn't you take any?" I asked.

"You believe me?" he asked, curious. "That I didn't take any?"

"Yes," I answered without hesitation.

"Why?"

"Because even if you did take them, I would still be standing here. I would still love you just as much."

"I think that's why I didn't take any," he confided, glancing between me and the pills. "That night I came to Alex's. The night I crawled in bed with you?"

I nodded.

"I was close that night. So close to swallowing a few."

My stomach ached thinking of it. Picturing him standing upstairs in the bathroom, staring at the pills, internally debating if he should. "Why didn't you?"

"I was at my breaking point that night. Instead of taking the pills, I came to you."

"You didn't say anything," I whispered.

"I didn't have to. Being beside you was enough." He twirled the length of my hair around his hand.

A tear splashed over my cheek. "I've been so worried about you." I wrung my hands together. "At first, I thought you hated me. And then I found the pill, and I was terrified you relapsed. I wanted to ask so many times."

Liam let go of my hair and shifted closer. "I will *never* hate you." A low sound vibrated his throat. "You should have said something. All that stress on you and the baby. I'm sorry, sweetheart. I'm so fucking sorry."

I shook my head. "I'm just glad you didn't relapse."

"And I'm not going to." He confirmed. "You know why?"

"Why?"

The silver-gray of his eyes was mesmerizing. The way it changed and flashed with every emotion that went through him.

"Because I have you," he murmured, brushing a thumb over my cheekbone. "Because I don't need an escape from any of this. Because escaping would mean running away. I don't want to be anywhere you aren't."

A sob broke out of me. "That's my line," I wailed.

Liam hooked the arm not holding the pills around me and tugged me close. His lips kissed my hairline and then the center of my forehead. I looked up, and he kissed a tear off my cheek.

"I can handle anything as long as I have you." He pulled back, brushing his hand over my stomach. "This little guy, too."

I watched as he dumped all the pills into the toilet. The white tablets floated around before he reached over and flushed.

"Wait," I said and rushed from the room. I found the pill I'd had in my pocket and brought it to him as well.

He plucked it out of my fingers and flushed it, too.

When all the pills were gone, he exhaled and smiled as though a giant weight had just been banished from his shoulders.

"I'm so proud of you," I said, going forward and hugging him. "I can't even imagine how hard that was. But you did it."

"I did it for you."

"No." I pulled back quickly. "You do that for *you*. No one else. You are worth being sober for, you and you alone."

"Hey," he crooned, taking my hand. His voice was almost shy considering we were standing in front of a toilet naked, holding hands. "This doesn't mean I'm cured," he said, cautious. "I'm always going to be an addict. There's always going to be that... *urge* inside me. I was strong enough today, but I might not be strong enough a year from now. It might not be the last time you find a pill in our bed."

"I said it outside. I'll say it anywhere. I'm with you. No matter what. I'll always be here."

"I love you, Bells."

"I love you, too."

Out in the bedroom, I pulled the shirt Liam had been wearing over my head, letting the fabric fall past my thighs.

"You feel like a shower?" he asked, wrapping his arms around me from behind. "I'll wash your back."

I reached up and fisted my hand in his unruly hair. "Mmm, yes, please."

The sounds of Charlie's low growl seemed to echo through the entire house. My body went taut, and I jerked away from Liam, eyes wide.

There was a loud knocking sound, and the dog started barking ecstatically.

Heart thumping all the way into my neck, I tugged at the shirt I was wearing. "Liam?"

His body was tight as he listened. The dog continued to bark, and then the doorbell rang.

Liam relaxed instantly and came to me. "Someone's at the door. That's all." He assured as Charlie continued to bark. "Mom will get it."

"Your mom isn't here. She ran an errand."

He flashed a smile. "Well, I guess that's good, considering the show we put on out on the deck."

I knew he was trying to make me feel better, that the fear on my face had probably been intense. I blew out a breath and tried to smile.

"I'll get it. It's probably just someone with another damn casserole."

Suddenly, the idea of being down here alone was very unappealing. "I'll come with you."

"You aren't wearing pants," he pointed out.

"You aren't wearing a shirt."

He shrugged. "It's a double standard, sweetheart. What can you do?"

I stuck my tongue out at him as he left the room, hollering for Charlie to shut up. I grabbed a pair of yoga pants to pull on beneath Liam's shirt and then pulled my hair up into a messy topknot.

By the time I was done, my heart had returned to normal, but I was still shaken.

Between my reaction out on the deck earlier and then again with the door, I was beginning to realize something.

I still didn't feel safe.

I was beginning to wonder if I ever would.

22

Liam

Did I ever mention I'm not a fan of casserole?

Kinda wished it was a casserole on the other side of the door right now.

"Joiner," I said, regarding my trainer/coach. "I didn't know you were in town."

"Mattison," he replied, looking me up and down. I wasn't offended. It was kinda his job to assess how I was.

Rather, it used to be.

"I came to pay my respects to your father. I was hoping to see you at the reception, but you, ah, left early."

"You went to my father's memorial?" I said, oddly touched.

He cleared his throat. "I know we, uh, like the snow and all, but you mind if I come in?"

"Shit, sorry, Tom," I said, shoving open the door and letting him in. When I turned from the door, he was already taking off his coat and boots.

Guess this wasn't going to be a quick visit, then.

When he was done, he regarded me. "Of course I came. Renshaw was a hell of a man. I had no idea he was sick. You should have told me, Mattison."

"I told you I was having some personal problems," I muttered.

"Your father dying goes beyond that."

"It wasn't the cancer that killed him," I said, my throat tight.

"I heard. No need for you to rehash it all now."

I relaxed a little. "Beer?"

"I could do with a beer."

I led him to the kitchen where I tossed him a longneck and then grabbed one for myself. I would probably need one for this conversation. Seeing him was like a kick in the nuts.

Tom Joiner was a visible reminder of all the years I spent working toward something and how quickly that something got smashed to hell.

Oh, wait, that was my knee.

My dreams and life just followed suit.

I popped the top off the beer and took a long pull, the cold liquid sliding down easily. There was some movement in the doorway, and my mouth kicked up a little. "Bells, come here."

Joiner lowered the beer from his mouth, suddenly interested.

Charlie walked in first, Bellamy close behind. She was still wearing my shirt with some pants on underneath it. Her cheeks were a little pale, which concerned me, and I wondered if it was the baby kicking around her stomach or the scare of the sudden visitor.

The dog sniffed in Joiner's direction, but when he held out his hand, Charlie stuck by Bells.

That led me to believe it wasn't the baby. She was nervous, and Charlie sensed it.

I held out my arm, and she walked into it, fitting herself at my side. "Bellamy, this is Tom Joiner," I said. "My old coach."

"Current coach." He corrected.

"Oh, hi!" Bells said, going forward to shake his hand. "I've heard so much about you. It's nice to meet you."

"Wish I could say I've heard a lot about you." Tom slid a sly glance my way.

I gave him a look that said I wasn't too happy with his remark. She took his comment in stride, though, merely shrugging. "Liam is a man of few words."

"Well, that's the truth," Joiner quipped.

"Bellamy is my girlfriend," I explained. Once again, I was annoyed that I had to use that word to describe her.

Joiner smiled. "I know. I might not have seen you at the service, but I saw everyone else. You might be a man of few words, but everyone else in this town likes to talk."

"Thank you for making the trip for the service. I'm sure Ren would appreciate it," Bellamy said.

Joiner smiled wistfully. "He was a real one-of-a-kind."

I wondered if it would ever get easier. Talking about my dad. Remembering him. Not being so fucking angry about the way he was taken.

As if she sensed it, Bellamy shifted closer, her hand covering the back of my neck and rubbing soothingly. I glanced at her, thinking about the time we had just before Joiner rang the bell. *So fucking grateful.* I was so lucky to have her in my life.

I knew if she wasn't, I probably would have fallen into the bottom of a pill bottle by now.

Bells said I had to stay sober for me, that I alone was worth sobriety. I supposed she was right, but the truth was I loved her more than myself. I loved my son more than myself.

They were powerful fucking motivators to keep the pills out of my gut.

They were also very powerful motivators to make sure nothing like what happened to Dad happened to them.

I haven't forgotten you, Crone. Oh, no. Your time is coming.

"I was hoping we could talk," Joiner said after a few beats of quiet and some more of his beer.

"Sure." I agreed. I mean, the man came all the way to Caribou to pay his respects to my father. And he was a huge part of my daily life for over eight years. As much as I didn't want to, the least I owed him was a conversation.

My hand settled at Bells's waist and tried to pull her along with us. She resisted lightly, saying, "Go ahead. I'm just going to make some tea. I'll be right there."

I swung around completely, blocking out my coach and focusing solely on her. Cupping her cheek, I asked, "You feeling sick?"

Her lips turned up. "Just a little."

I frowned. "Was before too much?" Fuck, I knew better. I'd been keeping my hands off for a reason.

Both her palms rested on my bare chest. "Definitely not. I'll be right there."

I led Tom out of the kitchen to the living area, where we sat across from each other. I hadn't seen him over a year. He looked the same, though, short, dark hair peppered with white, clean shaven, and trim build. He was dressed in what I thought of as his uniform, athletic pants and a pullover.

"I understand now why you've been so adamant about not returning to the pros," Joiner said, getting right to it.

Actually, you have no clue.

"It's not just my father." I began, kind of bitter. I shouldn't be bitter, not with Tom. He was operating on barely any information. In his eyes, there wasn't much standing in the way of me and the pros. He just didn't get it. And I couldn't tell him. Part of me wanted to, you know?

Just drain this beer, sit back, and spill every last dirty detail of the past few months. Wouldn't his face be a sight then? He'd probably get up and leave without any other conversation.

Then I could really kiss boarding good-bye.

I wouldn't do that, though.

Not because I was clinging to hope of returning. Well, maybe a small part of me was. It was selfish to involve an innocent man who'd been like a second father to me half my life. I couldn't drag him down with my problems.

Plus, there was the pesky gag order the FBI was choking me with.

"Level with me," Joiner said, sitting forward. "How bad is the knee?"

"Weak," I replied, short.

"Operational? Trainable? Returnable?"

"It doesn't matter."

"The fuck it doesn't!"

"Why are you pushing this?" I exploded, standing. "Jesus, Tom. My father just died, and you're riding my ass like a horny gay man."

"Liam!" Bellamy gasped.

I spun, seeing her standing nearby with a white mug cradled in her hands and the tag on the end of the teabag fluttering against the porcelain. Her cheeks were still pale, and I knew her insides were all twisted up.

"Sorry, sweetheart," I muttered, making my way to her side to escort her to the couch.

"I'm not the one you should be apologizing to." She admonished.

I glanced at Tom. "Sorry," I muttered.

After she sat down, Bellamy leaned around me to look at my coach. "We don't care if you're gay."

"I'm not gay," he answered, bewildered. "But thank you…?"

I chuckled and sat beside Bells. Just having her in close proximity made me feel a little less… hotheaded.

"Ren called me," Joiner said, his voice quiet and serious.

"What?" I perked up. "When?"

"Right after the last call you and I had, you know, when you quit on me."

It was the last day of my father's life. Joiner was one of the last people to speak to my dad.

My voice was hoarse when I spoke. "What did he say?"

"He wanted me to give you a little more time. He, ah…" Tom picked up the beer and took a pull like he needed a minute.

I did the same because it seemed like a pretty good idea. At the small of my back, Bellamy's hand rested, just above the waistband of my jeans. Her palm was warm, probably from the mug in her hand.

"He told me he was dying."

Shock rippled through me. No, it wasn't a secret, but it wasn't something we went around announcing either. "He told you?"

Joiner nodded. "He asked me not to give up on you. He was worried you were giving up boarding because of him. Because you're stubbornly loyal."

Bellamy laughed beneath her breath. "So true."

"Is not," I grumped, emotion swelling so forcefully in my chest it made me squirm.

Tom continued. "He believed in you. The way he talked about you… He was so proud."

I picked up the beer again, draining it. The glass made a hollow thud when I plopped it back on the coffee table. Shoving to my feet, I prowled over to the windows overlooking the ski slopes and whitecapped mountains.

God, I loved it. Every day that went by that I wasn't out on the powder, I felt like a piece of me got smaller.

"I've got a team of the best sports medicine and physical therapists lined up. They're all willing to come to you. I just have to make the call." Joiner pressed.

"No."

"You're one tough son of a bitch," Joiner said. I could hear him rise from his chair. "I figured you'd say as much."

I didn't say anything or turn around.

"What's your opinion on all this?" Tom asked Bellamy.

I stiffened. He had some balls, trying to drag my girl into this. Pivoting, I was about to call him out, but Bells replied first.

"It's not my job to have an opinion on this. My job is to support Liam, and if he says he's done, then he's done."

Joiner pursed his lips, then looked over at me. "I'll see myself out." He went to the door, and I trailed behind, stopping a few yards away.

Hand on the front door, he turned and glanced back. "You were the best boarder I ever worked with, probably ever will. If you ever need anything, just call. I hope all the ass riding I did didn't hurt our friendship."

My stomach flopped, and the beer I downed suddenly felt kinda bubbly. "It would take a lot more than that."

He half smiled. "Good to hear. Hey, I'll be in town through tomorrow. If you want to grab a bite, give me a call. No more shop talk. Just a meal between friends."

I nodded. "Sounds good."

Joiner glanced past me to where Bellamy stood. "It was nice meetin' ya, pretty lady."

"Nice to meet you, too."

I stared at the door after he'd gone, unable to do anything but mourn something I'd already thought I lost.

23

Bellamy

"Come with me."

I hadn't even known he was awake until his deep, sleepy voice filled the dim bedroom.

We were spooned together, my back to his front. I'd been lying awake for a while, just feeling him wrapped around me, listening to the sounds of him breathing.

He'd been solemn after the visit with his coach. I wanted to push him, to ask him why he kept denying he wanted to return to snowboarding.

But I knew why.

Liam had a list of a thousand reasons. The very bottom was his own knee. It seemed like talking it to death wouldn't change his mind. It would take something more than words to convince him.

I just wished I knew what that was.

Rolling toward the sound of his voice, I smiled sleepily at him. "Hi."

He kissed the tip of my nose. "Hey there, beautiful."

Reaching out, I scratched the underside of his chin. His scruff was quickly turning into a beard.

"So how 'bout it?"

Of course I'd go with him. "Where are we going?"

"To the reading of the will."

My hand fell away from his face. "Am I even allowed?"

He made a rude sound. "You're family."

"Not technically."

He scowled. "I want you there."

"I'll be there, then," I replied, secretly praying his mom didn't take offense.

Liam smiled and began running his fingers through my hair. "How you feeling this morning?"

"Ask me after I get up and move around."

He leaned in and kissed me tenderly, drawing it out until a haze of desire relaxed my limbs. "How about that shower we never took last night?" he murmured, drawing back.

I nodded, and Liam nearly leapt out of the bed, scooped me up, and carried me into the bathroom. I made it through the shower, getting dressed and doing my hair before a wave of nausea hit.

I managed to swallow it back but took a mug of ginger tea to go.

The reading of Renshaw's will was located on the executive floor at the main lodge of the resort. The attorneys thought it might be more comfortable for everyone to do it there.

I didn't think it mattered where it happened; it would be emotional either way.

Liam grew more tense the closer we got, and by the time we sat down in the boardroom, he was visibly agitated.

"Hey," I whispered, going to his side in front of a large window. "What's going on?"

"It just seems to soon. Dividing up Dad's stuff like it was never his."

"This place will always be Ren's. And he wanted this meeting. These are his final wishes."

"It's hard," he whispered.

"I know, sweetheart."

I saw him half smile in his reflection in the window. "There you go again, calling me sweetheart."

"You like it," I teased.

The door opened, and two lawyers walked in, dressed impeccably in their suits and ties. They went around the large conference table and sat down, then gestured for Liam, Holly, and me to take a seat across from them.

"Thank you for agreeing to meet today," one of the lawyers said.

"Like we had a choice," Liam muttered.

I slipped my hand into his, and we sat down. Holly seemed less anxious than Liam, but she was certainly subdued. Her pale cheeks seemed even paler with the black ensemble she was dressed in.

Liam wore jeans and a white dress shirt, the sleeves rolled up on his forearms. He'd trimmed his beard and combed his hair so he looked more put together than I knew he felt.

"Where is Mr. Alexander Carter?"

I perked up.

"What the fuck does Alex need to be here for?" Liam asked.

"I tried to call him. He didn't answer," Holly added.

Liam glanced at her sharply. "Why didn't you tell me he needed to be here?"

"I figured I would call him myself."

"I can call him now." I offered, pulling my cell out of my bag.

Liam put his hand over. "He's out of town."

Surprise raised my voice. "He is? But we just saw him."

"Something came up," Liam replied, cryptic.

"What came up?"

"Do we need to postpone?" he asked the lawyers, sounding hopeful.

And no. It didn't escape me he avoided my question.

"That isn't necessary," the lawyer answered. "You can fill him in, and he can come into my office when he returns."

Liam leaned toward his mom. "Dad left something to Alex?"

"I believe so."

"Let's get started," the lawyer replied, and both he and his partner opened up some folders.

The house, the cars, the bank accounts, and most everything went to Holly. It really wasn't a surprise.

"In the matter of BearPaw Resort, which includes all the property, buildings, business accounts, and any holdings of BearPaw Resort..." The lawyer went on. "Controlling interest of my shares and holdings are hereby transferred to my son, William Mattison."

Liam sat forward. "What?"

"Eighty percent of BearPaw Resort is hereby yours," the lawyer said. "The other twenty percent, Mr. Mattison has transferred to Alexander Carter."

Liam blew out a breath and sat back. "Alex."

Holly leaned toward her son. "Your father thought it was important to acknowledge Alex and his role in your life. You understand?"

Liam was shell shocked. "But what about you?"

"Me?"

"You founded this place with him. You worked alongside him in the executive suites. You know this resort and its workings a hell of a lot better than me."

"We built this place for you, Liam. As a legacy for you. BearPaw Resort isn't mine. It's always been yours."

Liam pushed out of his chair, walking to a cart filled with crystal glasses and a large water pitcher. I watched as he filled up a glass, looked at it, then set it down.

"Did you really think he wouldn't will this place to you?" Holly asked.

"No, I..." He glanced at me, and I nodded, encouraging him to continue. "I guess I didn't think of it at all."

Holly said, "You're taking over. It's only right it goes to you."

"Running and owning are two different things."

I wasn't sure about that, but I kept the thought to myself because it didn't really matter how I felt about it. Liam had his own thoughts and feelings.

The lawyer cleared his throat. "There's also the matter of the trust."

"Trust?" Liam asked, wrinkling his brow.

"Five million dollars. It's also been willed to Liam."

I sucked in a breath and stared at him.

"Five million," Liam echoed and looked at Holly. "Did you know about this?"

"Of course. We've been putting money into that account for you since you were just a little boy."

"You take it," he told her.

"I don't need it. Your father made sure I was taken care of. That money is yours."

"I don't want it," Liam burst out. "I don't want to get paid because my father was murdered."

"Liam!" Holly gasped.

I got up and went to him, placing a hand at his back.

He looked at me with steady, serious eyes. "I don't want it."

I knew he would feel that way. After our talk last night, I knew Liam didn't want anything he felt he didn't earn. He most especially didn't want anything that made him feel he was gaining something from the death of a parent.

"Then don't take it." I assured him, letting him know I understood.

"Your father wanted you to have that!" Holly gasped. "He wanted to be sure you were always taken care of."

"I have money, Mom."

"Yes, but…" She sat back. "This was from your father."

Liam frowned.

The lawyer spoke up, and it struck me how unfair it was a stranger was in the room, listening to such personal conversations. "If I may interject. It really doesn't matter if you want it or not. It's yours. It's in your name and is legally already yours. You can always choose to donate it if you truly don't want it."

"You can't!" Holly exclaimed.

"Put it in a new trust," Liam announced, touching my stomach. "One for my son." He glanced at Holly. "Dad would like that, knowing he made sure his grandson was taken care of."

"It's a boy?" Holly whispered, touching her throat.

"We aren't sure yet," I replied gently.

"I can arrange to have the money put into a trust for the child once he or she is born." The lawyer agreed.

"Mom?" Liam asked.

She nodded. "Yes, your father would like that. A way to be part of the baby's life since he isn't physically here."

"This baby might not have been here if not for him," I said, covering Liam's hand still on my midsection.

"Do it," he told the lawyer.

The quiet one nodded and began writing on his legal pad.

It was kinda surreal to know that my baby was a multimillionaire before he was born. It was a luxury, yes, but as a mother, it gave me a sense of peace because I knew he would always be taken care of.

"Is that it?" Liam asked, anxious to be finished.

"One more thing."

He sighed. I rubbed my hand over his, making him glance down. His pained eyes softened when they touched my face.

"The north section of land on BearPaw property, deeded to Renshaw personally, is hereby to be retitled at his request."

"North section of land?" Liam muttered. "That part of the resort isn't even developed. Nothing is out there."

"Not nothing," Holly answered.

We both turned to stare at her.

"The title is to be transferred to William Mattison, heir of Renshaw Mattison." The lawyer who previously hadn't spoken at all put in.

"What title?" Liam asked.

"I hope you will understand," Holly said. "He just wanted you to live your dream."

"Mom," Liam ground out. "What the fuck are you talking about?"

"Liam." I admonished. "Do not cuss at your mother."

He made a face.

Holly looked at the lawyer, who withdrew a white envelope from his pile of papers. "Mr. Mattison instructed me to give this to you in the event of his passing."

Liam glanced between the lawyer and the envelope he extended before going to take it. "This is Dad's handwriting," Liam said, staring at his name scrawled on the front. He tore his eyes away and looked at Holly. "What is this?"

"I'll let your dad be the one to tell you." She gestured to the letter.

Liam turned to face me, holding the letter between our bodies. "He wrote me a letter," he whispered.

"You should read it," I whispered back.

He swallowed so hard I heard it. He didn't look at anyone else in the room. Part of me wondered if he remembered they were even there. Still clutching the letter, he pulled me along to his chair and tugged me into his lap.

Once I was against him, he reached around me, ripped open the seal, and pulled out the piece of paper filled with Ren's writing.

His chin rested on my shoulder, but even though the words were in plain sight, I didn't read them. This wasn't for me.

This was one final conversation between Liam and his father.

24

Liam

Liam,

If you're reading this, then unfortunately, I'm not there to give this to you in person. I want you to know that of everything I've built in my life, my greatest accomplishment by far is you. I know you probably often wondered why you were an only child, and we often told you it was because we were so busy with the resort there had never been time.

That was partially true.

The real reason, my son, is because your mother and I never needed another child because you were more than we could ever ask for. You brought us more pride and love than five children ever could.

I know I've told you how proud of you I am, and I hope you know I truly meant it. You inspired me your entire life in ways you will never understand. You've always been so sure of yourself and who you are. You knew from the time you could barely walk that your feet belonged on a board. I know I pushed you at times, and at times you might have hated me for it, but it's only because I wanted you to reach the dreams I saw in your eyes from the minute you first touched snow.

I never expected you to run BearPaw Resort. Yes, I hoped you would always return home and that someday I might have you here at my side. This past year has been a dream come true in that sense, even though it came at a heavy cost for you.

I never wanted my dream to be realized at the cost of yours.

I can't be sorry that I had this time with you here, though. I love you, my son. So very much. Your strength and pride amaze me. I know you've committed to running this resort, something I know in my heart you will excel at, but I want you to have it all.

You don't have to choose.

Going back to boarding is not a betrayal to me. If anything, you __not__ going back is. I might have built this resort. I might own all these buildings… but, son. Son, you own the very mountain this place sits on. And not because you bought it. Not because you developed it.

Because this place is in your veins.

Take what's yours. Put aside your anger, your guilt, and even your fears. Go out of snowboarding in the same fashion you entered it. With passion. With heart and with determination.

Your mother and Alex can hold down the fort at the resort. It will be there after you've made your triumphant return.

I've built something to make it easier. To hopefully prove just how much I believe in you. It's my gift to you, my way of being there cheering you on, because it seems I won't be able to be there in person.

I hope you aren't angry with the liberty I've taken. Perhaps someday when you have a son of your own you will understand.

Whether or not you utilize the property that is now solely yours is up to you. Please understand, regardless, I am so incredibly proud to call you my son and wherever I am right now, I am watching over you and your mother with love.

Dad

I heard his voice as I was reading as if he were speaking right beside me. These final words meant more to me than any amount of money or property ever could.

For a moment suspended in time, it was as if he were still here. As if he wasn't gone. My heart knew peace, and the gaping, painful hole I'd been living with was blissfully gone.

I glanced up from the paper when the last word was read, the pain of his death assaulting me all over again.

Warm hands brushed over my cheeks, and I focused on Bellamy, who was wiping away my tears.

"Did you read it?" I whispered, voice raspy and low.

"No, those words are for you."

I nodded, drawing in a shuddering breath. "He built something," I said, trying to wrap my head around it.

"What?"

I shook my head and looked at Mom. "What is it?"

"Would you like to go and see?"

I stood, taking Bells and the letter with me. "Right now."

Mom glanced at the lawyers. "Could you call down and arrange a ride?" When she looked back at me, she said, "You're going to need a coat."

"I need some signatures on these documents to finalize everything." Lawyer number one cut in.

I swung around, Bellamy still in my arms. "Later."

"We're here now."

"I said later," I bit out.

He relented. "Of course."

"You'll need to go to the roof," lawyer number two said, hanging up the phone.

"The roof?" Bellamy echoed.

"Coats." Mom reminded me.

"We'll meet you at the elevators," I said and left the boardroom.

I was well aware of people staring as I walked along the executive floor. It was their first glance of me since the service and the first sight of me back in the office.

No one stopped to offer condolences, which was probably good news for them. I wasn't in the mood for that shit. This day wasn't about them. It was about my dad, his words… and how he'd somehow managed to make me feel a little less pain.

My assistant bolted up from behind her desk when I strode toward my father's office. "Mr. Mattison—"

"Liam." I reminded her.

"I wasn't expecting you today."

My feet stuttered. "Then why are you here?"

She glanced at Bellamy, who I was still carrying, and then at me. "It's my job to be here."

"Take the day off. Go home. Spend time with your family."

"Liam?"

I smiled because her confusion was kinda funny. "If someone told me to take the day off, I wouldn't still be standing there."

"Right," she said, still standing there.

I chuckled. "I'll be in tomorrow. But not too early. I gotta make sure my baby isn't torturing my girl."

Her eyes went wide. "Baby?"

"Liam," Bellamy whispered.

I put her down on her feet, keeping one arm anchored around her body.

"Baby." I agreed, rubbing her stomach.

"Oh! Congratulations." Her shock was pretty priceless.

"Thanks. Now go home. I'll see you tomorrow."

She grabbed her things and made a move for the elevator.

At the door to the office, I hesitated. A rush of emotion befell me as I stood there, hand on the handle.

Technically, yes, this was my office. But it would never really be. Not in my heart. In my heart, it would always be Dad's, and I would always picture him sitting behind his massive desk with the impressive view of his kingdom at his back.

You own the very mountain this place sits on. Dad's words echoed through me, and I admit it was the first time ever I felt like maybe I wasn't a king by default.

Shoving open the door, I swept my eyes over the place. It was filled with ghosts. The last conversation we had here. The ones we never had.

"You okay?" Bellamy asked at my side.

I glanced down at her, noting the patience and love in her eyes.

"I'm good," I murmured, kissing her hairline.

Before stepping over the threshold, I took her hand. Inside, I went right to the closet and pulled out a heavy coat and hat. Then I reached in for more and tugged a white BearPaw beanie over Bells's head.

"That coat is going to be huge on me," she said, peeking up from beneath the hat.

She looked cute as hell with all her hair falling around her shoulders. The blue logo on the hat made her eyes even bluer. "You're wearing it," I said, no nonsense in my voice. "You and my son are not going to freeze."

"We're going to the north section of the resort?" she asked, curious, as I pulled the coat around her.

It definitely was huge, but it would do.

"Seems so."

"What do you think it is?"

"I have no idea," I replied, pulling on my own coat and hat.

"That letter meant a lot to you," she said, stepping so close our shoes bumped together.

"Yeah." I agreed. After making sure the coat was zipped up around her and the hat covered her ears, I reached for her hand. "You ready for a helicopter ride?"

"A helicopter!" she squeaked.

I smiled. "The helipad is on the roof, sweetheart."

Her cheeks paled. Concern had me wrapping my arms around her. "Is it the baby?" I worried.

"No, it's the helicopter!" she said. "The one morning I'm not plagued with morning sickness and you drag me on a tin can with a propeller!"

Relieved, I laughed. "I can assure you our helicopter is not a tin can."

She didn't seem convinced.

"You want to stay here?" I offered.

"No!" She gasped. "I want to see the surprise."

"Helicopter it is," I declared, and we made our way up to the roof where the BearPaw chopper was already waiting.

Mom was strapped into the back, and I lifted Bellamy in, making sure all her straps and buckles were firmly in place. Then I put a headset over her head and kissed her on the mouth.

She gave me a wobbly smile as I climbed in the front seat beside the pilot.

The aerial view of the mountain and resort was impressive and honestly awe inspiring. It was a whole 'nother perspective of everything my father had built.

The sky was a cloudless blue, and the impossibly tall mountains rose into it like uncut diamonds glistening beneath the rays of the sun. Despite the pure blue of the sky, the predominant color even from up here was white. Snow blanketed the terrain impeccably, not a single blemish on the untouched landscape.

The pilot flew us away from the resort, away from the buildings, people, and ski runs. We went past the lift, and I couldn't help but glance down at the place where the men had forced Bellamy and tried to kill her, which had left us outrunning an avalanche.

You wouldn't know it by looking down now. It looked peaceful and pure from up here.

I glanced behind me, and our eyes locked. I knew she recognized where we were, and her memories mirrored my own.

"Approaching the north," the pilot said into our ears through the headsets.

Another mountain peak, seemingly bigger than the last, rose into the sky, and the pilot pulled back, flying us higher. In my ear, Bellamy gasped, and I grinned, glancing back at her again. She gave me an evil look that promised retribution when we were back on the ground.

I liked it up here. There was something about being in the sky that left me feeling weightless. Maybe I just felt closer to my father up this high, or maybe it was because of his letter and the fact we were going to see something he'd left behind.

When we crested the peak and flew through a white, puffy cloud, the landscape before us changed, flattening out to acres of untouched land, all covered in glistening white.

"Just up ahead," the pilot said and pointed.

I leaned forward, staring out the windshield as something large came into view. I glanced at him as if I thought maybe I was seeing things.

He grinned, his chuckle floating through all our ears.

I looked back, blinking.

We drew closer, and the pilot lowered the chopper a little, giving me the perfect aerial shot.

"Holy shit," I swore.

"I've never seen anything like it." He agreed.

My eyes were glued below us. I could hardly believe what I was looking at. My hand splayed across the freezing-cold glass as I pressed closer.

The pilot chuckled and circled around, making a large ring around the massive structure.

It was pristine. Perfection. A fucking living dream.

Suddenly, I spun, pinning my mom with a stare. "You knew about this?" I yelled over the engine, though we all had connected headsets.

She smiled, tears in her eyes. "I knew, but this is the first I'm seeing it. He was very secretive… This was a labor of love for him."

I glanced at Bells. She was crying.

My eyes flew back to the window, and I stared in wonder.

Holy. Fucking. Shit.

My father built me a superpipe.

25

Bellamy

I might not have known what it would take for Liam to allow himself to embrace his dream.

But it didn't matter.

Because his father did.

26

Liam

I stood there staring, blinking, then staring again.

My own private superpipe.

And my God, it was a sight to behold.

I knew just by looking at it the pipe was approximately eighteen feet tall, and an experienced boarder could get up to a fifteen-foot jump on it. The walls were so perfect, the snow packed to such perfection, I would wager half my bank account that I would be able to get up to twenty-eight MPH on this thing.

It was so fucking impressive I was speechless. My limbs literally quivered with the urge to grab a board and break it in.

I could practically taste the satisfaction, the adrenaline, and even the spray of the snow as I cut through it.

I mean, I literally had a hard-on right now. My dick was fucking rock hard.

"Jesus," I prayed, staring up at it. It was lined with massive floodlights so I could totally practice at night. There were American flags waving along its perimeter, and the silence that reverberated around this acreage would echo with the sound of a board cutting into snow.

There was even a small cabin off to the side, probably for storing gear and getting out of the elements. You know, if anyone wanted out of the snow.

I didn't understand those types of people.

The sound of a snowmobile coming up behind me made me turn. A few moments later, one of the men who ran the slopes for the resort climbed off and grinned at me. "Ain't she a fuckin' beauty?"

"You in on this, Glasko?" I asked, still freaking in shock.

Jon Glasko worked with my father my entire life. He was pretty much an expert at keeping our slopes running and packed with snow.

"You're damn right."

I held out my hand, and we shook. "This is a damn fine sight," I said, looking back at the pipe.

"Ren didn't skimp on this at all. It's top of the line. Some serious time and money went into this thing. It's fit for an Olympian." He paused. "Well, it's fit for you."

"How?" I asked, still staring.

"Time and money, my friend. Time and money."

I glanced around at Mom, who was standing close by, taking in the sight. "When did he have time to do all this?"

"Right after your accident. You were still in the hospital."

"I thought he was undergoing cancer treatments."

"He was. He was doing this, too. I've never seen a man more determined to get something done—and done right, I might add. He insisted this had to be ready when you were."

"Or maybe he wanted to get it done before the cancer got him," I murmured, glancing back to the structure.

"That, too." Mom agreed, sober.

All those months Mom and Dad had not been around so much when I was in the hospital. All those months I spent being angry about it.

This was what they were doing. Dad was battling cancer, but he still made time for this.

For me.

For something that would live on after him.

I threw out a hand, waving my fingers in the air. Bellamy stepped out, slipping her gloved fingers against mine. "Can you believe this?" I asked her.

"Sure makes the sweater I was going to get you for Christmas look lame," she quipped.

I laughed.

"This baby takes nine million gallons of H^2O to pack it with snow," Glasko said, proud.

I was proud, too. What a goddamn masterpiece.

"He trucked in a Zaugg machine to make sure it was done with absolute precision."

I whistled.

"What's a Zaugg machine?" Bellamy asked.

"It uses lasers to sculpt the pipe into the perfect shape," I replied.

"This is how sure he was," Mom said, coming to stand beside me and Bells. "He was so sure that you would return to boarding that he had this entire thing constructed, here at home, for you to use privately and to your heart's content."

"I could train here," I murmured. "I could practice and still check in on the resort. Still be here with my family." I glanced down at Bellamy.

"It's all right here." She nodded. "Yours for the taking."

No. It was mine for the earning.

I could prove I did in fact own this mountain. That snow was in my veins. I could leave my legacy on my own terms and step into a new one all on BearPaw territory.

Oh my God, I was tempted. Passion and fire burned in me brighter than it had in a lot of years. A renewed sense of energy and adrenaline coursed through, and the craving to win pounded in my chest.

The letter my father wrote sat in my pocket, the gift he built spread out before me.

"My knee might not hold up." I hedged.

"You won't know unless you try," Bellamy answered.

I stared at the pipe, still amazed my father believed in me just this much. Enough to bring my dream to me.

All the reasons I'd been denying myself sort of up and vanished. All the reasons I should do it suddenly reappeared.

"Do it, Liam." Bells urged. "Do it for yourself."

I dug into my pocket and pulled out my cell and hit a few buttons. The call went through, and seconds later Tom Joiner answered.

"Liam? You want to meet for dinner after all?"

"Forget about food, Joiner," I said into the line. "I've got something a hell of a lot better."

Bellamy made an excited sound and hugged me hard.

I couldn't help the wide smile that split my face.

Fuck yeah, I was doing this.

27

Bellamy

It was so good to see him like this.

It was something I honestly didn't think I would see so soon, but here we were. I smiled as I watched him, curled up in the center of the big bed with Charlie at my feet. He was a cross between an excited little boy and a man buzzed on really good liquor.

"I'm gonna have to get all my gear, make sure it's all still good," he said into the phone. "Hell, maybe I should get new gear."

He paused, listening.

"Yeah, yeah. Maybe call them up." He stopped mid-pacing and made a face. "You think they would do that? I don't know."

He glanced up at the ceiling as if he was surprised as Joiner said whatever he was saying in his ear. Liam began pacing again, a caged animal wanting to run.

"No shit?" he swore, turning and glancing at me. "All my old sponsors still want to work with me. Under Armour is making me some custom shit for my knee."

I grinned widely. "They know a sure bet when they see it."

His teeth flashed, and he chuckled. To Joiner, he remarked, "No, I'll call Chevy myself. They've been too good to me."

I listened to him and Joiner prattle on about everything humanly possible that was related to snowboarding and marveled at the fact they'd already spent several hours together at the pipe. They acted as though they had to plan everything in one night.

I sighed loudly, and Charlie lifted his head to stare at me. "Little boys and their toys," I told him, scratching behind his ear.

The phone Liam had been talking on landed on the end of the bed with a thump. "Whachya say about me?" he asked, raising a brow.

"Nothing," I replied sweetly.

My body bounced when he leapt on the bed and near tackled me. Charlie jumped up with a bark, and we all ended up in a pile on the mattress with me on the bottom. Of course, Liam made sure he held his own weight and the weight of the giant dog.

I squeaked and squirmed, making Liam chuckle and tickle me.

"Get him, Charlie!" I wailed, and the dog slobbed up Liam's arm good.

"That's nasty!" he insisted and sat back on his haunches. Charlie stood over me, wagging his tail and drooling everywhere.

Liam tugged the shirt he was wearing over his head and used it to mop up his arm. I lost interest in the game when his bare chest entered the equation. I didn't know how someone could look so warm and smooth when they had snow in their veins.

Liam noted how I stared, and a knowing smile transformed his face into a smug expression. Both hands planted on either side of me, and he leaned down.

Just as he was finally about to kiss me, his face screwed up and he drew back. "What the fu—" His voice fell away when he picked something out of the bed and made a face. "Woman, you're leaving them nasty raisins in my bed," he said, showing me the wrinkly fruit.

I giggled.

Charlie leaned over and ate it out of his fingers.

"Good boy!" I crooned as he went around sniffing for more.

"Probably gonna give him diarrhea," Liam quipped.

I smacked him. "They aren't that bad!"

"What else you got hidden in this bed?" he purred, leaning down to scoop me against his chest and roll. "Anything for me?"

His mouth covered mine before I could say anything, making the rest of the world fall away for a few quiet moments. Our legs entwined against the blankets, my hair sliding over my shoulders and brushing against his face. Liam didn't brush it aside or move against it. He put a palm against the back of my head and pulled me closer.

Liam was pretty much an expert with his tongue. He turned a French kiss into a dance, into seduction. With every stroke and lick, I became more electrified.

As he pulled back, he tugged my upper lip with him, not so committed to ending the kiss. I felt a little fuzzy when I blinked down at him, our gazes hidden from the rest of the room thanks to the curtain of my hair.

"It's good to see you like this."

"Like what?" he murmured, stroking my cheekbone with his thumb.

"Happy."

Shadows moved over his face, robbing just a little of that peace I'd seen before.

"It feels like a betrayal to feel anything but sorrow."

I smiled gently and rubbed over his stubble. "I know. But your father wouldn't want that. *This* is what he wanted. You filled with energy and determination. You living your life."

"Can you believe that pipe?" he asked, wonder coming into his stare. His lips curled up a little.

I almost felt a little jealous of that pipe. At its ability to bring him back to life like this. At the same time, I was so grateful. I wished Ren could be here to see him light up.

I smiled. "I'm so happy you're going to be using it. That you finally admitted how much you needed to do this."

Liam deserved so much more than to spend the rest of his life wondering *what if.*

Quickly, he rolled, coming over me, his steady, intense stare looming over mine. "You know I never could do this without you, right?"

I rolled my eyes. "You, *Mr. To The Extreme*, could do this in your sleep."

His grin flashed quickly. "You know what they used to call me, do you?" Then he whisper-sang, "Stalker."

I laughed low. "I told you I followed your career."

Liam leaned down and kissed my forehead, allowing his lips to linger against my skin. My eyes fluttered closed, and I wondered how the hell I lasted eight years without him.

When he pulled back, there was a serious note in his eyes. "Once, I could have done this in my sleep, but not now. Too much has happened. It's so fucking intimidating,"

I tilted my head. "*You*? Intimidated? Of what?"

"Going back. Worrying that I won't be able to live up to the name I held before. To the boarder I was. What if my days of being the best are over? What if my knee just won't perform, and instead of going out because my knee took me out, I go out because I just don't have it anymore."

I made a soft sound and wiggled until my arms were free and could loop around his neck. "I have never met anyone harder on themselves. I've never known anyone to be so confident yet at the same time fight for control."

"To the extreme," he quipped.

I smiled 'cause it was funny.

And true.

I closed one eye and squinted at him through the other. "Wanna know what I think?"

"Duh," he mouthed.

"Let go. Do this for the love of it. Because it feels good." I reached out and touched the sides of his lips. "Because it makes you smile like nothing else does."

He frowned. "That's not true." He grasped my hand and turned his face to kiss the palm. "You make me smile like that, too."

I smiled, but his frown intensified.

"I will not have you thinking that boarding makes me happier than you," he demanded.

"I don't—"

Liam cut me off. "Because I could never board again, and I would still be happy as long as I had you." He gripped me tighter. "I mean it, Bells. I wouldn't even be going back if you weren't here to support me. You make me feel like anything is possible."

I melted beneath the words, and I admit it was nice to hear because sometimes Liam seemed so hard to reach I couldn't tell if I loved him enough.

A low swear floated over my head. "Baby, you are more than enough. I'm sorry as hell I ever made you feel like you weren't."

I gasped, feeling my eyes widen.

He smirked. "Yeah, you said that out loud."

"I didn't mean to."

"I'm glad you did because it's how you feel, and I need to know this shit."

I rolled my eyes. "You have enough on your plate without worrying about my hormonal thoughts."

"The *only* thing on my plate that matters is you and my baby."

"I just want—" Stupid tears sprang into my stupid eyes. I blinked them away, not wanting them.

"What do you want?" he whispered, kissing my cheek.

"I want you to know how much I love you. How much I've always loved you since that first moment you found me staring up at the lift, scared as crap."

He laughed. "You were practically green with fear."

"I was not." I protested, even though I totally was. "I feel bad for everything I've cost you," I whispered, sharing one of my most painful thoughts. I knew we talked about it before, but this was just so hard to let go of.

He dropped his forehead to mine. "You've given me so much more than I even thought you could."

My voice wobbled with emotion I tried to hold back. "I watched you reading that letter today from your dad. It bruised my heart, watching the emotion play over your face. I took that from you."

"Can I tell you something? Something that will make me sound like a terrible man."

"You can tell me anything."

"Sometimes I wonder if Dad dying this way was better. If having it be fairly quick was easier than watching him slowly waste away with cancer."

My throat constricted. "Oh, Liam, that's not terrible. That just shows how much you love him."

A distressed sound broke from his throat. "You mean being glad he was murdered?"

"No!" I said firmly. "Being glad he suffered far less than he might have. Being glad he died on his own terms, not because of some horrible disease."

"It wasn't on his terms. It was Crone." Frosty was a kind way to describe the sound of his voice.

Chills raced up my spine, and I shivered. "You scare me when you talk about him."

His eyes flashed, and he glanced away, blowing out a breath. "I hate him, Bells. I hate him, and I won't lie and say anything else."

"I hate him, too." I confessed. "He took both our fathers."

Liam's jaw clenched and the skin around his eyes tightened. "I'll be damned if I let him take anything else from either of us."

"He won't. He said so in the note he sent."

Liam made a rude noise. "Yet you still practically jump out of your skin when the wind blows sideways or someone knocks on the door."

"I spent a long time running. A long time looking over my shoulder. Part of me wonders if that reflex will ever go away." I rationalized.

"It might be over," Liam murmured, hunching around me like a shield. "But you're still suffering."

"We all are," I added.

"It's exactly what he wanted," Liam intoned.

"So you believe him?" I asked. He pulled back and stared down at me. "Do you believe Crone will finally leave us alone?"

"Yeah, I do. The bastard gets off on knowing we have to live with the mess he made."

"Well, you know what they say," I said, dragging a hand through his soft, messy hair.

"What's that?"

"The best revenge is a life well lived."

Liam didn't say anything. Instead, he kissed me. I wasn't sure if that meant he agreed or if perhaps he was trying to distract me.

28

Liam

The best revenge is a life well lived.

Was it? Was it really?

It wasn't that I didn't plan on living my best life or making sure Bells did, too.

I just couldn't shake the feeling it wasn't good enough. Not for someone like Crone. For most scum, death was far too easy.

But then there were these special cases. The kind where death was the only option. It was the only way to be sure someone like him didn't keep coming back. The only way to make sure we *could* live our best life.

In truth, I wouldn't be able to fully relax until I knew this was well and fully over.

Yeah, I told Bellamy I believed the debt was paid. It wasn't a total lie. Part of me did believe it. Or wanted to.

And the other part?

It whispered that only a foolish man believed the promise of a man who lied for a living.

29

Bellamy

When the doorbell rang, I glanced up from my bowl of cereal.

Raisin Bran, of course.

Beside me, Liam set down his coffee and looked at me.

"Maybe we should just give Tom a bedroom here," I quipped, shoveling more of the crunchy flakes into my mouth.

"And why's that?" Liam wondered.

"Because if he's going to be coming over before I'm even finished with breakfast, he should just sleep here."

Liam chuckled. "It's not Joiner."

A fissure of alarm shot through me, and my spoon lowered to the bowl. Taking a deep breath, I reminded myself that people rang doorbells all the time. It was a common occurrence and didn't mean someone was about to try to kill me.

A warm, sure palm settled over my bare thigh. "Everything is fine. You're safe," he vowed, reading me without even trying. "It's for me. I have a delivery coming."

I perked up. "A delivery?" Then I remembered. "Snowboarding equipment? I know you're like a snowboard god, but that was fast, even for you."

Laughter filled the room, and the doorbell rang again.

On his way to answer, Liam called out over his shoulder, "It's not boarding shit. It's something for you."

"Well, why didn't you say so?" I exclaimed and jumped up to follow along behind him.

At the door, Liam winked. "That would just ruin the surprise."

He pulled open the door and smiled. Before he could say anything, Alex's dark head poked inside. "What's going on up in here? What took you so long to open the door?"

"Alex!" I called, giving him a wave.

"Hey there, baby girl. Long time no see."

"Feels like forever." I agreed.

"*Baby girl*," Liam intoned, staring between us. He pivoted toward Alex. "What the fuck did you just say?"

"Touchy." Alex grimaced.

"Do not call her that. Ever. Again." Liam fumed.

Alex glanced at me and winked. I giggled.

"If you hadn't just done me a solid, I would throw you the fuck out."

"You better watch your mouth," Alex said, pointing dramatically to something behind him.

I leaned around, trying to see, but the door and two large men standing there blocked my view.

Liam's shoulders relaxed. "You know I appreciate this. And so will *Bellamy*." He enunciated my name as if Alex might not know what it was.

It made Alex snicker.

"Appreciate what?" I asked, curious. "What are you doing here so early, and why haven't you come inside yet?"

"I got a special package," he replied, glancing at Liam.

Liam looked at me and smiled.

"What is going on?"

"Step aside, boys." A voice floated through the door.

I froze. I knew that voice. It had been a while, but I knew it well.

"Mom?" I called, thinking I was surely hearing things.

Liam grabbed the side of the door and pushed it wide.

"So much for ladies first," she said again and stepped around Alex.

I gasped, putting a hand up to my mouth as my vision turned wavy and unfocused. "Mom!"

"Bellamy!" she said. Her voice was exactly as I remembered it. And so was her face.

I went forward at the same time she did. We met in the middle, nearly colliding in an embrace. A sob broke out of me, and I buried my face against her shoulder and cried.

Oh my God, she smells the same.

She patted my back, running her hand down the length of my hair. "It's so good to see you. I've worried so much and missed you."

I clutched her tighter, hardly believing it was real that she was here and we were actually allowed to be in the same room.

"Mom," I said again. It sounded more like a sob. It was like my brain was broken and that was the only word I knew.

"Yes, honey," she crooned, hugging me a little tighter. "I hope you don't mind, but I brought my things. Thought I might stay."

I cried even harder as I nodded vigorously against her.

"I really hope that's the hormones," Alex said rather loudly to Liam. "Otherwise, you gonna need to buy some stock in Kleenex."

Mom pulled back a little to look at me. "Hormones?"

"I'm pregnant," I wailed.

Mom started crying, too.

Once the tears subsided just a little, I looked up over her shoulder at Liam, who was watching with a bemused expression on his face.

I pulled away from Mom and went to him. He opened his arms instantly. Fitting my face into the crook of his neck, I sniffled. "Thank you," I whispered. "You have no idea how much this means to me."

"I think I might," he murmured, brushing the hair away that was sticking to my tears.

I kissed the side of his neck and pulled back. "I love you."

He chuckled. "I love you, too."

"What about me?" Alex cut in. "I'm the one that went and picked her up."

I pulled away from Liam to hug him. "Thank you, Alex," I said. "This is the nicest thing anyone has ever done for me."

"I gave you a baby, but whatever," Liam muttered under his breath.

I laughed.

"Some people be so greedy. Can't share the spotlight." Alex tsked.

"You hugged my girl long enough," Liam deadpanned. "Time's up."

I stepped back from Alex and smiled. "I'm going to make you breakfast."

Alex's light-blue eyes lit up. "For reals? You got any biscuits and gravy? I could go for some of that."

"You can have Raisin Bran," Liam intoned.

Alex made a face. "That's just mean."

"You've been with these two these last few months?" Mom asked.

I turned around and nodded dramatically.

"You poor girl. Come tell me all about it."

"But you making them biscuits, right?" Alex called behind us as we went to the kitchen.

"I can't believe you're here," I exclaimed as we went.

"I could hardly believe it when your beau called me and invited me to come to BearPaw. He even sent that nice young man to make sure I made it here safe."

I stopped partway to the coffee maker and turned. Liam was just stepping into the kitchen. "You did all that for me?" I whispered.

"You missed her, and there's no reason she can't be here with you."

When I rushed him, he rocked back on his heels but managed to hold us both steady.

"There they go again," Alex cracked. "They do this kinda thing a lot. It makes everyone uncomfortable," he told my mom.

She laughed.

Stepping back from Liam, I took his hand and led him over to where my mom was standing. "Mom, this is

Liam. He's…" I didn't know what to say. I mean, how did I sum up in a single sentence how much he meant to me? "He's the one."

"It's nice to meet you, Liam."

"Ma'am," Liam said. "I appreciate you coming all this way."

"There's nowhere I'd rather be," Mom said, linking her arm with mine.

I still couldn't believe she was here. I could see her and talk to her, all without having to be afraid.

"So is breakfast still happening?" Alex wondered, hopeful.

"There's cereal on the table." Liam pointed.

Alex grimaced. "You were serious? What is happening here, Liam?" His eyes widened. "Are you constipated?"

Liam put a hand to his chest. "That is a *very* personal question."

Alex dropped a hand on Liam's shoulder. "You can tell me anything, bro."

"Maybe we should let them catch up." Mom offered, steering me farther into the kitchen while I giggled. "I'll help you make breakfast. We have catching up of our own to do. Lots of it."

"We definitely do." I agreed, sweeping my eyes over her face one more time. "I missed you."

"Oh, honey. Me, too."

Behind us, Liam and Alex were still bantering as I pulled out all the ingredients for the breakfast Alex requested.

"I want to hear everything, Bellamy. Starting with the baby." Mom encouraged.

"Everything." I promised, feeling so full inside I could burst.

I glanced over my shoulder at the same time Liam did.

We did that thing where we had a conversation without any words.

He was happy.

I was happy.

It was a good day.

30

Liam

The sound of a board cutting through snow was unmistakable and so was the thrill of being out in it. I was flying. Not even the cold temps could deter me. The bitter wind parted as I cut through.

Being back on a board, back on a halfpipe, taught me a few things:

1) There was no giving this up. Thinking I could was stupid.

2) My God, I fucking loved this.

And

3) Snowboarding came as naturally to me as breathing.

The second Joiner touched down in the chopper and his eyes took in this beautiful mountainside pipe, we were off and running. The chain inside me broke. I couldn't keep this part of me on a leash any longer.

I had to do this.

I had no idea how it would turn out. I just knew I had to try.

I eased into training, though adrenaline pounded in me, creating urgency that left me frustrated. Joiner was a hawkeyed hard ass who insisted on doing everything with the pace of a granny.

Learning to walk before I ran was the equivalent of sitting in a traffic jam on the way to claim a million in cash when, before, I won marathons.

Weeks began to pass. The near-full-time commitment I put into recovering the ability and strength I'd lost was paying off. Two months in and I was resembling the boarder everyone dubbed Extreme.

Granted, I wasn't twinning with the old me yet. But I would.

"I'm going again!" I shouted to Joiner, who was watching my latest run, who nodded with approval.

Before I could set up, the phone in my pocket started vibrating. Using my teeth, I pulled off the gloves I was wearing and answered without glancing at the screen.

I always had this phone with me. I might be committed to boarding and making another run with the Olympics, but it still took a backseat to Bellamy and my son.

My son, confirmed by her recent ultrasound.

Yes, I hogged all those pics, too.

"Yeah?" I said into the line, hunching down a little so the wind didn't muffle the sound.

"Liam Mattison?" said a voice I didn't recognize.

I straightened. "Who's this?"

"You should turn on the TV," the voice answered. "There's something you should see."

"Who is this?" I demanded again. "What do I need to see?"

No one answered because the call went dead. Pulling the phone away from my ear, I looked down at the screen, which went dark.

"What the fuck?" I muttered, calling up the number on my history. *Unknown.*

My first thought went to Bellamy and my unborn son. The board wedged beneath my arm fell into the snow, and I hit the screen a few more times.

After a couple rings, her voice filled my ear. "Liam, is everything okay?"

Everything inside me relaxed. *She's okay. Thank fuck.* "Why wouldn't everything be okay?"

"Because you're calling me in the middle of the day, at work."

I frowned. I called her at work. *Oh shit.* I barely ever called her at work. At least since I'd been hitting the training hard. I used to call her all the time.

"Can't I just call my best girl to see how she's doing?" I asked, putting on the charm.

She giggled lightly, and I smiled to myself. A wave of homesickness slammed into me, catching me off guard. I'd just seen her this morning.

It wasn't enough.

"Of course you can," she purred into the line. The loud sounds of a kitchen and Chef D'alessio's voice filtered behind her.

"He better not be yelling at you." I growled.

"Chef's on the war path." Bells sighed. "But not at me."

I made a sound.

"How's training going?" she asked.

"Gnarly."

Bellamy paused. "Is that good or bad?"

I laughed. "I miss you."

Her voice dropped a little, and it turned me on. "I miss you, too."

"You're sure everything is good with you? Baby okay?"

"Everything's fine. Baby, too." She hesitated, and some anxiety came through the line. "Why?"

I felt like an ass for making her worry. She'd finally started settling in, finally started feeling safe, and here I was calling out of the blue and making her second-guess herself.

"No reason." I soothed. "I just wanted to hear your voice."

More commotion sounded in the background. Bells sighed again. "I have to go."

"I'll see you in a bit, sweetheart."

"Love you."

"Love you, too." I confirmed.

When I pulled the phone away, Joiner approached. "What's going on?"

"I'm not sure," I said, mulling over the call I'd received.

In my hand, my cell went off again. I glanced down, half expecting to see Bellamy's name on the screen. It wasn't her. It was Alex.

"Alex?" I answered.

"You seen the news?" he asked. The tone of his voice made my heart rate skyrocket.

"No. I'm on the mountain."

"You better go turn on that rigged-up TV you got up there."

"Hang on," I said and jogged to the small cabin near the pipe. It had a small TV with limited channels. I left the door open when I strode inside, flipping the power instantly. "Turning it on," I told Alex. "What am I looking for?"

"You'll know," he said cryptically.

The screen and sound came on. The red "Breaking News" banner at the bottom of the screen caught my eye and then the journalist's voice filled the silence.

"Welcome back. If you're just tuning in, we've interrupted your usual programming to bring you coverage of what some are calling the biggest criminal justice upset in decades.

"It has been announced that modern mobster and well-known criminal Perry Crone, who was sentenced to life in prison nearly two years ago, has been granted early release from the state prison where he has been serving his sentence."

"What the fuck?" I roared.

"While many people are scrambling and confused as to how this could happen, our sources tell us that a high-level judge signed off on the release due to Crone's good behavior and prison crowding. Crone is said to have agreed to several stipulations upon his release and—"

"This has to be a joke," I spat. "There's no fucking way the FBI would let him out of his cage."

Alex whistled. "He buttered someone's biscuit with those deep pockets of his. Can't help but wonder how much his freedom set him back."

His freedom could cost Bells her tentative grip on normalcy and safety.

Fuck.

Crone's freedom could cost Bells her life.

"No!" I shouted and shoved at everything on the small counter nearby. Shit scattered everywhere, and the sound of shattering glass filled the space my heavy breathing didn't.

"Where's Bellamy?" Alex asked, his voice calm but not complacent.

"Work. I just talked to her. She's safe." I growled. *"For now."*

"What do you wanna do?" Alex asked, knowing damn well we couldn't just let this happen.

"Meet me out front of The Inn in twenty," I said brusquely.

"Will do."

I cut the call and turned to leave. My steps stuttered as Joiner came inside. "What the hell happened?" he asked, taking in the mess.

"I'm done for the day. Something came up." I started past, and he put a hand on my shoulder, restraining me.

I glanced down where he touched and back up.

Joiner pulled his hand away but didn't step aside. "What happened?" he repeated.

"We'll talk later," I answered and started forward.

"Call if you need anything!" he yelled out the door.

I kept going, hopped on my snowmobile, and fired it up.

Bellamy

For a while, I thought I was winning over most of the kitchen staff. I did actually win over a few. However, it seemed what acceptance I'd gained during my weeks working at The Inn was somehow lost during my time off following Ren's death.

I couldn't really understand why.

I mean, as far as everyone knew, I was the victim of a brutal robbery and present when Ren was shot. Not to sound callous or even that I wanted it, but one would think that might get me more acceptance, if only due to sympathy, rather than the opposite.

When I'd come back a couple months ago, people smiled tentatively and avoided my stare. I'd never been one they included in the "kitchen gossip," but it was less so now.

Then the bump happened.

You know, my little baby boy stopped torturing me with all-day sickness and Liam started plying me with food.

Feed my son. Feed my son. The man acted like I wouldn't know to eat if he wasn't hounding me about it.

As a result, I began showing. Because that's what happens when you're pregnant. According to Liam, I wasn't big enough. He seemed to think I needed to grow to the size of a house. Personally, I think he equated the size of my stomach to his success at making a baby.

He was utterly absurd.

He made up for it, though, by being unbelievably sweet. He still carried around a pocket full of pictures, every single day. He touched my stomach more than I did and let me eat Raisin Bran in bed.

So far, I was mostly a small, round belly, but I was only halfway through my pregnancy. I knew that would change soon enough.

The undeniable proof I was carrying Liam's baby seemed to put me on a pedestal. The very one I'd worked tirelessly for weeks upon weeks to get off of in the beginning. It seemed as though just when people were starting to see me as a person, not just Liam's girlfriend, Ren died, and I became a walking reminder that I was linked to the Mattison family.

And all that kitchen gossip? I was pretty sure most of it was about me.

It didn't bother me. Okay, it bothered me a little. I still subscribed to the fact that this stuff was small considering everything I'd been through and, therefore, didn't matter.

Guess my feelings were a little harder to convince because, I admit, sometimes coming here gave me a stomach ache. I tried to tell myself that was the baby, but when the daily sickness wore off, it was kinda hard to keep lying to myself.

I was just emotional. It was a pregnant woman's right. Right? That was the lie I was telling myself these days.

Truth was things were finally starting to settle down. At least for us. No one had tried to kill me or Liam. No one was leaving me creepy rubber toys, the FBI wasn't breathing down my neck, and we were doing our best to adjust to life without Ren.

Liam was in his element and seeing him without so much weighing him down was honestly the best part of it all. Well, that *and* my mom.

Having her back in my life was a dream come true. I teared up thinking about her even now. She was staying at Holly's house with us, which made it so easy to spend all my extra time with her. Even though she'd been here two months, it seemed we were still catching up. We were able to do all the things I missed so intensely after my father was murdered, and it was all because Liam found her and brought her to BearPaw.

I had my life back. A *full* life right down to my dream job.

Except... honestly?

This job wasn't so much a dream anymore.

And more honestly?

I was still sort of holding my breath that something would take away all this happiness.

I squeezed my eyes shut because even thinking like that made tremendous guilt assail me.

"Hey, Jess?" I said, glancing up from what I was doing. The girl working nearby made a sound and kept on working.

With a suppressed sigh, I walked the short distance between our stations and stopped beside her. "Jess."

"Yes?" she said without looking at me.

I mean, really, how hard was it to look at someone when they spoke directly to you?

"Are you almost finished there? I need all this prepped so I can start tonight's specials."

"I'm not done yet."

"You knew I needed this stuff hours ago. You should have had it done already." It was accusatory. I admit it. It was also authoritative because, technically, I was her boss.

And she was being a disrespectful bratty turtle on purpose.

Jess glanced up, giving me a surprised side eye. Usually, I just asked for stuff fifteen thousand times and never got testy about it.

"What are you going to do, call baby daddy and tattle?"

I sucked in a sharp breath. "What did you just say to me?"

"Nothing." She feigned innocence.

"Insulting your superior is not nothing," I snapped.

"You wouldn't be my superior if it wasn't for who you slept with to get here."

"You're right," I tossed out. "My culinary experience has *sooo* much to do with my sex life."

"Someone's hormones are working overtime," one of the other girls quipped.

"No." I said. "I'm just tired of being surrounded by jealous bitches."

I was fuming. Like the tolerance rope I'd been gripping the past few months was frayed and about to snap.

"I wouldn't worry too much, Jess." The girl who spoke before walked up behind me, making me the middle of a mean girl sandwich. "There's no ring on her finger, which means as soon as she pops out that kid, Liam will get bored and kick her to the curb. Then you can have the job that should have been yours."

Wow.

I was stunned speechless for a moment because I was surprised at the big ol' balls these girls had. I mean, of all the nerve!

My brain scrambled to catch up, to push back the fierce anger and shock, and come up with a scorching reply.

"Aw, don't have much to say now, do you?" she taunted.

"I sure as fuck do." The low, angry voice cut through the kitchen and silenced everything.

You could have heard a pin drop for several seconds, which felt like minutes. My eyes fell closed briefly for two reasons:

1) I loved the sound of that voice.

And

2) He was royally pissed.

I glanced around just in time to see Liam move gracefully through the kitchen. He was dressed for the slopes and had a dark-blue beanie pulled down over his head. Intensity and fierceness rolled off him in waves. So much so people actually stepped back as he moved, even if they weren't in his path.

The only one who dared standing close enough was Alex, who prowled along beside him like a wingman from hell.

One had flashing silver eyes, and the other's were cold as ice.

"Liam," Jess said, her lips practically puckered to kiss his ass.

"That's Mr. Mattison to you," he said, turning the weight of his gaze on her. She wilted instantly, and he flicked his stare to the other girl.

When his eyes turned to me, everything about them softened as he assessed me for damage. I wanted to roll my eyes, but secretly, I was kinda relieved.

His clenched jaw loosened and his lips turned up. "Bring my baby over here," he said gently, crooking a finger in my direction.

I did roll my eyes then and walked toward him, cheeks flaming with embarrassment.

The second I was within reach, both his palms covered my belly, engulfing it, and a small part of me swooned. I died a little every time he did that. Every time he held our baby in his hands.

Despite literally vibrating with anger and silently daring anyone to speak or move, Liam dropped down on his haunches in front of me and pressed his lips to my belly. "Plug your ears, pumpkin," he murmured. "Daddy has to take out the trash."

"Liam." I warned. He stood swiftly, raising to his full height and slipping back into that beast mode of his. He cupped the back of my head, kissed my hairline, and then gently but deftly pushed me behind him.

I glanced at Alex, widening my eyes. "Do something."

"He's got this handled," Alex said, crossing his arms over his chest.

"That's not what I meant," I muttered.

"You're fired." The words were lashes from Liam's mouth.

"But, Mr. Mattison!" Jess exclaimed. "It was a misunderstanding."

"You're right," he intoned. "It was. You never should have been hired in the first place."

"We were just joking." The girl beside Jess jumped in. "Bellamy knows that. Tell them," she implored.

Alex nudged me. "Girl, why didn't you tell me this was still going on?"

Liam whipped around. "*Still* going on?"

"They've been giving her a hard time since she got here, bro. Even after all them dishes she washed and vegetables she cut."

Liam's eyes flared, pinning me. "What's he talking about?"

I gave Alex the stink eye.

He shook his head. "Girl, I gave you time to handle it. Clearly, this needs a heavier hand."

"Have you been doing other people's work in here?" Liam asked me, quiet. Deadly.

I balked. "No. I just help where it's needed."

Alex leaned in toward Liam. "She was washing dishes the night I came to pick her up…"

Realization flashed across his face, and I knew he was thinking back to the night I was attacked here, realizing I'd stayed late to pick up kitchen duty.

Chef D'alessio chose that moment to walk into the room. "What's going on in here?" he bellowed. "Why isn't anyone working? Of all the impertinent—" His words died the second he stepped around a station and saw Liam and Alex. "Mr. Mattison. Is something wrong?"

Liam turned his head to pierce the chef with his cool stare. "Actually, yes. I'm wondering what the fuck kind of kitchen you're running here."

"I beg your pardon," he replied, terse.

The rest of Liam rotated so he was fully facing the chef. "It's come to my attention that you've been allowing your kitchen staff to blatantly harass another, *and* you've been allowing her to pick up the slack of your other employees."

"I can assure you—"

"I would be very careful with whatever words you choose right now." Liam advised very quietly.

"Jess? Monica?" Chef looked between the two pale women. "Are you involved?"

"They no longer work here." Liam informed him.

"Y-you fired my staff?"

"They're *my* staff." Liam cut him down. "And yes, I did." He turned back to Jess and Monica. "Get out."

"Please." Monica stepped forward, about to beg.

"*Out!*" Liam roared.

Someone off to the side jumped at his sudden yell and knocked a pan off a table. It clattered against the hard floor.

Both girls raced for the door.

"Oh, and, ladies?" Liam beckoned.

The both stopped, turning back, wary.

Liam took a step forward. "Telling a pregnant woman she is going to be kicked to the curb as soon as she has her baby is the epitome of disgusting. If I ever see either of you on BearPaw Resort property again, I will have you physically removed."

One of the girls let out a cry as they both raced from the room.

When they were gone, a collective breath seemed to fill the room.

But Liam wasn't done.

"And for the record." He spoke loudly for everyone to hear. "I want this baby, and I'm in love with his mother. If I hear anyone whisper anything remotely resembling anything but that, you will join those two idiots in exile."

"Liam." I admonished.

"And…" He continued, ignoring me. "Bellamy did not get hired here because of me. She got hired because of her talent and culinary skills. To suggest otherwise is demeaning and insulting to both her and me."

Liam stopped talking, but no one moved. Not even the chef.

After a moment, Alex cleared his throat. "Any questions?"

No one said a word.

Liam made a sound. "Back to work!"

Just like that, the kitchen started up again. Nervous energy buzzed through the place, and I let out a shaky breath.

Liam stepped up to Chef. "I would suggest taking a hard look at the way you're running this kitchen, because what I walked in on today makes me wonder if you're suitable to run a gas station eatery, let alone this five-star restaurant."

"Liam!" I gasped for like the fifteenth time.

Chef D'alessio stuttered, his face flushed.

I wanted to find a giant pot to crawl into.

Liam reached out behind him, found my hand, and wrapped his around it.

"C'mon, Bells. We're going home."

"I'm in the middle of my shift!" I hissed.

Liam lifted an eyebrow at Chef, who cleared his throat. "Take the rest of the day… er, as much time as you need. I'll make sure your duties are covered."

"That's not really necessary," I said, face flaming.

My God! I spent months trying to avoid not being seen as the spoiled girlfriend of Liam Mattison, and now look! Just look!

Liam started walking, towing me along with him. I tried to dig my heels in, but Alex closed in behind me.

I was outnumbered. Not to mention embarrassed, exhausted, and fuming mad!

When we made it outside, winter wind picked up my hair and whipped it around. I yanked my hand free of Liam's and glared. "What the hell?" I cried.

Liam looked at me and frowned. "Where's your coat?"

"Inside, with all my other belongings I couldn't grab because you were beating on your chest and acting like a caveman!"

Liam glanced over at Alex, who sighed dramatically. "I'm on it."

Alex disappeared back inside, and Liam peeled off his coat and tucked it around me.

"I cannot believe you," I said through gritted teeth.

"Those bitches got off easy in there," he intoned. "And I'm still not sure Chef will be keeping his job."

"You can't just fire everyone!"

"The hell I can't."

"Stop it," I said, weary.

Gripping the collar of his jacket and holding it closed beneath my chin, Liam regarded me with serious gray eyes. "I won't ever stop protecting you. I won't ever tolerate anyone saying such degrading shit to you." Gently, he grasped my jaw and lifted my face. "You know none of that shit is true, right?"

I nodded. "I know."

Liam cursed, hooked an arm around me, and directed my body into his. I fit against him perfectly, and the fresh snow scent he always carried rose around me and filled my senses. It didn't seem to matter I was angry and upset, because my body relaxed into his almost instantly.

"That's my girl," he murmured, holding me a little tighter.

"This doesn't mean I forgive you," I said against his chest.

His low laugh floated overhead, and my eyelashes swept down.

Alex came back outside, carting my coat and bag, and Liam ushered me into Alex's Hummer. When I crawled into the back, Liam grabbed my waist and gently tugged me into his lap.

"There are a ton of seats," I pointed out.

"I know."

"What are you even doing here anyway?" I asked after Alex started driving. "Both of you."

"We need to talk," Liam replied, pushing me down against his chest.

"About what?" I said, a fissure of worry moving through me.

"Just give me a minute, huh?" he whispered. "Just let me hold you."

I relented because being held by Liam was something I loved.

Still, I couldn't help but worry if that inkling of fear that happiness was fleeting wasn't about to turn into full-blown reality.

32

Liam

I might have to start mandatory drug testing for the resort staff, because those bitches had to be high as kites.

Of all the crack-headed, moronic yapping I heard in my life, I think what I just heard those women say to Bellamy took the cake.

As far as I was concerned, firing and banning them from this resort for life had been kind, because what they really deserved was my size twelves up their asses.

I was feeling some kind of way right now. And not just murderous either.

Protective, possessive… *guilt-ridden.*

I raced down off my private strip of mountain, already incensed, to get to Bells and make sure she was safe. The sudden and unexpected release of Crone was not good. Not good at all. Walking into The Inn, a place she wanted to work, and overhearing those cows dumping their insecurities all over her and finding out she'd been silently enduring this treatment from day one?

Oh, fucks no.

How did I not know about this? Why did Alex? What else had I been overlooking and not shielding her from?

And fuck, them pointing out the fact my girl didn't have a fat diamond on her finger wasn't Bells's fault. It was mine.

What kind of message was that sending to everyone in this town? Bellamy was good enough to screw and impregnate, but not good enough to marry?

Maybe *I* was high, 'cause that shit was unacceptable.

Holding on to her tight, I leaned my head against the seat inside the Hummer. Last time things blew the fuck up, it drove a wedge between us. It had been hell, and I wasn't making that trip again.

Alex pulled up in front of his A-frame, and I nodded in approval. Without turning around, he shut off the engine. "Figured talking here might be better."

"What's going on?" Bellamy asked, fear creeping into her voice. "You never cut training early."

I frowned. "Maybe I should have."

She lifted her head off my shoulder and wrinkled her nose.

God, she was beautiful. I reached up to the base of her neck and pulled out the pins holding all her sunny hair into a bun. It fell down her back as I pushed them all into the pocket of my coat she was wearing, then dragged my fingers through it, spreading it out.

Her blue eyes made me think of tropical waters, and the very light sprinkle of freckles over the bridge of her nose made me smile. Her face was smooth, skin baby soft. She didn't have any makeup on, and it was the way I preferred her.

"I love you," I whispered, still taking in all her features.

Alex was already out, moving around the side of his ride toward the back door.

"You're scaring me." Her lower lip trembled.

I sat forward and brushed a kiss over the wobbly lip. "Don't be scared, sweetheart. I'll take care of you."

"I don't want you to take care of me," she announced, stubborn.

The door beside us opened, and Alex peered inside. "Y'all done making out?"

"We aren't making out." Bellamy grumped.

I held her out, and Alex lifted her down to the ground. The three of us went inside. Bellamy barely had the coat off before she said, "I take it you didn't pull me out of work because of that little incident."

"It wasn't a little incident," I snapped. Then I blew out a breath. "But no. We came for another reason."

"Just tell me what it is."

Alex and I glanced at each other, then back at Bellamy. "Perry Crone is being released from prison."

She blinked as a stunned look crossed her features. Instantly, her hand went to her belly and rested on the round bump. God, I fucking loved that belly.

Seeing her walking around pregnant was the biggest stroke to my ego. I was damn proud of her pregnant state, damn proud that was my kid she was carrying around.

"He-he's getting out of jail?" she echoed. "But I thought he was in there for life."

"He was," I spat.

"Money talks, Bells," Alex quipped. "He probably paid off quite a few people."

"I don't understand." She worried. "Could he really pay off that many people? What about the FBI? What about the fact that he killed my father...?" She looked at me. The shock was wearing off and now panic was setting in. "And yours…"

I went to her, put a hand on her back, and guided her to the couch. "Sit down," I instructed.

"I don't want to sit down!" she exclaimed. "I want to know how this happened!"

"I don't know yet," I replied. "I haven't made any calls."

"How do you know?" she demanded. I saw the hope in her eyes that maybe I was wrong.

"It was on the news this morning," Alex said.

"Oh my God." She fretted, eyes seeking out mine. "He's going to come for me." She gasped. "My baby. He can't hurt my baby."

She stood up from the couch as if she planned on running. Like escape was her only option. It was her default setting it seemed. It was how she'd stayed alive this long.

I wrapped my arms around her from behind, holding her against me, hoping she felt the strength in my body and heard the promise in my words. "No one is going to hurt you or our baby."

Her hand clutched my arm. "Alex?" Bellamy whimpered.

"Same, girl who got away. Not only will that man have to get through Liam, but he'll have to go through me, too."

That didn't seem to make her feel better. "I don't want either of you to get hurt."

"The only way I'll be hurt is if you or my son are."

She was shaking. Keeping my arms around her, I backed us toward the couch, lowering until I was sitting with her in my lap. One hand moved to her stomach, splaying out over the baby in a defending gesture.

"He's out now?" Bellamy asked.

"No, he's still locked up. He's not out yet."

Alex went to the TV and switched it on, putting it on the news station, hoping the story would play again and we might get some details we missed before.

"That's good," she said, relaxing. Then she sat forward, as if an idea just came to her. "Maybe he won't care." She hypothesized, glancing at me with a new light in her eyes. "He already said the debt was paid. It's been months and nothing's happened. Maybe he was serious. He'd been angry I'd gotten him sentenced to life, but now he's getting out. There's no reason to hold a grudge anymore."

My eyes met Alex's over her shoulder. Neither of us wanted to disagree with her or take away any kind of peace she might find.

But damn. I didn't believe that, and neither did my best friend.

Bellamy's eyes searched for mine, pulling me from the silent convo I shared with Alex. "What are we going to do?"

I pursed my lips. "You're going to go make some hot cocoa while I try and get some answers."

"Hot cocoa!" she exclaimed as though I were being preposterous. "This is no time for that."

"I could use some." Alex put in. "I was so busy at work today. I haven't had time to eat."

Bellamy's mothering instincts kicked in. "You haven't eaten?" She made a sound. "I'll make you a sandwich."

I rubbed her belly. "Make me one, too, sweetheart?"

She kissed my cheek.

On her way into the kitchen, she informed us, "By the way, I know you're totally distracting me while you call the FBI."

"You're my favorite girl," I called after her.

Pretty sure she muttered something about charming cavemen.

"Someone called me before you did and told me to turn on the news," I told Alex, keeping my words quiet.

His eyes narrowed suspiciously. "Who?"

"Unknown caller."

He made a rude sound. "Let me see the number."

I called it up and handed my phone to him. He took a screenshot and texted himself the photo. "Give me a few."

I nodded and dialed up my good buddy Agent Frost. When he answered, I said, "You didn't think a heads-up was warranted?"

"Mr. Mattison," he surmised immediately.

"What the fuck, Frost?"

"I take it you've seen the news."

"Is your FBI badge real?" I questioned.

"We were blindsided by this just as much as you were."

"Oh, did that dickwad kill your father, too? Try and kill your girlfriend? Send you letters from the slammer?"

"Letters?" he asked, emphasizing the plural.

I made a sound. "It was just the one."

"Look. I know this is very upsetting. Crone managed to bankroll some people in some very high places. We've been scrambling all morning since this shit broke."

"And?" I pressed.

"And he's got his business dealings zipped up tight. So far, all we know is he's being released early next week. The paperwork is already in processing."

I paced to the opposite side of the room. "What's it going to take to stop it?"

"We're still working on that." He hesitated and then confided, "Truthfully, it's not looking good."

"Jesus H. Christ," I swore. "Do you have any idea what kind of stress this puts on Bellamy and my baby?"

Frost paused. "Bellamy is expecting?"

"Forgot to mention that, did I?"

"Well… I suppose there hasn't been a need for us to be in contact. But a heads-up would have been nice."

"Now you know how I feel," I muttered.

Frost sighed dramatically. "Witness protection is always an option. It's the only way the FBI––"

"No," I ground out. "You know she won't go for it." Besides, how the fuck did they think they could wipe out my identity? I was known around the world. The country of Thailand gave me a truck, for God's sake.

I glanced at Alex, who was speaking quietly into his phone on the other side of the room.

Our stares collided.

He knew and I knew this was beyond the FBI now. These assholes hadn't even known about Crone's release before we did.

Incompetent. Unreliable.

Definitely not up to the task of keeping my family safe.

Without another word to Frost, I pulled the phone away from my ear and hung up.

Alex lifted his chin.

"They aren't going to be any help."

That subzero part of him that he rarely let anyone see slipped to the surface. "Then I guess we'll have to handle this ourselves."

I nodded.

A voice in his ear turned his attention away, and the phone in my hand went off. It was Frost. I debated not answering, then figured it would be stupid to alienate any source of information I might have.

"Yeah?"

"If it's any consolation, Crone will be heavily monitored and is only authorized to be in his home state of New York."

"It's not," I deadpanned.

"I didn't think so." Frost sighed. "If I find out anything, I will let you know ASAP, okay? And you know the FBI will do whatever they can to protect you and your family."

"If that was the case, that fucker wouldn't be walking free next week."

"We've been keeping close watch on his organization. As far as we can tell, Crone has made no plans of coming after you."

"If he comes after me and I kill him, self-defense stands. Correct?"

"Mr. Mattison, I would advise that if Perry Crone or any of his people come near you, call 9-1-1 immediately."

"And if he attacks me or mine while I'm waiting for the police?"

There was a pregnant pause. "Self-defense stands."

"I'll talk to you later, agent."

I didn't wait for him to say anything else, ending the call.

I looked up as Bellamy approached, carrying a plate filled with food. "Was that Frost? What did he say?"

"Thanks, sweetheart," I said, taking the plate, then squeezing her hand. "Sit down with me."

She did, and I couldn't resist sliding my hand over her round belly.

"Liam." She reminded me gently.

I was tired of Crone getting in the way of my life. "The FBI doesn't know much more than us. But Crone isn't allowed to leave New York."

"Shouldn't we have been notified? In movies, the victims get to testify at hearings before criminals are let out of jail."

"I don't think things operate like that where Crone is concerned, sweetheart."

"Got it," Alex exclaimed and came over. His plate in one hand and his phone in the other. It made a sound, and he hit the screen.

"You know this dude?" he asked, turning it toward me.

Bells and I both leaned forward to look.

"I've never seen him before," Bellamy noted.

I had. "It's the guard from the prison. He was there the day I went to see Crone. I had a conversation with him."

"Well, you must have made an impression because he felt compelled to call and warn you," Alex mused, set his phone down, and picked up the sandwich Bellamy had delivered.

He made a sound as he chewed and nodded, shaking the food in her general direction.

"He called you?" Bellamy inquired.

I nodded. "To warn me about Crone's release."

"Why would he do that?" Bellamy wondered.

"I got him winter Olympics tickets for next year," I said, offhand.

Her voice held a note of wonder. "You did?"

I shrugged. "It was minor. He recognized me, we had a conversation, so I did him a solid."

"Minor?" Bellamy asked. "Why do you two always say that?"

Around his food, Alex answered, "It's minor. You know, no big deal. Nothing to worry about. It's not major—"

"It's minor." I finished.

"So it's bro code." She surmised.

"No bro code is something else entirely," Alex said.

She made a face, which I thought was cute as hell, then changed the subject. "If you didn't know him"— she pointed to the pic on Alex's phone—"how did you find out who he was?"

Alex shrugged. "Skills."

Her nose wrinkled. "What kind of skills?"

"Skills an innocent like you don't need to know nothing about."

"You think I'm innocent?" She seemed surprised by this.

We both laughed.

"I'm hardly innocent."

"Don't worry. We like you that way." Alex assured her, and I nodded.

"I killed a man! I emptied an entire clip into him!" she declared as if I needed a reminder.

I dropped the half-eaten sandwich on my plate and glanced at her. "Which is exactly why you don't need to be worrying about any of this."

"Liam Mattison," Bellamy declared and stood, towering over me because I was sitting. Her hands went to her hips, which molded her shirt to the baby growing inside her. "I've had just about enough of your egotistical, macho, chest-beating ways!"

I lifted an eyebrow. "Is that so?"

"Army skills," Alex said, still eating. We both looked at him.

"What?" Bellamy asked.

"It was some army skills. I made some calls. I know people."

"And you think I'm too innocent to know that?" She scoffed.

Alex's eyes shuttered a bit as he shoved more food into his mouth.

Bellamy felt the change and glanced at me.

I grabbed her hand and tugged her down. "Alex doesn't like talking about his years in the army, sweetheart. You know that."

"I'm sorry." She apologized to Alex.

"Don't be sorry, baby girl. It's all good."

I let out a rumble, and Alex grinned because he knew what he did. I let it go, though, because he just dipped back into the dark waters he left behind.

"That call cost you anything?" I asked, serious.

He paused in chewing, then shook his head. "Naw. It's cool."

"You'll tell me if it did?"

"Yeah, bro. I'll tell you."

Bellamy looked between us. I felt her questions, but she didn't ask in fear of upsetting Alex.

"I think I will make some cocoa after all," Bellamy said, heading toward the kitchen.

I watched her go and began to worry. Just when things started calming down, Crone had to go and stir them up again.

33

Bellamy

The near-dark bedroom lured me like ocean waves crashing against a solitary shoreline. Sleep would have pulled me back under if Liam hadn't moved against me.

An innocent touch, just the brush of his leg against mine. But it was enough. The contrast of the hair on his leg versus my smooth one enticed me in a way sleep never would.

In a world of unknowns and days that could change at the drop of a dime, there was one constant I could always rely on. The pure chemistry that tethered Liam and me together, invisibly but so permanently.

My reaction to him was ingrained in me, something I likely had been born with and was lucky enough to discover. It didn't matter how hard life pushed us apart. The way my skin sizzled when he was close would never change.

The sound of blustery wind pushed against the house, making beams creak and the urge to push closer against him all that more enticing. This bed was cozy and Liam's body my safe haven.

I slipped beneath the covers, gliding down his body, dragging my fingers across his warm, supple skin. He inhaled deeply in sleep and shifted unconsciously, spreading his legs a little, and I smiled. He didn't have to be awake to react to me. We were like two planets with the perfect orbit. Two planets destined to circle each other for the rest of our lives.

Taking the quiet invitation, I settled between his thighs and began kissing up the front of his bare leg. Liam hadn't slept in clothes. He rarely ever did. I liked that about him. I liked that he wanted to put the most amount of bare skin against me as humanly possible, even when we weren't making love.

Shifting over, I repeated the kisses on the opposite leg and then settled my palms against each thigh and rubbed gently. In sleep, Liam moaned, and I rubbed a little deeper, slipping up toward the center of his body.

The skin on his sack was delicate and soft. Carefully, I weighed his balls in my palm and massaged lightly. Liam moaned again, and I dipped my head and smiled against his thigh.

His hips thrust upward just slightly. Just enough to push his sack a little farther into my hand. I fondled him while my other hand skirted over his lower abdomen and brushed over the tip of his stiff cock.

His ab muscles contracted, and his dick jumped with anticipation. Very softly, I nibbled his sack and then sucked part of him between my lips.

Liam's hand scooped up some of my hair, which was falling over his body, and wrapped it around his fingers. After lavishing attention on his boys, I licked upward from the base to his tip and then slid my lips over his shaft, taking him deep.

A hissing sound filled the room, and I smiled against his dick. Holding firmly to the base of his rod, I began working it. Slipping my mouth up and down over the rigid length, enjoying the way he jerked against my tongue when I hit just the right spot.

His hand moved from my hair to the back of my head and pushed gently, encouraging me. I picked up the pace a little, then took him deep, allowing his head to hit the back of my throat. His legs tightened around me as I pulled back slowly and caressed his balls.

I lifted my lips, replaced them with my hand, and jacked him while nipping the inside of his thighs with my teeth.

His sack was drawn tightly against his body, and his dick was so hard it began to quiver. The salty taste of him coated my tongue, and my lips felt swollen from sucking. Craving more, I planted both hands on either side of his hips and dipped my head, taking him between my lips again. My body rocked against him, and a small sound of pleasure filled the space over my head.

Liam moved, slipping his hands beneath my arms and sitting up. I lifted my head, taking in the sight of him above me and how his eyes flashed in the dimness of the bedroom.

I knew just from one look that I wasn't going to get to finish. No, Liam had other ideas.

With a beastly growl, he lifted, pulling me up his body and draping me across his skin. His lips crashed over mine, and he took control, though I was the one on top.

We kissed deeply, tongues nearly fighting, and my breasts ached with need. Almost as if he heard their silent plea, Liam ripped his mouth away and pushed me up slightly so he could latch on.

I cried out as intense pleasure shot through me, moving all the way to my core and making it almost hurt. He sucked my nipples until between my thighs was dripping and I was trying to straddle his cock.

Before I could sink down, he rolled, taking all his weight on his arms, and settled between my thighs. I looked up, dizzy with need, and he smiled. Just when I thought he would come inside, he disappeared.

I made a sound of distress and pushed up onto my elbows just in time to look down my body and see him brush a few tender kisses across my rounded belly.

My heart turned over, and the love I felt for him battled against the extreme need pounding in my veins. After one last kiss and caress over my belly, he reached between to slip one of his thick fingers into my entrance, testing to make sure my body was ready to accept him.

I bit into my lower lip and shivered.

He grunted. The sound only made me want him more as he rose over me. His head met my entrance, and I held my breath, anticipating that first push.

His lips dipped low. "Breathe," he whispered, his mouth so close it brushed against mine.

I inhaled, and Liam entered my body. In a single gentle push, he was sheathed inside me completely. I felt my body contract around him and my back arched off the bed.

His lips latched onto one of my nipples and tugged as his hips began to move. My fingernails dug into his hips as he fucked me.

Liam kept up a steady, gentle pace, and it seemed no matter how hard my nails bit into his skin, he wouldn't hammer into me any harder.

I knew he wouldn't. There was no way he'd be rough while our child lay between us.

His lips unlatched from my breasts, and I sagged against the mattress when he pushed deep.

"Look at me," he rasped, his voice groggy from sleep and sex.

I forced my heavy lids open to do his bidding, and my breath caught again. His stare claimed me in a way even his body couldn't. Liam didn't just own my body; he owned my soul.

And by the look in his eyes, he knew it.

He knew and he reveled in it.

"You're everything to me," he whispered.

I came apart beneath him, shattering into a million tiny pieces. My body strained against his as I shook and shuddered. Liam scooped me up close and held me while rivers of pleasure flooded my body. When I finally started to settle, he tilted his hips, and I began to shudder all over again.

His lips moved in my hair. I clung to him until my limbs went limp. Laying me out on the mattress beneath him, Liam rose again, pulled free, and then surged back in. The girth of him seemed to swell and his strokes became quicker.

Moments later, the cords in his neck stood out and his body went rigid. I felt his dick pulse with release, and my muscles tightened around him, milking every last drop.

When the throes of a powerful orgasm finally loosened their grip, he shuddered and glanced down, sweeping his gaze over me, assessing to make sure I was okay.

I smiled and reached up, trying to pull him close. He refused to give me his full weight, and when I made a pouty sound, he chuckled and moved to my side. Liam cupped my face with his hand and pulled it gently toward him.

We kissed softly and lazily, until he pulled away and kissed my shoulder.

"Hey," I murmured.

"Hm?" He nudged the side of my neck with his nose.

I giggled and grabbed a handful of his hair right above his forehead and pulled so his eyes would meet mine. "You're my everything, too."

Liam lay against me, nuzzling my neck and entwining his leg with mine. These were the kind of moments that made all the terrible ones worth it. This was the reason I fought even when the fight seemed like a losing battle. Liam was worth it. Love was worth it.

An unfamiliar feeling shot through my stomach, and my eyes flew open. Another one followed close behind, and I gasped.

"Bellamy?" Liam said, alarm creeping into his voice.

The strange sensation happened again, and I sat up, instinctively putting both hands against my bare belly.

Liam burst up, hit his knees on the bed, and held his hands out so they hovered close by. "What's happening?" He stressed. "Jesus Christ, Bellamy, what's wrong?"

I glanced up, tears in my eyes, and whispered, "The baby."

Liam

I thought I'd known fear. It definitely wasn't an emotion I was unfamiliar with.

But this?

Seeing my girl grip her pregnant belly as tears flooded her eyes… It was too much. If a man could die by fear alone, this was what would take me out.

"We're going to the hospital," I bellowed and lunged out of bed. I raced around, searching for a damn pair of pants until I saw a pair lying right there at my feet.

I tugged them on, trying to put both legs on at once and nearly falling on my ass while doing it.

"Liam…"

I cursed and righted myself as I yanked them up my body. "I got you, sweetheart. Just sit there and breathe. Everything's going to be okay." *Dear God, please, please, let everything be okay.*

Not my son. Please, not my son.

I raced to her side, only to realize she was naked.

Bellamy caught my hand before I could rush off in search of clothes. "Liam, stop."

I spun back. "What hurts? Tell me."

She smiled as a tear tracked down her cheek. "Nothing hurts," she whispered. "Feel."

She guided my hand to her stomach, pressing hers flat over mine.

I stood there, heart hammering, as I tried to make sense of what she was doing.

"Bells, we need to go," I said, trying not to sound cross with her.

"Wait!" she urged. "He's moving!"

Oh, holy shit… He's—wait. *What?*

I looked at Bellamy again as she lay back and pressed her hand over mine. I waited, heart still pounding, and nothing happened.

"I probably hurt you," I spat. "I probably was too rough."

"There!" She gasped and pulled my hand to another spot.

Nothing happened.

I frowned.

She looked up at me, love shining in her eyes. "Talk to him."

When I hesitated, she nodded encouragingly. I dropped to my knees beside the bed and leaned toward my son. "Hey, pumpkin," I said. "What's going on in there?"

Something bumped against my palm. Bellamy's eyes widened with excitement. I glanced at her, shocked. "Was that him?"

She nodded vigorously.

"Shaw?"

There was another knock against my hand. And then another.

I jolted back, staring between Bellamy and her stomach. "Is he supposed to do that?" I demanded.

She laughed. "Yes! I've never felt it like that before. Usually, it's just flutters, like wings… but this…"

"I felt it," I said, stunned. "I felt him move."

Bellamy smiled soft. "He knows your voice."

My eyes snapped to hers. "He does?"

She nodded and made a sound between a laugh and a sob.

My hand covered her belly again and rubbed lightly. "So everything's okay? I didn't hurt you. The baby is okay?"

Bellamy covered my hand with hers. "Yes, everything is perfect. I didn't mean to scare you. I just hadn't felt it like that before. It's amazing."

"You're fucking right it is," I declared. "That kid is a goddamn genius!"

Another light nudge hit my palm.

"See!" I exclaimed. "I told you!"

Bellamy laughed and nodded.

I released her stomach and swooped in, capturing her lips. When I pulled back, she wiped at the tears on her cheeks. "You really need to stop cussing. He can hear you!"

I kissed her stomach and laid my cheek against it. "You're sure you're okay?"

"I promise."

I crawled back in the bed, wrapping my arms around her. I sat there for a while, marveling in the fact that we created a life together, a life that grew and changed with every passing day.

Thank you, Dad.

"That was quite the wake-up call," I murmured after the ruckus inside me calmed and I was able to think. She settled a little farther against me with a contented sigh. "What are you doing up so early?"

"I'd rather spend an extra hour with you than sleep in and wake up to you already gone."

Since deciding to try for the Olympics next year, I jam-packed as much training as I could into my day. That meant early mornings so I could spend the nights with my girl.

"You still okay with all the hours I'm putting in?" I asked, checking in.

"Of course."

"Bells." I warned, worried she was holding back.

"I'm okay with it, really. I'm so proud of you. Sometimes I just miss you. And yesterday was a lot."

I kissed the top of her head, making a sound of agreement. Between the revelation about Crone and then walking in to The Inn to find another situation, yesterday pretty much sucked.

It was also eye opening. I had some decisions to make.

"Why didn't you tell me about the bitches at work?"

"I was handling it."

I made a rude sound. "Were you, really?"

"I was, at least for a while. Then it got hard again." She admitted.

"What do you mean?"

"I mean, my baby bump is a visual reminder that I'm shacking up with the boss."

"We are not shacking up," I snapped.

Bellamy pulled back and looked at me. "It was just an expression."

I scowled. "I heard what they said to you,"

"And you fired them for it." She sniffed.

I raised an eyebrow. "And you don't approve?"

She shrugged. "It's definitely not going to win me any points with the remaining staff."

"What is this, high school?" I muttered, rubbing a hand over my face.

"Can I ask you something?" she whispered.

Dropping my hand, I met her eyes. "You can ask me anything."

She nodded and glanced down at the bed. Her long hair fell over her shoulders, concealing her bare breasts, and her pregnant belly rounded out, displaying my genius son.

"Do you think dreams can change?"

"I know they can."

She lifted her chin. "Yeah?"

I nodded. "People change and grow. It only makes sense their dreams change with them."

"But you've always had the same dream."

I shook my head slowly. "Snowboarding is a passion, and yes, at one time, it was my dream to be the best. I accomplished that, and you know what I realized?"

"What?" she asked, hanging on everything I was saying.

"A man cannot survive on one food alone."

Her face went blank, and she blinked. Blinked again. "How does this relate to food?"

I laughed. "Think about it. You can't just survive on one thing. Like a steak. I need sides to go with that steak. Some potatoes, some veggies... a little sugar." I winked, and she giggled.

"I was only eating steak for a long time. It starved me of a lot of other things. Then one day, my steak got burned. I couldn't eat it. Maybe if I'd had some sides, I wouldn't have almost starved to death."

Her head tilted to the side. "That actually makes sense."

I scoffed. "Where do you think my son gets his genius from?"

She rolled her eyes.

I picked up her hand to link it with mine. "When I blew out my knee and was lying in that hospital, I fell into a bottle. Maybe if I'd had more than just boarding, it would have been easier."

"So your dream changed." She surmised.

I nodded. "Yeah. And it was hard to let it. It felt like letting go."

"And that's why you were so scared to let it back in, to go back to boarding."

I smiled softly. "Maybe he gets his genius from you."

"From us." She corrected.

I lifted our hands and kissed the back of hers.

"My dream isn't boarding anymore, Bells. It's you and my son. It's this resort and our family. Yes, I still want snowboarding to be a part of that. I always will. But it's not my entire life anymore. You are."

"You got some pretty words, Liam Mattison."

"They aren't words, sweetheart. They're the truth."

"That's what makes them so pretty," she replied.

"You're not happy at The Inn," I said, laying it out bare. From the moment I walked into that kitchen and felt the vibes competing with the scent of food, I knew. Bellamy was too good for that place.

She hesitated and swallowed thickly, then tucked some hair behind her ear. "I feel ungrateful to say so."

A strangled sound erupted from me, and I sat forward, tucking my fingers beneath her chin and lifting. "Why on earth would you feel ungrateful?"

"Because I yearned for a job like this for years. And before that, I worked toward it in school. I thought that dream had been taken forever, but then I came here and Ren offered me this job."

"Changing your mind doesn't make you ungrateful."

"I think it does."

"Sometimes you have to get a burned steak to realize you need some sides," I quipped.

She choked on a laugh. "Well, I guess if I hadn't gotten this job, I would still be dreaming of it."

"And you aren't anymore." That kind of made me sad for her. I knew how much it hurt to let go of a dream. To think it wasn't yours for the taking anymore.

She shrugged, then gasped quietly and implored me with her baby blues. "I am so appreciative of the opportunity, and I want you to know I will still put out my very best effort so The Inn won't suffer."

I made a sound. "I don't give a rat's ass about that place."

"You should! You own it."

I gestured to her with my chin. "Tell me why you don't like it." Her shoulders slumped, and I knew I wasn't going to like the answer. "The truth, Bells."

"I don't fit in," she confided. "It doesn't seem to matter how much I smile, how helpful I am, or even how stern I get. They don't respect me. I'll always be the girl who slept with the boss to get her job."

I was just going to fire them all. Problem solved.

She made a sound. "You can't fire everyone, Liam."

"How'd you know I was thinking that?" I wondered.

She tapped her finger against the side of her head.

I sighed heavily. "You can't be a queen and work among the commoners."

An offended look crossed her face. "I'm not a queen, and they are not commoners!"

"It wasn't an insult, baby. It's fact. How many times have you said I was royalty? How many times did you tell me I was a king."

"That's different," she murmured.

I grabbed her chin. "No," I said forcefully. "It's not. Truth is I'm the boss around here. I own this place, and with it comes a certain… position. You're mine."

She narrowed her eyes, and I backtracked a little.

"I'm in love with you. Completely. You're carrying my child. That gives you a certain position."

"They whisper behind my back. The call me a *Belladonna*."

I felt my temper rise. "You should have come to me!"

"That would have made it worse."

"You're worried about going back today. After yesterday."

She wrung her hands in her lap. "Sometimes going there gives me a stomach ache. I just… I feel unwelcome. And I'm just…" She paused. "Tired."

I gathered her against my chest and stared over her head, grateful she couldn't see the anger in my eyes. It was hard for me to sit here and listen to this. Hard for me not to react and yell. I didn't care what she said. Chef D'alessio's days were numbered.

"You aren't going back." I decided.

She made a sound and looked up. "It's my job."

"And it makes you physically sick. Did you really think I'd let you go back there? That kind of stress is not good for you or Shaw."

The stubborn glint in her eyes melted. "I like it when you use his name."

I leaned down and kissed her.

"I can't just not go back." She informed me. "But if you're okay with it… maybe I'll give my notice."

"There's no need to give a notice."

"Yes!" She insisted. "There is. Not showing up and having you quit for me is disrespectful and unprofessional. I am neither of those things. I might not want to work there, but I still love to cook, and someday I hope to find a place where I can have some steak with my sides."

My lips tugged up in a smile. I had to force myself to keep to the matter at hand. "Three-day notice." I bargained.

"A week."

"Fine." I sighed heavily. "But if you start stressing out—"

She laid a hand against my lips. "I won't. Just knowing there's a solution is enough. But I want you to know it means a lot to me that you gave me a chance there."

I snorted. "I'd let you run the place if I thought you'd take the job."

"Not going to happen."

"Yeah. I didn't think so."

She laid a hand across her stomach. "I was, um…" Her blue gaze lifted. "I was kind of thinking it might be nice to be at home with Shaw."

My throat constricted with emotion. Visions of her rocking him, feeding him, and playing with him filled my head. "Yeah?"

She nodded, then hurried to add, "At least while he's a baby. If you're okay with that?"

A wide grin cracked my face. "Nothing would make me happier."

"Really?" she implored. "I have some money, but it's not very much."

"I have enough money for all of us." I promised, laying a hand beside hers. The baby moved, and my heart tumbled over.

"I don't want you to think—"

"Stop right there," I intoned. "I do not, nor will I ever, think you give two shits about my money. Having you home with our son and happy is worth way more than any amount of cash."

"Thank you," she whispered sincerely.

"You know what?" I said, suddenly inspired.

Her brow wrinkled. "What?"

"I'm taking you on a date."

"A date?"

I nodded. "Just me and you. I've been training. You've been working… We live with our mothers." I stuck out my tongue, and she laughed. "We haven't had much time for dating."

"We've been sort of busy." She agreed.

"Which is exactly why I'm taking you out." I picked up her hand and gave her my best charming smile. "Will you do me the honor of going on a date with me?"

"Shouldn't we have dated before I got pregnant?" she asked, facetious.

I gave her a bland look. "I'm trying to be romantic."

"Oh. Sorry." She giggled. "Of course I'll go on a date with you."

A wide smile graced my face.

"So where are we going on this date?"

I smirked. "Guess you're just going to have to wait and see."

35

Bellamy

The day of my date with Liam arrived. He was being incredibly secretive and sneaky about it, which made me wonder what it was he was planning.

I pretty much resigned myself to an entire day of waiting and wondering until he was supposed to pick me up.

Yep. He was picking me up even though we lived in the same house. This whole surprise date night might be maddening, but it was also so incredibly sweet.

Truth was Liam and I didn't really have many actual dates. We'd had tacos when I first arrived in town, which probably didn't count, but it was as close to a date as we'd ever gotten. That and we made out like horny teens in the back booth.

That's what people did on dates, right?

I didn't even know. Sure, I'd been out here and there over the past eight years, but that all seemed so far away, so unimportant.

I guess the last actual date Liam and I shared was when he took me to the winter carnival all those years ago.

He was already up and gone to training for the day. His dedication was something I really admired. I'd wanted to go up to the pipe with him, but he turned me down. It wasn't my most becoming moment, but I pouted about it.

He thought it was cute, then declared I couldn't go because my mom had booked us a stay day at the resort spa. Personally, I think he enjoyed torturing me and letting the anticipation build. And build it did. Even Liam seemed a little nervous about it. Every time I would try and pry some detail out of him, he would almost blush and turn shy.

Liam was the least shy man I knew, so it was just proof something was up.

"A girl could get used to this kind of pampering," Mom said from the pedicure chair beside mine.

I smiled. "Thanks for booking this. It's been nice."

"You deserve a little relaxation after everything."

I glanced her way. "So do you."

"How have things been going?" Her question made us both look at the women giving us our pedicures and then back.

"Good. Nothing new to report," I replied generically. I knew she would understand that meant there was no more developments in the release of Crone.

Unfortunately.

It didn't seem to matter how many calls Liam or I made. It was roadblock after roadblock. It gave a girl serious doubts about our legal system. I just couldn't fathom how all his money was so much more important than the safety of innocent people.

It was sickening how much money actually bought.

Liam had even called the mayor of New York. He got put through, too. Apparently, phone calls from a United States Olympic Medalists were quite an honor. Too bad they weren't enough to keep a criminal behind bars.

Liam was so incensed after that call it had taken several hours for him to calm down. I even suggested maybe we postpone tonight, but he wouldn't have it. In fact, I almost felt like the more definite Crone's release became, the more he wanted this date.

"So what do you know about tonight?" I asked Mom, a gleam in my eye.

She laughed and shook her head. She had chin-length brown hair she used to keep highlighted with a beautiful honey color until she went into witness protection. I hadn't been the only one who lost everything when I witnessed my father's murder. Mom hadn't even been there, but she'd lost everything, too.

"You should get your hair highlighted," I suggested. "Like it used to be."

She tilted her head, fingering the straight strands. "You think?"

I nodded. "Definitely."

"I don't know," she mused.

"Oh, do it," I exclaimed. "My treat! Maybe they can fit you in while I'm getting a blow-out."

"I can go see while your polish is drying," her tech replied.

I nodded vigorously.

"Well, okay." She agreed.

The woman finished applying the polish and then went off to see if there was some availability. I glanced down at the bright, glossy red on her toes. "It's beautiful."

Mom glanced at mine, which was pure white. "So is yours."

"It reminds me of the snow," I said. *And snow reminds me of Liam.*

"I really like him," Mom said, as if she knew it wasn't the snow that made me choose the color.

"You do?"

She smiled. "I don't know many men who would live with his girlfriend's mother and his mother," she teased. Then she turned a little more serious. "He makes you happy and I see the way he looks at you. It's what every mother wants for her daughter."

"I can't imagine my life without him." I confided, glancing down at the white polish adorning my fingernails as well.

"That's good," she mused.

"Good?"

"Of course. That's how you know you found the one."

I reached my hand out, and she surrendered hers. "I'm so glad you're here. When I found out I was pregnant, you were the first person I wanted to call. Just thinking my baby would never know you was devastating."

Her eyes turned misty, and she smiled. "That's all over now. We're here together, and that won't change."

I glanced off in the direction the two nail techs went and lowered my voice. "What if he comes for us?"

"He won't. He's not going to do anything to jeopardize his freedom."

I wondered if she believed that or if she just wanted me to. She squeezed my hand and smiled. "No thinking like that, not today. Today we are being pampered and relaxing."

"So are you going to tell me where Liam is taking me tonight?"

"What makes you think I know?"

"Do you?"

"Nice try." She laughed. "My lips are sealed."

I let out a frustrated groan, and the women returned to usher us over to the salon so we could get our hair done.

Before I moved off toward the stylist's shampoo bowl, Mom caught my hand. "Bellamy."

I glanced around.

"I love you, and I'm so glad we're together again."

I rushed forward and hugged her. "Me, too, Mom."

After that, we were both whisked off, me to get a shampoo and blow-out, and Mom to get her highlights.

After our facials, nails, and hair, we headed back to Holly's. I loved the house, but even after a few months, it still didn't feel like home. As the baby inside me grew, thoughts of a place of our own became more frequent.

I didn't say anything, though, because there was enough going on already. Adding house hunting and a move into the mix wasn't wise. Besides, if we moved out, Holly would be here alone, and I didn't want to say I was ready for our own place and make Liam feel he was abandoning his mom.

"So..." Mom began, following me into our bedroom. "What are you going to wear tonight?"

Charlie was bouncing around in front of me, and I knew he wouldn't stop until I gave him my undivided attention. Dropping down, I scratched behind his ears as his tail beat against the carpet. He tried to lick me with his massive tongue, but I ducked just in time.

I stood and sat on the bed. Charlie plopped his massive head in my lap. I shrugged, thinking about my wardrobe. "Liam said something warm. So probably jeans. I don't have much to pick from."

I'd been here long enough to have a dresser full of clothes, but they were all casual. Nothing about me was fancy or even dressy. I didn't really have any "date wear."

Thinking about it made me grimace. "Maybe I should have gotten something…"

"Hold on," Mom said and disappeared from the room. A few minutes later, she came back with a large white paper bag and set it beside me on the bed.

"What's this?" I asked.

"I saw it the other day when I was in town, shopping with Holly. I thought of you, so I bought it."

"You didn't have to do that," I said, touched.

"I wanted to. There was a long period of time I wanted to give you gifts and couldn't."

Reaching into the bag, my hands closed around impossibly soft material. I lifted the item and held it out. "It's beautiful," I said, staring at the thick white cardigan. It was one of those oversized styles that I could put on over a thick, long-sleeved T-shirt for added warmth. The material was so soft and thick I wondered if perhaps it was handmade. The neck and front opening was lined with white faux fur that was almost downy to the touch.

I pulled it in, hugging the material against my chest and letting the fur tickle my cheek. "I love it. Thank you so much."

"When I saw you pick white for your nails today, I knew I had to give it to you because it matches."

I smiled. "It does."

I set aside the sweater and hugged her. Mom squeezed a little tighter than usual and whispered, "I'm so proud of you."

Sniffling, I pulled back. "So what are you going to do tonight since I won't be home?"

"Holly and I are having dinner."

I nodded. Our mothers had become good friends since Mom came here to stay. I was glad because the baby made us all family, and I wanted nothing more than for all of us to get along.

"Speaking of. We're going to be leaving soon, so I better go get dressed!" On her way out, she stopped and turned back. "I'm going to want all the details tomorrow."

"I'll take notes." I promised.

"You better not! Enjoy your time with him. Pretty soon, you're going to have a baby vying for your attention."

I rubbed a hand over my stomach and smiled to myself. He moved beneath my hand, and it made my smile widen. Since that first kick, Shaw had been very active.

A little while later, I dressed in a pair of thick black leggings, because none of my jeans would button anymore, a plain white long-sleeved shirt that was also a little snug around the belly, and added the cardigan Mom gifted me.

Since Liam said warm, I put on the boots he'd bought me when I first arrived, letting a pair of tall white socks stick out from the top.

The spa day had been really good timing because I didn't have to do my hair. It was so long, it would have taken forever to blow it out and then flat-iron it into its straight, glossy style. I loved it like this, sleek and done. I rarely ever did it this way because, well, who had time for that?

Charlie got up from the bed with a woof and raced from the room. Seconds later, Liam's voice reached me. "Bells?"

Butterflies erupted in my stomach and made me smile. "In here!" I called and turned from the dresser to race out of the bedroom. I knew I'd seen him this morning, but it felt like days ago.

He was walking across the room, on his way from the door leading into the garage, when I saw him. My footsteps faltered when our eyes met, and so did his.

We stood there on opposite sides of the room, just staring. He didn't really look any different than any other day, dressed in dark jeans, dark waterproof boots, and a heavy coat. He wasn't wearing a hat, though, and his hair was tamed, combed back and pushed into a style.

He looked the same, but there was something different, a certain air of anticipation in the way he took me in with his gray stare.

He was nervous, and it was absolutely adorable.

"I was, uh, gonna ring the doorbell." He began, offering up a sheepish smile. "But I was afraid it might scare you."

I nodded, understanding. I didn't have the best track record with opening the door to strangers.

"Are those for me?" I asked, gesturing to the huge bouquet of roses in his hand.

He glanced down as if he'd forgotten they were there. "Oh, yeah," he answered and walked toward me.

"You look," he said, sweeping his eyes over me once more, "really beautiful."

"Thanks," I said, reaching for the bouquet. There had to be two dozen roses, all of them snow white.

Fingering the silky petals, I smiled. "These are gorgeous. Thank you."

"I wasn't sure what your favorite flower was," he said, scratching behind his ear.

I whispered, "Any kind you bring me."

He reached out and pulled his fingers through a long strand of my hair. "I like this."

"I know," I said, shy. Liam loved my long hair, and as much of a pain in the ass it was, I probably would never cut it because of that.

We stared at each other for a few more quiet heartbeats, and then he cleared his throat.

"I'll put these in water. Then we can go," I said, a giddy feeling sort of rising up in me. I felt I was in high school and being picked up on a first date with a guy I had crushed on for so long and thought he hadn't even known I was alive.

But he did. And he was here. With roses.

After I found a large glass vase, I filled it with water and slid the entire bouquet inside it. I would arrange it later when we got home. For now, I was too excited.

He was waiting at the bottom of the stairs when I came down and offered a hand so he could help me the rest of the way.

I stepped down, and he didn't move back. Undeniable attraction pulsed between us, as well as anticipation. Liam reached down. I thought he was going for my hand.

Instead, he caressed the baby sandwiched between us.

His other hand came out, and I stood there as Liam cradled our child while basically making love to my face with his eyes.

My knees began to feel like Jell-O, and it was as though I were hypnotized by his presence.

The side of his mouth kicked up, and he finally let go. "Just had to get that out of the way for the night."

I smiled.

Then Liam reached for my hand. "You ready to go?"

I nodded vigorously, making him laugh low.

Right before we stepped out into the garage, I hesitated and tugged him around. "What's wrong?" he asked, stepping close, so close I had to tip my chin back to look up at him.

"I just wanted to tell you this is the best date I've ever been on."

His teeth flashed. "We haven't done anything yet."

"It doesn't matter."

He groaned and touched our foreheads together. "I'm kinda nervous," he whispered.

The confession endeared him to me even more.

"Don't be," I whispered back.

Gripping my hand, he started walking again. Leading me out into the winter's night as anticipation swirled around with the snow.

36

Liam

This wasn't just a date. It was what I hoped was the first night of the rest of our lives. Bells had no idea, but I'd put a lot of work into tonight, and so had a few others.

I was unsure how she would react. I was pretty sure tonight would go down in one of two ways:

1) Really fucking epic.

Or

2) Giant ass failure.

I was really praying it would be number one.

It wasn't a lie when I said we needed to date more. We needed more simple times, more time to just be a couple. We spent far too much of our time together trying to survive and climbing over massive obstacles.

It hadn't been easy. But it was proof. Proof we belonged together and could literally overcome anything as long as we had each other.

Even so, nerves bunched inside me, twisting my stomach and filling my head with scenarios of how badly this all could end. I was used to taking risks in my life. I mean, *To the Extreme* was my motto. Yet it was a lot different to take professional risks than it was to take personal ones.

The sky was dark when we stepped out of the staff quarters and onto the snow. Night skiing was in full swing. The mountain was lit up with large lights, and the ski lifts were all running.

All of them but one.

"Outside?" Bellamy asked as I led her over the snow toward the ski runs. "You know I can't snowboard right now."

"We aren't going boarding."

People skied past. T-he scent of snow tinted the air, and the energy of the mountain gave me some courage.

Bellamy's steps faltered when we drew closer. "Oh no," she said. "Is that lift broken? Do you need to look at it before we do whatever you have planned?"

I smiled. "It's not broken."

She wrinkled her nose. "It's not?"

I shook my head. "It's reserved."

"You can reserve a ski lift…?" She wondered, then realization lit up her eyes. Her kissable lips formed a small O. "For us?"

Bellamy stopped and leaned her head back, staring up at the lift and reminding me of the day I'd met her eight years ago.

Slipping my hand around her waist, I stepped close. "This is where it all began for us, remember?" I spoke low. "I figured this was the perfect place for it to continue."

"Continue?" she echoed.

"What do you say, Bells? You up for a ride?" I held out my hand, mimicking that day long ago. "I'll hold your hand."

A knowing and bittersweet smile graced her face. The white ball on the top of her knit cap bounced when she nodded. "I'll go anywhere with you."

I helped her into the seat, then sat beside her and made sure she was secure. Blowing out a nervous breath, I lifted my hand and signaled to the guy I had working in the lift booth. The car jolted a little when it lifted but quickly smoothed out.

We held hands as the carriage went up and up until we were suspended over the snow and trees, not quite part of the sky, but not low enough to be part of the ground.

"It really is an incredible view," she observed and laid her head on my shoulder.

"Makes you feel like anything is possible up here."

"Mmm." She agreed and gazed out over the treetops.

As the chair continued up the mountain, we left behind the night skiers as we traveled toward the black diamond run.

"You closed down the run, too?" she asked, noting the giant lights were off up here and people weren't skiing.

"There's a private party up there tonight."

"A private—" Her words cut off when she gasped and sat forward.

The chair rocked, and I anchored my arm around her tightly. "Easy." I reminded her.

"Look!" she said, not even hearing. She pointed below, and I smiled.

"What is that?" I asked, even though I knew.

"Someone lit up the black diamond run with…" She leaned out a little farther, and I pulled her back. "Is that candles?"

"They're in big jars," I informed her. Both sides of the trail (near the top) were lined with candles.

She gasped again, looked at me, then hurried to glance back down. "Oh, it's beautiful!" she murmured, watching them flicker below. "Is that for the private party?" she asked, still staring as we moved over them. "I didn't know you rented out ski trails."

"We don't," I said, reaching into my coat.

"Then what's that for?" She puzzled, finally looking away from the view at me.

"It's for you," I said, holding an open velvet box between us,

Bellamy put her hands to her mouth, her blue eyes going wide.

"You're the only girl I'd shut part of this place down for," I said, gazing into her eyes. "You're also the only girl I want to spend the rest of my life with."

Her stare dropped to the box and the ring nestled inside. Her hands fell away, and she whispered my name.

"Marry me," I said. "Put this ring on your finger and never take it off."

She reached over and gripped my thigh. Her other hand lay on my wrist.

"You want me to marry you?" she asked.

I laughed, but it was because I was so damn nervous. "Oh yes," I said, swallowing. "From the minute I saw you standing beneath the lift, looking terrified but determined, it was always you. No one else could ever come close to you. I loved you then, I love you now. . . and I even loved you all the years in between when I thought I'd lost you. Don't be the girl who got away, Bellamy. Be the girl who stays."

Tears rolled down her cheeks, and I hoped that was a good thing.

"Will you marry me?" I asked again, just so she was totally clear.

A low sob broke from her lips, and she nodded. "Yes. Yes, of course I will marry you."

I let out the breath I was holding and plucked the ring out of the box, then pitched the empty velvet over my shoulder.

She gasped and watched it fall from the sky. "Liam!"

"We don't need that. I won't be returning this," I quipped, feeling much more confident.

"What if I don't like it?" she asked, sassy.

I paused. *Well, shit.* What if she didn't like it?

Her giggle floated around, her hand over mine. "I was kidding. I don't care what it looks like. I love it."

"If you don't—"

She made a sound and cut me off. "Can I see it?"

I held it up between my fingers so she could see the diamonds.

"It's a snowflake," she whispered, gazing at it. "How in the world did you find an engagement ring in the shape of a snowflake?"

I made a sound. "I know people."

"It's gorgeous," she said, still gawking at it.

I gestured for her hand, and she tugged off her gloves and held her left one out. With the ring poised to slip over her ring finger, I paused and looked up. "Thank you," I said. "Thank you for making me the happiest man alive."

She nodded and made some sounds I hoped were happy, and I slipped the thin silver band over her finger.

The center of the snowflake was a two-carat round diamond, and all the other diamonds that clustered around it to make it into a snowflake were of smaller size.

I was shocked the jeweler I called made it so quickly, but, hey, being Caribou royalty definitely had its perks.

"I know it's not really a traditional style..." I began, nerves taking over again. "But, ah, snow is kinda my thing, and given where we live..."

"It's perfect." Bellamy held her hand out and studied the way the snowflake gently lay against her finger and sparkled. "It's the only snowflake that will never melt." She looked up and smiled brilliantly. "I love it, and I love you."

I lifted my head and let out a loud *whoop* into the sky. Then I kissed her.

She pulled back first, gazing down to the ring and then over the side of the chair. "You did all that down there? You put out all those candles?"

"I had some help."

"I can't believe you did all that just to propose to me."

"Oh, sweetheart, that wasn't for the proposal."

She wrinkled her nose. "It's not? Then what's all that for?"

I smiled. "That down there is for our wedding."

37

Bellamy

"I think this ring is making me hallucinate."

Liam laughed. "I can assure you it's not."

"I could have sworn you just said wedding."

"I did."

I blinked and glanced below at the lines of candles leading up the mountain. "You want to get married? Right now?"

His teeth were very white against the night sky behind him. "I should have married you eight years ago."

"But you just asked me," I said, still trying to catch up. This was amazing. Never in a thousand years would I have expected this tonight.

"You said yes."

I laughed. "Usually couples need time to plan a wedding."

"I don't know why. It was easy." He scoffed.

"You planned our wedding," I said, unbelievably.

"I want to marry you. Right now."

"But," I said, glancing down. My goodness, those candles flickered so beautifully against the snow. It was almost as if Liam and I were flying into another universe, one filled with starlight, magic, and glistening snow.

Liam put a finger against my cheek and pushed my face so I would look at him. "No buts. Up there at the end of this line, there's a minister, our mothers, Alex, and even Charlie. They're waiting for us to arrive so they can watch us pledge forever."

"They're all here?" I whispered, awed. "They know about this?"

"They helped plan it."

"Oh my gosh."

"Look." Liam took both my hands between his. "I know this is unconventional, but I don't want a long engagement. I don't want some stupid society wedding that the press will get wind of and hound us for months about. I know the bride normally picks out everything—"

"This is perfect." I cut him off. "I don't need to pick out anything. I don't want anything but you and our family."

He grinned crookedly. "So you'll do it? You'll marry me right fucking now?"

I laughed as excitement surged inside me. "Right fucking now."

He wagged his eyebrows. "I love it when you say naughty words."

Suppressing a smile, I lifted a finger. "There is just one thing," I said.

"I have rings. I have the paperwork. Everything is taken care of."

"I can't believe you did this," I mused, still absolutely blown away. "How did you manage this so fast?"

"I got skills," Liam replied, cocky.

I had to give it to him. "You clearly do."

"Look," he whispered, motioning below.

The lift crested the hill, and the platform came into site. What was beyond it, though, made me gasp. Up at the top of the black diamond run was a small pergola with enough space for two people to stand beneath it. The top was draped with pine greenery and more jars suspended from the wood with lit candles inside.

Just on the other side of it stood who I assumed was the minister, wearing a thick black dress coat and a thick scarf around his neck.

A few large lit jars and lanterns were perched in the snow around the area, along with a few massive bouquets of white roses. Nearby, my mom, Holly, and Alex waited, while Charlie rolled around in the snow.

"The black diamond run seemed most appropriate," Liam said quietly as I took it all in. "Because, you know, the black diamond trail is the most challenging of all. I figured with all the odds we've beat to get here, this black diamond had nothing on us."

My vision blurred a little as tears filled them. I blinked them back and then swiped at my eyes, only to have my attention caught by the gorgeous ring Liam slipped on my finger.

Everyone saw us coming, and they all began to wave. I waved back as more tears flowed. Turning to Liam, I sniffled. "I just... I don't know what to say. This is incredible."

"You don't have to say anything but yes."

I leaned forward and kissed him, my tongue nudging against his lips. He opened for me, and our tongues stroked only briefly before he pulled back. "Landing is coming up." He gestured. "Careful now."

He guided me off the chair and lifted me off the platform before the chair behind us could sweep by. He saluted the guy working the booth and then stepped so close our bodies touched.

"Are you ready to become my wife?" he murmured, staring into my eyes.

I nodded.

He grinned and started away, but a moment of doubt ensnared me and I resisted, tugging him back. "Liam."

He glanced around, a wary look crossing his features for whatever he heard in my voice. "Bellamy?"

"Before we do this, I have to ask," I said, swallowing thickly. "I need to know."

"What is it?" he said, coming back to stand in front of me.

"Are you sure this is what you want, too?"

38

Liam

I made a sweeping gesture with my hand, indicating everything I set in motion. "You seriously need to ask me that?"

"I just want to make sure you don't feel pressured. Because of the baby." She hedged, and I crossed my arms over my chest and glared. "And because of things people might be saying."

Ah.

I made a rude noise. "You think I give two shits what some fired bitches have to say?"

"Well, you exiled them for saying it, so yeah."

"I exiled them because of the way they treated you."

An impatient sound filled her throat. "I don't want to argue. I just want you to be sure. I know you love me and our baby."

"I do, which is exactly why I want you to have my name." Softening my tone, I cupped her jaw, imploring her with my eyes. "I want this. You. More than anything else. I would marry you even if you weren't pregnant, even if I wasn't famous and women weren't being jealous hags."

She rolled her eyes, and I smiled. "I will admit I'd like to be married before my son is born. He deserves that."

"Yes." She agreed. "He does."

"Good. Can we get married now?" I asked. Geez, I never had to work so hard for anything in my life.

"Yes, please."

I scooped her up and made her shriek and laugh. "Liam!" she exclaimed, patting my shoulder. "You're supposed to carry me over the threshold, not to the altar!"

"I'm doing both, sweetheart. To the extreme."

"'Bout time y'all got here. I was about to become a snowman," Alex heckled.

"You guys!" Bellamy exclaimed. "You all knew!"

"It was so hard keeping the secret!" Bells's mom exclaimed.

"Liam has been hard at work."

I set her down beside me as our family stepped close. Bellamy looked up. "How did you have time to do this and train?"

"I'm a motivated guy."

"I did it all." Alex lied.

I punched him in the shoulder. "He did not," I told Bells.

"I'm so happy for you both," Holly said, reaching for our hands. "All a mother wants is for her child to be happy."

Stephanie nodded. "It's true."

"I just wish your father was here to see it."

"He's watching." Alex assured her and looked to the sky. "He has the best seat in the house."

My throat tightened, and I glanced overhead. I hoped Dad was watching. I hoped he knew how grateful I was for his sacrifice.

"Shall we begin?" the minister said from near the awning thing. It had a fancy name, but damn if I remembered it.

I held out my hand to Bellamy, and she reached for it. Alex smacked my arm away. "That is not how this shit works!"

I spun on my best friend and glared. "Dude. I'm trying to get married here."

"And I'm trying to be the best man."

"Being best man requires you to stand over there and shut it."

"Liam!" Bellamy hissed.

"I've taken it upon myself to walk Bells down the aisle," Alex announced.

"There is no aisle," I pointed out.

"Don't you think your girl deserves a proper ceremony?"

I relented. "Yeah." I agreed. "I do."

"Doesn't anyone want to ask me what I want?" Bellamy wondered.

Both our mothers snickered.

"That boy is a handful," Stephanie told my mom.

"Is he ever."

Alex and I turned to Bellamy. "What would you like, sweetheart?"

"Go stand over there." She directed me.

Alex made a triumphant sound. I leaned in to kiss her, but she pulled back. "You have to wait until we're married."

Alex cackled, and I resisted the urge to give him the finger. I figured it wouldn't be proper in front of a minister and all.

The snow crunched beneath my boots as I went over and stood under the lights and pine near the minister.

Bellamy's cheeks were flushed and her eyes were bright when she turned to my best friend. "I'm very honored that you would do this for me."

Alex offered Bellamy his arm. "Girl, the pleasure is all mine."

She tucked her hand in his elbow, and he leaned down to kiss her cheek. She looked so happy I couldn't yell at him.

"He ever gives you any trouble, you just come to me," Alex told her.

"I'm waiting down here," I called out.

Bellamy giggled and started forward with Alex. Her mom gasped quietly and hurried over and handed her a bouquet of roses. She accepted, and then they started toward me again.

There was no music except for the rustling of the wind in the trees, and the only light was from the millions of stars overhead and the candles we'd placed all around.

Honestly, it wouldn't have mattered if it was this or a million people standing watch. The only two people who existed in this moment were her and me.

Our eyes never strayed as she closed the distance between us, and I savored every step she took because in just moments, she would officially be mine.

Alex stopped in front of us, and Bellamy rushed forward. A pulled her back, though, saying, "Whoa, girl, slow your roll."

"Bro," I growled in warning.

"Go ahead," Alex said to the minister, ignoring me.

"Who gives this woman to this man?" the minister said clearly.

Bellamy giggled, and even though I was annoyed, my lips twitched.

"That would be me," Alex replied dutifully.

I reached for my girl, and Alex grabbed my hand. "Take care of her."

"You know I will."

He nodded and dropped my hand, came forward, and hugged me. "Congrats, man. You deserve this. It's good to see you happy."

I forgot how annoying he was being and hugged him back. "Thanks, Alex," I replied. "Wouldn't have wanted to do this without you at my side."

"Always." He pulled back and smiled at Bellamy, then moved over to my side.

Mom and Stephanie were already crying as I pulled Bellamy to me. She smiled up at me, candlelight reflected in her eyes and glistening off the sleek strands of her hair coming out from beneath her hat.

I honestly couldn't think of anything more perfect… more us. Standing on the top of the mountain with the people we loved most.

It moved me in ways I honestly hadn't expected.

"I love you," she whispered, reaching up and stroking my cheek.

"Love you more," I mouthed back.

The minister cleared his throat, and we turned to face him. Our vows carried with the wind and echoed through the trees. Rings were exchanged, and a long kiss was shared.

It didn't take very long to bind us for eternity, which somehow seemed appropriate because in truth, Bellamy owned me from the very first moment we met.

39

Bellamy

Holy cow. *I am married.* I was Mrs. Liam Mattison.

Best date *ever.*

I wanted to pinch myself; this was all so unreal and amazing. Instead, I glanced down at the snowflake adorning my finger and the newly positioned diamond wedding band.

Butterflies flapped around in my stomach while pure joy split my face with a smile.

"Are you happy?" Liam asked, lifting my hand and kissing the rings he'd just put there.

"So happy," I replied, returning the gesture and kissing his newly adorned hand.

"Wait!" Alex called out just before the lift operator could send us back down the mountain.

Liam and I both glanced over our shoulders as Alex came bounding through the snow with Charlie hot on his heels. He was carrying a huge white poster with a couple white balloons attached and trailing behind him.

I laughed. "What in the world are you doing?"

"It's tradition," he exclaimed and spun the huge sign around.

JUST MARRIED

Liam nodded. "Good call."

Alex attached it to the back of our chair, and the balloons floated around behind us.

"Fly free, love birds! Fly free!" Alex said, stepping back.

Mom and Holly clapped and cheered as the chair jolted forward and carried us away from our wedding spot.

"I'm sad to leave," I said, taking in the candles and the view before it was out of sight.

"The night's not over yet," Liam promised in a voice that made my thighs squeeze together.

"It isn't?"

He shook his head, eyes like melted silver. "We have the honeymoon suite at the resort."

I glanced toward the huge lit-up building down the mountain and smiled. "You seriously thought of everything,"

"Oh, sweetheart, I'm just getting started."

"What could possibly be left?" I wondered.

"You'll see," he murmured, lowering his lips.

He kissed softly but deep. I was lightheaded with happiness as my body grew heavy with need.

I don't know how long we kissed, but when he finally pulled back, I noted the resort seemed a lot closer than before.

Liam glanced around, and a slow smile lifted his lips. "You ready for your wedding present?"

I gasped. "A wedding present! My word, Liam, the wedding was more than enough."

He made a noise, not agreeing or disagreeing, then dazzled me with a smile. "Well? Are you?"

"I don't need any more presents."

"You're going to like it," he teased.

"Where is it?" I asked curiously, reaching into his coat. "In here?"

His chuckle loosened more of my lower half, and I groaned. Liam put an arm around me and gazed out over the landscape. "See that over there?" he asked, pointing.

I leaned around him to look. "What?"

"That down there. It's a light."

It took a moment, but then I saw a lit-up X down below. "That X?" I asked.

He nodded.

"What is it?"

"That, sweetheart, is the future location of our new house."

I gasped. "A house!"

"Mm-hmm. It's a good lot, private and not too close to the resort, but still close enough I can take a snowmobile to work."

"You built us a house!"

"Oh no. Taking over our wedding is one thing, but I would never build an entire house without you picking everything you want inside."

I started to cry. I mean, really. How much happiness could one girl get in a single night before she dissolved in a puddle of tears and amazement?

"It's okay." Liam soothed, pulling me into his chest. "We can find some other lot."

"No!" I said, jerking back. The lift starting rocking, and Liam reached to steady us. "I love it. I don't want anything else."

"Then why are you crying?" he asked warily.

"Because I'm so happy, and I just love you so much!" I wailed.

He pulled me back into his chest. "I think the cold is getting to you."

I sniffled. "No, it's not. You are!"

"Me?" He wondered.

"You're perfect!" I wailed again. In that moment, it was unfathomable how I could ever show him how much he meant to me, how much the life we were building meant.

For a long time, I existed in a tiny apartment, afraid to go out, closing myself off from any friend I might have, cut off from my family and life.

And then I ran here to hide.

I found home.

I found love that could withstand death. That could rival fear. I found a reason for everything and rediscovered my heart.

I found it all within a single man.

The lift began lowering from the sky, and the lights from the resort seemed so bright compared to the candles we'd just left. Liam practically lifted me off the chair and platform.

"Wait here," he said and kissed me on the forehead.

I watched him jog over to the booth where his helper was sitting. He slapped some cash into the guy's hand and said something. They both laughed, and then Liam jogged back to me.

We went up the staff elevator in the hotel, all the way to the top floor. Liam already had the room key, so we didn't have to stop and speak to anyone on the way.

The elevator opened to a small hallway with one wide door on one end and a large window offering a stunning view on the other. Before even making it to the door, Liam grabbed me by the waist and pushed me against the wall, claiming my mouth. I moaned and kissed him back, raking my hands through his hair. He moved suggestively against me, and I wrapped my leg around his. With a grunt, he pulled back and picked me up, my legs anchored around him instantly. Still kissing, Liam carried me down the hall and stopped in front of the door. It took a few tries for him to dig the key out of his pocket, but when he did, he pulled his mouth free and licked over his lips.

"Marriage tastes good on you, Bells."

"Open the door," I urged, husky.

When it was open, he shoved it back with his foot and strolled inside. It slammed behind us, but the sound was lost on me.

The exquisiteness of the space drowned out everything else.

"*Oh, Liam*," I whispered.

"I think I owe some people a raise," he murmured.

The suite was filled with buckets of white roses and candles. Soft music played through the space. The curtains on the large window were open, and the illuminated resort lay below like the kingdom it was.

Liam set me down, and I went around trailing my fingers over the delicate rose petals and gazing at the extravagant decoration.

"Every rose in the entire town must be here."

"The next town over, too." He admitted.

"Oh, look!" I said, rushing over to a table with a small white cake on it. It was one tier, all white, with a simple white ribbon around the base. On the top was a statue of a bride and another of a snowboarder. It made me laugh. "It's us!"

Liam came up behind me and nuzzled the side of my neck. "Cute," he said.

"I take it you're not hungry."

"Not for cake."

I swiped my finger up the side of the cake, coating it with icing. Holding it up, I asked, "How about now?"

Liam closed his hand around my wrist and pulled my hand back. His lips slid over my finger to suck the icing off. The sensation of his tongue licking over me made me sway back against him.

He sucked even after the icing was gone, slowly dragging his lips up until pulling back completely. "Best cake I ever had," he murmured and pulled me around to kiss me passionately.

I was breathing heavy when he lifted his head. My brain was fuzzy, and the room was scented with roses and vanilla. Taking his hand, I led him through the suite toward the bedroom. On the way, we passed a massive bedroom with flickering candles and rose petals scattered across the tile floor.

"Look," I said and changed course, stepping inside. In the center of the floor was a giant white tub, large enough for four people. It was filled almost to the top with water. More rose petals floated on the surface, and a huge arrangement of them sat beside the tub. "That looks heavenly."

Liam walked toward the water and dipped a finger in, making the water and petals ripple and wave. "Water is still warm. How about it, wife?" He beckoned, pulling at his coat. "Want to soak?"

I started shedding the layers I had on, aware of Liam watching with heavy-lidded eyes. I stripped deliberately, putting on a show for him in the candlelight.

He'd stopped pulling at his own clothes in favor of staring at me, so I made it worth his while and dipped my fingers below the waistband of my leggings and let out a low moan.

No longer patient, Liam came forward, his palms cupping my bare breasts and kneading the flesh. My head fell back, and I sighed. It felt so good. They'd been growing larger and aching. He worked down my body, pulling off the rest of my clothes.

"Open for me," he whispered, still on his knees in front of me.

I spread my legs, and he kissed across my inner thigh as his fingers delved into my folds. I grabbed his hair to steady myself as one finger dipped in, teasing, then pulled back out.

"Liam," I panted.

He stood and swept me off my feet, cradling me against his chest and kissing me dizzy. Next thing I knew, I was being lowered into the bath, the warm water slipping over my skin like silk and taunting my already humming body.

"Touch yourself," he told me, backing up to start pulling at his clothes. My hand went below the water and stroked across my clit. Visibly, I shuddered, and Liam chucked his clothes faster. His dick stood out from his body, thick and proud. I watched as he wrapped a hand around it and stroked.

The second he was within touching distance, I lifted my hand and let water glide over his stiff cock, enjoying the way it pulsed when the liquid trickled over it. I did it again, then leaned forward and sucked it all off.

The water level rose when Liam lowered into the tub, some of it splashing out on the floor, but no one cared. He picked up a white rose petal and dragged it across my collarbone as his free hand rolled my nipple between his fingers.

The ends of my hair soaked up the water and trailed behind me when Liam pulled me closer. The tub was so big he could easily stretch out his legs and lean against the side. I straddled his waist and rocked against him. He grabbed my hips and urged me into a rocking motion. He wasn't inside me yet, but it didn't matter. I was so turned on, just rubbing up against him had the power to make me quake.

Liam's head leaned back against the edge of the porcelain, and his eyes drifted closed. Candlelight flickered, creating a play of shadow and light over his strong jaw and cheekbones.

Tired of playing, I lifted slightly. Liam adjusted, bending his knees and grabbing my ass. I slid down over his cock deliciously slow, making us both moan loudly.

When he was fully sheathed, I held still for long moments, just feeling him inside me. He cupped a hand beneath the water and lifted it, pouring water over my shoulder and over my chest. I closed my eyes, and he did it again.

I started rocking, riding him beneath the water. He made a satisfied sound and leaned his head back again, exposing his neck. I bent down and latched on, sucking him gently and then licking over it. His hips thrust up, meeting mine, and more water splashed over the side, splattering on the floor.

My breasts tingled when he covered them, massaging and stroking, making the nipples vibrate and shoot tingles of pleasure down to where his dick was.

I started riding him harder. Water splashed around and rose petals stuck to his chest.

"That's it, sweetheart," he purred, gripping my ass and pushing up.

I moaned and bore down, gasping when he hit the perfect spot.

"Liam," I said, restless, still moving, searching.

He sat forward quickly, locking me against his chest and digging his hand into the hair at the base of my neck. With a single rotation of his hips, my body tightened, and then he thrust up and rocked.

I cried out, white light exploding behind my eyes as pure bliss rolled over me in waves. I collapsed against him even as the sensations continued and his dick milked my body for every last ounce of pleasure.

I was still riding the wave of elation when he made a sound and grabbed my shoulder. I swiveled my hips, and his teeth sank into my skin. He shouted when he came and kissed across my shoulder as the aftershocks rippled through his limbs.

Afterward, we washed each other tenderly, and I lay in his arms until the water turned cold.

40

Liam

I was pretty damn happy with myself.

It was a damn good wedding I pulled off and an even better wedding night. I knew marriage wouldn't be all fun and games, but damn, we were off to a pretty epic start. I kept my wife up past her bedtime, so it was no surprise she was sleeping late.

I was already awake, having grown used to crack-of-dawn training times, but I'd been content to lay there curled around her body. My hand cradled her stomach, and a sense of peace I'd never quite achieved before filled me.

I guess putting a ring on it truly made it mine. At least officially.

And honestly?

I fucking loved Bells having my name. It was just another layer of protection, another way of making sure she was safe. I had no intention of going anywhere, but life taught me to be prepared. My father's untimely death hammered home the lesson.

Perry Crone was set to be released literally any day now, and all my attempts at blocking that son of a bitch failed. Crone owned a lot of people in high places. Either that or a lot of people were really terrified of him.

If something happened to me, as my wife, Bellamy would be taken care of. Everything would go to her. On top of that, the Mattison name would shield her, open doors that might otherwise remain closed.

I knew I told her it didn't matter what people around here said, and it really didn't, not to me. But like it or not, there was another level to it. Life's politics were in effect even in this wintery resort town. By slipping that ring on her finger, I put a barrier around her. I sealed her position and basically silently demanded she have the respect she deserved.

Not to mention, my son would be the rightful heir to all of this.

Call it archaic. Call it staking my claim. I didn't give a fuck because I was doing what I had to do to protect me and mine.

Life was short. Life was difficult. Why not grab on to some joy, too? Bells was my joy, and being married to her was better than winning an Olympic medal.

She stirred and slowly rolled to her back and smiled. Lifting my hand up over her head, she fingered the steel band wrapped around my finger.

"It wasn't a dream," she murmured, pulling my hand into her chest and holding it there.

"Nope. You're stuck with me for life."

"I can live with that."

I leaned down and kissed her, then pulled back and snagged the phone off a nearby table and called down to the kitchen.

"It's Liam," I said when they answered.

"Congratulations on your marriage!" the person on the line sang.

I chuckled and glanced at Bellamy lying there looking at me. "Thank you. You can go ahead and get my order ready and sent up."

"Right away," they replied and then hung up.

"Your order?" Bellamy inquired, stretching like a cat.

"Part of my duties as a husband is to make sure you are fed. Breakfast will be up soon."

"You're a pretty good husband."

I flashed a smile. "Just pretty good?"

She pretended to think it over, and I leaned over her, brushing a kiss across her lips.

"Pretty great." She amended against my lips.

My tongue slid against hers, coaxing a deeper kiss that lingered for several long heartbeats. Bellamy turned her face, breaking the kiss, and I moved down her cheek and jaw.

"Epically amazing," she murmured.

My hand closed around her breast.

"Best ever." She went on.

"That's better." I agreed.

We made out until the bell on the door rang, and I groaned. "Wait." She cajoled, wrapping her legs around my waist when I tried to get up.

I chuckled and let her have some of my weight again, making her sigh, content.

"Don't you want some French toast? Bacon? Hot chocolate?"

"I'd rather have more of you." Her hand slid down my body and landed on my bare ass.

"Your body needs a break, sweetheart. I went at you more than once last night. And you need to feed my son."

Her lower lip stuck out in a pout, and I sucked it between mine. We kissed another moment. Then I slipped out of bed and grabbed my boxers off the end of the bed.

"Hurry back," she called.

I paused to look through the peephole, making sure the staff just left the tray there and wasn't waiting on the other side.

No one was there, so I pulled it open, expecting to find a large room service cart.

It wasn't there.

Instead, there was a small white gift on the floor in front of me, a large red satin bow tied around the package. Even though the hallway was empty, I glanced around anyway, as if the person who left it would just be hanging around.

I bent and picked it up, noting there was no tag.

The elevator dinged, and I glanced up. A large cart draped in white linens emerged from the elevator first, followed by a young woman in a pressed uniform. She jerked to a stop when she saw me there. Her cheeks went bright red as she tried to avert her gaze.

I have to say, she must not have tried very hard because her eyes fastened on my abs and chest like glue.

"Morning," I said, not bothering to jump around and try and cover the fact I was only wearing boxer briefs. I did move the gift down in front of my package because I was still rocking a semi hard-on.

She cleared her throat and forced her eyes down to the cart. "Good morning, Mr. Mattison."

I usually told people to call me Liam, but it seemed pretty inappropriate to correct a girl who was not my wife to call me by my first name while I stood there in my skivvies.

When she drew close enough, I grasped the end of the cart and pulled it close. "Did you leave this outside the door?" I asked.

She glanced at the gift and shook her head. "No, sir."

"Do you know who did? The staff maybe?"

She shook her head. "Not that I know of."

"No worries," I said, but inwardly, I was wondering where it came from. I mean, no one knew we were staying here last night except our close family and the minister.

I set the box on the edge of the cart, noting the arrangement of red roses in the center. "That's a nice touch."

"That is from the staff. Along with the cake in your room."

"My wife loves that, by the way," I said, picking up the service tab and signing my name. Then I added a generous tip.

When I looked up and held it out, she glanced away quickly, having been caught staring again. "Thank you."

Keeping her eyes averted, she took the slip and scurried toward the elevator.

I pulled the cart into the room and shut the door.

Bellamy came out of the bedroom, a thick white robe tied loosely around her. "I'm starving," she said, going straight for the cart.

"Oh, what's this?" she asked, distracted by the gift. "Liam, you've already given me far too much."

She reached for it, smiling. A sick, wary feeling washed over me as she did. Moving fast, I snatched it out of reach. "It's not from me."

She frowned. "From the staff, then?"

"It was in the hall when I opened the door. The room service girl said it wasn't from the staff."

"A surprise?" she said, a little excitement in her eyes, but very quickly, it changed, wilting and dying a swift death.

Bellamy looked at the gift as if it were a bomb about to detonate at any moment. My girl did not have a good track record of good things just showing up at her door.

And the way my instincts were screaming at me?

This wasn't a good thing.

"Is there a tag?" she whispered.

"No."

"Did you tell people about the wedding?"

"No."

"Liam…" she said warily, fear plain in her voice. I couldn't help but notice the way her hand went straight to her rounded belly.

There was only one way to really know what was inside and who it was from. In one swift move, I tugged the ribbon right off the box and lifted the lid.

Bellamy shifted nervously from foot to foot as I cleared away some of the white tissue paper and reached inside.

There were three cotton bundles tied together, so I pulled them out and set aside the box. I unrolled the first to reveal a black T-shirt in a size big enough for me. I held it up so we could both see the back.

KING
01

I unrolled the next, which was the same black T-shirt but in a size meant for Bellamy.

QUEEN
01

The third wasn't a T-shirt, but a black onesie for a baby.

PRINCE
01

"Is that all there is?" Bellamy asked, holding back any reaction.

I set aside the shirts and lifted the box, pushing around in the tissue paper. "That's it." I confirmed.

"Oh," she said, relieved. "Well, I have to admit it's all pretty adorable. She came over and picked up the onesie, and I had to fight not to snatch it away from her. Holding up the tiny garment, she cooed. "Just look how tiny!" She held it up to her stomach and mine lurched. "Someone sent you a present, pumpkin," she told the baby. "Someday, you'll be big enough to wear it. My little prince."

Bellamy glanced up at me, smiling with a soft light in her eyes. "It was probably from someone on the staff. I'm sure word got around last night that you were up here and why you had the black diamond run shut down. After all, everyone says you're the king."

"Yeah, probably," I said, taking the baby outfit from her and placing it with the other two. I added, "I'll ask around tomorrow."

"Yes, definitely. I'd love to send a thank-you card to who sent it. How adorable, our little family has matching outfits now."

She was standing there cradling her baby bump with a happy glow lighting up her face. *My wife.*

"How about some breakfast in bed?" I smiled, grabbing the handle of the cart.

I followed behind her toward the bedroom, stopping only long enough to toss the clothes on the counter on the way. We ate our fill of the elaborate breakfast I'd ordered the night before. Watching Bells lick warm syrup off her fingers and lips made me forget all about the gift.

After I'd given in and made gentle love to her on the pillows and blankets, I held her while she dozed back to sleep.

Slipping out from beneath her, I crept back into the main room, past the shirts, and to the box I'd said was empty.

Yep. I lied.

There was something else inside the box.

Something I didn't want to ruin Bellamy's wedding night. Christ, we hadn't even had a full day as a married couple. She looked so happy and at peace. I couldn't take it away from her.

It was my job to shield her from this shit. Her and my son.

After glancing behind me to make sure she hadn't followed, I picked up the note left in the bottom of the box.

William,

Much congratulations on the marriage and pending arrival of your son. It seems that living with the death of your father and the reason for it hasn't proved as difficult for either of you as I predicted. It's a shame your embraced happiness didn't make it easier for you to embrace mine. I was rather disappointed to hear of all the noise you've been creating about my release. Perhaps you should have focused more on your wife and unborn child, because if you had, I wouldn't have to.

Long live the king.

PC

I stared at the note a long time, reading the words over and over again. Correction. Not words. Threat. Perry Crone just threatened my family.

As smart of a man as he was, this was very, *very* stupid.

41

Bellamy

I woke with a smile on my lips. I was married. To Liam. If someone told me a year ago, while I was holed up in my crappy apartment alone and jumping at every noise, that this is where I would end up, I would have accused them of being cruel.

Back then, thinking I would have anything even remotely as amazing as this was painful to even dream of.

I didn't think life had anything good in store for me.

I was wrong.

I scooted back, expecting to come up against my new husband, but all I felt was empty space. Looking over my shoulder, I frowned to see he wasn't there.

"Liam?" I called out, sitting up and pulling the sheet with me.

He appeared seconds later, strolling in the doorway in nothing but his tight, black boxer briefs. God, he was an amazing sight. The past couple of months of intense training honed his body even more, defining every muscle that rippled whenever he walked.

"You like what you see?" he drawled, cocky, as my eyes lingered on his form.

"I'm pretty sure any woman with a heartbeat would like this sight. Hell, probably even a few without."

He grinned.

"Where were you?" I pouted, reaching out to caress his abs.

"Getting this." He held up a large manila envelope with a red bow on it. I looked at it, surprised, and Liam chuckled.

"You didn't even notice it, did you?"

"You expect me to see anything but you when you walk around almost naked?"

"Fair enough." He allowed. Swiftly, he reached out and tugged down the sheet covering my bare chest.

"Hey!" I said as cool air brushed over my breasts.

"It's only fair."

"Not really. I don't make as pleasing of a sight as you."

He smacked the envelope on the bed to plant his hands on his hips. It only served to draw attention to the sharply defined V that trailed beneath the waistband of his boxers.

"There is no sight on this planet more beautiful than you sitting in my bed with rumpled hair, naked breasts, and my baby on full display."

I felt my cheeks heat as his eyes appraised me. The urge to cover myself was pretty strong, but I liked the intensity in his stare. I liked the way his expression totally proved his words.

"What is that?" I asked, pointing at the envelope.

"Your wedding present."

"You got me a house."

"I got you some land to put a house on." He corrected.

"Same thing," I retorted and stuck out my tongue.

He swooped forward and sucked it into his mouth, making me melt toward the mattress. A strong arm wound around my back and supported me, holding me in place so he could suck and tease the tongue I'd threatened him with.

When he was done, he pulled back and smirked, completely proud.

"I really wish you hadn't," I said, indicating the packet.

"I don't think you will say that once you see what it is."

I was curious, sure. But I felt incredibly guilty and a little undeserving. "I didn't get you anything."

Liam reached out and caressed my stomach. "Yes, you did."

"You might say different when you're changing a diaper at three a.m."

He spread his hands in invitation. "Bring it on."

"It doesn't feel right. You giving me all these things."

He picked up the envelope and slid it in front of me. "I didn't buy this. I just made a call."

Curiosity won out. Did you really expect it not to? I pulled open the flap and glanced inside. There appeared to be several documents inside.

Wrinkling my brow, I looked up.

He nodded for me to keep going.

I slipped everything out and put it in my lap. Liam grasped the envelope, pulled it open, and held it upside down until a small card fluttered out and landed face down on the top.

I picked it up, turning it over, and gasped.

I glanced between him and the card, surprised. "How…?"

"You deserved this."

"But the FBI said it wasn't possible!" Tucking the card close in my lap, I lifted the papers and read the one on top.

The FBI said they couldn't give you your name back. The one you were born with. That's not what that is." He pointed to the line with my new legal name.

"It's better," I whispered, eyes becoming blurry.

Bellamy Michelle Mattison, the official documents proclaimed. I picked up the new social security card with the same name printed on it.

No more Bella Lane. No more being someone I wasn't. No more hiding and pretending.

"You were gonna have to change it anyway, with the wedding. So I called them. They agreed to put it through with your real first and middle name, adding my name at the end."

I flung myself at him, the papers trapped between our bodies.

"This means so much to me," I cried, hugging him tight. "I can finally just be me."

"You were always you, sweetheart. Now it's just legal."

I pulled back, tears falling. "I have your name."

He made a sound. "'Bout time."

"How did you get them to do all this without me."

"Frost owes me. He owes us both." He reached down between us and pulled out one of the papers beneath the top. "It's technically not official… You have to sign this first."

"I need a pen!" I exclaimed, pushing at his shoulder so I could get up and find one.

He reached behind him and pulled one out.

"Was that in your underwear?" I asked, widening my eyes.

"Lucky pen," he quipped.

I snatched it with a giggle and scrawled my signature across the document.

"It's official," I proclaimed, smiling wide.

Liam tucked some hair behind my ear and smiled. "Mrs. Mattison," he murmured before leaning down to kiss me.

I tried to pull him closer, but he wouldn't let me. "Hold that thought," he said, reaching for another document. "I need you to sign this, too."

I took the paper and glanced over it and smiled. "You already signed it," I observed, running my finger over his signature.

"I'm not playing around," he said. "You're mine."

"Right here?" I asked, pointing.

He nodded, and I signed the bottom of our marriage certificate, making that official, too.

He gathered them up, carefully placing them back in the envelope as though they were sacred and he was afraid they might get misplaced. "We have to get these filed today."

"We do?"

"I want it done as soon as possible."

My heart rose into my throat, and speaking was impossible.

"Hey, you okay?" he asked, bending to look into my eyes while swiping away a tear.

I swallowed my heart, forcing it back into my chest, and nodded. "Perfect."

Liam kissed my forehead.

"Want me to get dressed so we can go?"

His eyes swept over me. He pushed the length of my hair behind my shoulder. "Not yet," he murmured, leaning down to kiss my bare shoulder. "We've got some time."

It was time spent deliciously.

42

Liam

I'd been up for hours when a snowmobile came into view from the halfpipe. Joiner noticed as well, then gestured for me to go again, regardless.

Even though I had a compelling list of worries, I forced those thoughts out to focus. The only way I was able to do it was with practice. I had to condition the mind just as much as the body.

It was part of being a pro athlete. Part of the reason I was once the best snowboarder in the world. When my feet were strapped in, when I was on the pipe, there was nothing else. No one else. Being distracted could get me killed.

I blocked out Alex's arrival and positioned myself. Pulling the goggles down over my eyes, I blew out a breath and erased my mind. I pushed off, the board making a sound I sometimes heard in my sleep.

It was a solid run. I hit the landings and made the turns. Was it my best ever? Nope.

But it was good. It was progress. And my knee was hanging in.

"Looking good!" Alex yelled, and I started toward him, toting my board with me.

"I'm taking a few," I told Joiner when I passed him.

"Not too long. Don't let your muscles get cold."

"Yeah, yeah," I muttered and moved on. I was hitting it hard today because I refused to train yesterday. Like I was going to drag my ass out of bed and leave my brand-new wife to pound the powder. It was bad enough I was back at it today.

Joiner was acting as if I'd missed weeks instead of one day. It was going to be interesting to see how my knee was at the end of this all-day session because I had to basically fit two training sessions into one day.

I'd wanted to whisk Bells off on some tropical honeymoon. Trade the snow in for some sand. Ever since I opened the letter from Crone, I was wishing I had. It might be good to get her the hell out of here for a while.

Of course, our problems would still be here when we returned, or worse… They'd follow us just like they'd followed us to our honeymoon suite.

Crone was a bastard.

"Got your message," Alex said when I was close. "What's going on?"

I hitched a chin toward the small house. "Inside."

I left my board and boots by the door, tugged off my gear, and ran a hand through my hair on my way to the small fridge. "You want some coffee or something?"

"Haven't had any coffee yet," Alex replied.

I dropped a pod into the machine on the counter and hit the button, then moved by to get a bottle of the specially formulated drink I loaded up on when I was training.

"This is some dedication," Alex observed, waiting for his coffee to finish pouring. "If I got married the day before yesterday, I'd still be knee deep in my bride."

I chugged some of the drink and then set it on the counter to reach into my coat and pull out the note Crone sent. "We got a little wedding gift from Crone," I spat and tossed it beside Alex.

Snatching it up, he read it through quickly, then slammed it down on the counter. "What the fuck?"

"He sent matching shirts… including one for the baby."

"Oh, fuck no!" Alex roared. "What kind of scumbag threatens a baby?"

"The kind with a death wish," I replied, cold and calm.

"How's Bellamy handling this?"

"She doesn't know." I admitted.

Alex looked at me as if I'd grown an extra dick right in the middle of my forehead. "She saw the shirts, assumed they were from the staff, and I didn't correct her. That scumbag has taken enough from her. I wasn't letting him take her wedding night, too."

Alex nodded. "I get it. But you're gonna have to tell her. She has to know."

I let out a few curses and sat down. "I know."

"Where's she at?"

I made a sour face. "Work."

"What do you want to do?"

"Kill him," I said honestly.

Alex lifted the coffee and sipped it. "I can help you make that happen."

Letting out a frustrated growl, I shoved out of my seat and made a call.

"Agent Frost," he answered on the second ring.

"I need to get back in there."

"And where is that?" Frost replied, not surprised at all I didn't bother with a greeting.

He'd get a greeting when he got Crone off our backs.

"I need to see him again. Put me on the list."

"You can't see him—" He started to protest.

"He contacted me, threatened Bellamy and the baby."

Frost's voice grew a little louder in my ear, as if he sat forward suddenly. "How?"

I told him about the note and the clothes. Then I added, "And he left it on the doorstep of the honeymoon suite we were staying in that no one knew about."

"Okay, Liam, I need to know exactly what the note said."

"I'm going back to that prison," I declared. "And I want his release revoked." This time I wasn't taking no for an answer.

"I'm afraid that's not possible."

"You owe us this," I ground out, angry.

"He's already been released."

The words felt like a bullet ripping through flesh and pummeling right into my heart. "What did you just say?"

Alex perked up from where he was lounging.

"All his paperwork went through. He was released yesterday. He's no longer in custody."

"And you didn't think I needed to be made aware!" I yelled.

He cleared his throat. "I tried to call. You didn't answer."

Fuck me. Couldn't a guy get one damn day? "I got married. I was busy."

"Congratulations," Frost said, sounding more annoyed than happy.

Like I gave a flying fuck.

"Where is he?" I demanded, spinning around and looking at Alex. *He's out*, I mouthed.

Alex whistled low.

"In New York, at his home. He's being monitored. We have people in place to make sure he stays put."

"Spare me the shit. We both know it's not good enough."

"We're doing everything within the law."

I snorted. "That's the problem. You jack-offs are doing everything by the book while he has no rules."

"I did everything I could, Liam. The Bureau did everything we could. My hands were tied."

"Well, mine aren't," I inflected dangerously.

"I don't like the way that sounds, Mattison."

"Yeah, well, I don't like worrying that my pregnant wife is going to be killed by some animal you let out of prison!"

"I'll send some agents out. I'm going to need that note."

"What the hell for? So you can say you tried to do something when shit hits the fan again?"

"I know you are frustrated—"

"You have no idea," I growled.

"Please, Mattison. Let me do my job."

"Do it fast," I replied and disconnected the call. "What an asshat," I said, tossing the cell on the counter.

"You're right, you know. They're bound by a bunch of boundaries and laws. Crone isn't," Alex remarked.

"The only way this is going to be over is if I take him out."

"Killing a man changes you," Alex said, matter-of-fact.

"So does standing by and letting the same man kill your family."

Alex inclined his head. "I just want you to think about what you're doing."

I cocked my head to the side. "You think I would regret it?"

Her pursed his lips and rubbed a hand over his jaw. "No."

"Then why are we having this conversation?"

"Because it's my job to be your conscience just like it's yours to be mine."

I appreciated that. I really did. Alex was the best friend I would ever have. "You've kept me straight more times than I care to admit."

"Same. It's what we do."

I nodded, then asked, "What choice do I have?"

"You don't." Alex asserted. "If I was in your position, I would do the same."

It wasn't lost on me that we were standing around talking about killing a man like we sometimes talked about the weather.

This is what life had become.

This was the man I'd become.

No. This was the man Crone was forcing me to become.

Bellamy

My last day at The Inn was uneventful. Which was good. I liked uneventful. Not enough things in life seemed to be as of late. However, it would have been nice to see a little bit of a sendoff. Someone to acknowledge I'd done my job well.

No such luck.

Instead, all I got was the air tinged with the collective feeling of relief from everyone. Including Chef D'alessio.

It just proved my exit from this kitchen was for the best. I loved cooking and I loved working in the culinary arts field, but doing it in a place where no one liked me was far from a dream.

I still liked to think that perhaps *I* wasn't disliked, rather than the connections I had.

I caught a few people staring at the large diamond ring on my finger, nestled against the diamond band beside it. I knew people wanted to ask. They were so curious.

But it was hard to ask a personal question of someone you made very clear they were not your friend.

I didn't volunteer the info either. Let them wonder. Word was likely spreading around the entire resort like wildfire anyway. It was petty, I supposed, but it gave me a little satisfaction to know I had information they wanted and didn't give up.

I finished all my work an hour early, and instead of offering to help a few of the others with the jobs they seemed behind on, I didn't. I took off my chef's coat, made sure the station I'd been working in was pristine, and then turned in everything I had that belonged to the kitchen.

I clocked out early, aware the chef was standing in the doorway behind me, quietly watching. After I pulled my bag over my shoulder, I turned. "I just wanted to thank you for giving me the opportunity to work here at The Inn. I know it wasn't ideal accepting a hire you didn't have any say in, but working with you has taught me a lot."

Like how not *to run a kitchen.*

He straightened, a little surprise and, dare I say, embarrassment flashed over his features.

"Also, it will always mean something that my late father-in-law believed in me enough to let me work in his best kitchen." While what I said before was mostly out of politeness, this last part I said with heart and truth. I meant that. Ren gave me a chance when he didn't have to. When, honestly, it would have been better for him if he hadn't.

I would never forget that. And I would make sure his namesake didn't either.

Embarrassment did flush his face then. I guess feeling like you'd somehow let down the late and great Renshaw Mattison was an unpleasant reminder.

Chef cleared his throat. "I'm sorry this didn't work out. You do have many talents in the kitchen."

I didn't know if he actually meant that or not, and to be honest, his opinion of me didn't matter.

How freeing it was to realize that. To know with absolute truth that I just didn't care. I had a full, happy life, and it was okay to let this part go. It wasn't a failure so much as a lesson.

"Good luck," I bid and left the kitchen.

I knew luck wouldn't help him. As soon as this season was over, he was out. Liam was already quietly looking for a replacement. I didn't feel bad about it either, because this resort could do much better.

I knew the job could be mine, but truthfully, I didn't want it.

I had no desire to go to a place filled with people who resented me and would only do what I said because Liam would intimidate them. I still hoped for a career in food prep, but I didn't think a place like The Inn was the right fit for me. I wanted something a little more casual, something closer to the heart of the resort and the people who vacationed here.

Yes, that was my brain forming some ideas and dreams. But I would let them percolate for a while before I ever brought them up. For now, my focus was on my son and my husband.

Since I was a little early getting home and my creative juices were flowing—funny how they didn't start to flow again until after I left my "creative" job—I decided to make some of Liam's favorite pumpkin bread and then some dinner. Perhaps Liam's other favorite, chicken and beef tacos with homemade salsa and guacamole.

"How was your last day?" Mom asked, perched on a barstool at the island as I pulled out ingredients.

"Uneventful," I replied. "I'm glad to be done. Now I can focus on this little guy." I went on, rubbing my stomach. The baby moved beneath my touch, and I smiled.

"You've been through a lot, more than anyone should. I think you deserve some time off to relax and enjoy life."

"I'm lucky to have that ability," I said, slicing an avocado in half. I decided to make the guacamole first so Mom and I could snack on it while I baked. "Not everyone has a husband that can support that."

"That's true," Mom allowed. "I hope you don't feel guilty about it, though."

"I'm working on it," I said, honestly.

Once the guac was done, I popped a taste in my mouth and then added a little more seasoning. Afterward, I dunked in a tortilla chip and tried it again.

"Good," I said and pushed the large bowl toward Mom.

We munched on the dip for a while, talking and laughing, before I pulled back and started on the pumpkin bread.

"I've been thinking," Mom said, and I glanced up. "It's time for me to get my own place."

"So soon!"

She smiled. "It's been quite a while, honey. And you'll be moving out, too."

"Not for a while yet. We're going to stay on here until our house is built." That would be a while yet. Liam still had someone drawing up some preliminary plans.

"Well, I'm not saying I'm moving out tomorrow, but soon. Holly has been so generous with her home, but I'm not her son and daughter-in-law. I'm just a woman she didn't know."

I glanced up from the stand mixer. "Maybe when you first got here, but not now. Now you're friends."

"Yes, we are. Which is why I don't want to take advantage."

"I understand," I said, a little sad.

"Don't worry," she said, hearing it in my tone. "I'm not going far. I plan to be around as much as possible to see my grandson."

"I'm so glad you're here," I said, adding one more to the million times I'd told her that over the past couple months.

"Me, too, honey." She crunched another chip. "I just accepted a job in the accounting department of the hotel, so I'll be starting there next week."

"Mom!" I gasped, abandoning the bread and going over to her. "You didn't tell us you had an interview."

"I know."

"Why not!"

"Because I wanted to get it on my own, not because Liam or you put in a word."

"I completely understand that." I nodded. "Did you tell them who you are?" It worried me that my mom could be subjected to the same treatment I had been at The Inn.

"Oh, yes, they know. They're also aware I interviewed and applied without Liam knowing. They liked my qualifications and hired me."

I hugged her. "I'm so happy for you."

"Thank you. It will be nice to build a life here and have family around."

"Yes," I said. "It will."

Once I get a couple paychecks, I might rent one of the cabins around here. They seem cozy.

Liam would never let her pay rent, but I kept that little bit to myself. Today it was just nice to know things were coming together for everyone.

My phone rang, and Liam's name flashed across the screen. An instant smile formed as I picked it up. "Hi," I answered.

"Hey, sweetheart. How's my wife today?"

I spun away from the counter, putting my back to Mom because I didn't want her to see the way I madly blushed at just the sound of his voice.

"Good. How's my husband?"

"I'd be better if I was home with you."

"Are you almost done?" I asked, going over to where I was making his bread.

"Yeah. I'm finishing up now. You home?"

I made a sound of agreement. "I'm making us dinner."

"Didn't you work all day? You need to sit down."

"I left early."

"Someone giving you trouble?" he demanded.

"No. I finished, so I left. Last day perks."

He made a sound, beyond happy I was done there. "How was it? Any regrets?"

"None."

"There's something I need to talk to you about tonight."

"Oh?" I asked, pausing in the middle of what I was doing. "Is something wrong?"

"Everything's okay. I don't want you stressing out. There's just something I want to tell you."

"You can't tell me now?"

"I'd rather wait 'til I'm home."

"But you're okay?" I pressed.

"I'm fine." He assured me.

"I'm making pumpkin bread," I said, letting it go. If something was terribly wrong, he would have said so.

He moaned. "You know a way to a man's heart. I'm fucking starving."

"And tacos," I teased.

"I love it when you talk dirty to me."

I laughed.

"Mom there?" he asked, gruff. I could tell by that deep rasp it wasn't food he was thinking about. And the reason he was asking about our roommates was because he was starving for something he didn't want to share.

"My mom is. Your mom is still at the office."

"We need our own place."

I giggled.

"I'll be home in a few," he told me, smile in his voice. "I love you."

"I love you, too. Hurry."

I held the phone against my ear a few moments after he hung up because I wanted to hang on to that warm, fuzzy feeling he always elicited.

"Young love," Mom said once I did put my phone aside.

I poured the pumpkin batter into a loaf pan and carried it to the oven. "I'm making tacos tonight. That sound okay?"

"It sounds wonderful, but I won't be staying."

"Why not?" I frowned.

"Because you need alone time with your new husband."

"No!" I insisted. "You are always welcome. We love you."

"And I love you. Which is why I'm going to give you newlyweds a chance to have dinner as a couple."

"Mom."

"Don't mom me," she said, stern. "You better take every chance you have to be alone with him, because once that baby arrives, it will be a party of three."

I relented because she was right and because I wanted some time with Liam.

"Except, of course, when he's with his nona. Then you can have some alone time."

I smiled at the image of my mom and my son together. "Thanks, Mom."

"Of course. I'm going to head to the resort and do a little celebratory shopping. I think I need a few new pieces of clothes to wear to work."

"Ooh! Good idea." I told her the name of a few of my favorite boutiques, and she said she would check them out.

"I'll be back later on tonight, and if I don't see you then, I'll see you in the morning."

"Breakfast?" I asked.

She nodded once. "It's a date." She paused on her way out of the room. "Do you want me to stay until Liam gets here?"

"No," I said, waving her off. "He's on his way. I'll be fine."

She hesitated. I set aside the spoon in my hand. "I'm safe now, Mom. We both are. Crone is still locked up, at least for now. And even still, he said I was free, and we haven't heard anything from him for months. We can't live in fear forever."

"I suppose not." She agreed. "Some habits are hard to break."

I nodded emphatically. "I know. But we have to try."

When she was gone, I started working on dinner. The scent of baking pumpkin bread filled the kitchen and brought Charlie, in all his drooling glory, to my feet.

I gave him a chew bone, and he carried it to the other side of the kitchen and flopped down to slobber all over it.

I made the salsa while the chicken and beef marinated in my own special blend and added it to a bowl beside the guac. After I chopped up some fresh herbs and crisp lettuce, I grabbed some tortillas so I could warm them in the oven.

A thudding sound from somewhere in the house made me glance up. Immediately, I looked at Charlie to note he had perked up, too.

I listened, straining to hear any other sounds, but when none came, I tried to calm my racing heart and get back to dinner. Charlie seemed to have an easier time than me, having turned back to his bone ravenously.

The tortillas were wrapped when I heard the sound again.

This time, Charlie jumped up with a rumble and glanced around. Fear and panic assaulted me, reminding me of all the times I'd been in danger.

Charlie's nails tapped against the floor when he left the kitchen and started down the hall, as if patrolling for the source of the sound.

Another faint sound made me pause, this one sounding more like scraping than anything else.

Odd, it seemed it was coming from outside the house and not in.

Charlie barked, the hair on his back rising in an intimidating line. Flashbacks of the night I was attacked and he nearly got shot tortured me and made my fingers shake.

"Stay," I told him and started to back out of the bedroom without moving too fast.

Charlie came forward, as if he knew what I was about to do, but I was faster. I leapt out and shut the door quickly, trapping him in the room.

He barked and scratched at the door when I turned away. I felt bad, but I couldn't let him out, not until I was sure he wouldn't be hurt.

Backtracking, I went to the top of the stairs and glanced over the railing. I couldn't see all the way down, but I called out, "Holly? Is that you?"

She could have just gotten home from work and the sounds I heard was her coming in from the garage.

Holly didn't answer.

A very familiar, uncomfortable warning feeling made all the hairs on the back of my neck stand up, and I was unable to hold the panic at bay anymore.

Rushing back to the kitchen, I picked up my cell on the island so I could call for help.

Movement over by the giant sliding doors that led out onto the amazing deck caught my eye. I spun, telling myself it was just a shadow, while the other part of me retorted I couldn't see shadows when it was already dark.

God. It's already dark outside.

I froze when I realized that shadow I saw was actually not a shadow at all. It was a man, a large, looming figure standing just on the other side of the glass. I watched in horror as he lifted his gloved hands, cupping them around his eyes and leaning so he could peer directly in.

His eyes, which were visible through the wide holes cut out in the black ski mask he wore, looked like freakish, floating balls of white with dark dots in the center.

I screamed and lurched backward, nearly dropping my phone.

The phone! I was practically wheezing with fear when I unlocked the screen. Liam's contact info was still pulled up from when he'd called before. I hit the call button instantly.

As it rang, I glanced back up at the figure.

He was no longer peeping inside.

Instead, he was hunched over at the handle, picking the lock. Horrified, I watched the bolt on this side of the door begin to turn.

I yelled and lunged forward, forcing it back the way it had been.

The man straightened, shook his finger at me like he was scolding a child, then tried again.

I blocked the attempt. I would play this silly game all night.

Liam's voice came over the line, and I pressed the phone against my ear. "Liam!"

"…out on the slopes right now. But leave your info and I'll call you back."

A frustrated cry broke free when I realized the call had gone to voicemail.

In my distraction, the man unlocked the back door and started to slide it open. I fell on the handle, shoving it closed, and forced the lock back into place.

The man stiffened, clearly angry with this game, and reached around behind him.

I watched in horror as he withdrew a long-barreled gun and pointed it directly at me.

44

Liam

I felt my phone vibrating against my chest just after I started up the snowmobile. I hesitated, not going to answer because I was anxious to get home.

But then I realized it could be Bells.

Sitting back, I pulled the phone out of my coat and glanced down just as the screen switched to a missed call.

It was Bellamy.

A prickle of fear slid up my neck, and it had nothing to do with the fact I was outside on a winter's night.

I cut the engine and yanked off one of my gloves with my teeth. The bell on my phone sounded, indicating a voicemail.

I called it up and listened.

… No! … He has a gun! … No!

I nearly dropped my phone when the explosive sound of a gunshot ripped through my ear.

Sounds of commotion I couldn't even comprehend erupted, and then the line went dead.

I didn't bother with my glove or anything else for that matter. I restarted the sled, still gripping my phone, and tore down the mountain.

45

Bellamy

I had a warped sense of déjà vu.

I'd been here before, in this moment. It sucked then, and it sucked now. Villains kept finding small windows of time when I was alone and using them to their advantage.

It was really starting to piss me off.

What was it about me that sang, *I'm an easy target,* and, *I can't defend myself?*

My size? My gender? Something on my forehead I couldn't see when I looked in the mirror? Whatever it was, I was tired of it. I was tired of this.

And...

They were scaring my son.

I froze for a spilt second, which felt like a year-long trip to hell and back, when that man pointed the gun through the glass right at me. But then adrenaline kicked in and so did my will to fight.

"No!" I screamed. "Put the gun down!"

He didn't listen. Shocker.

But he did angle the nozzle slightly away and pull the trigger. The bullet slammed into the glass, sounding like a Mack truck going through a wall. The window cracked and shattered, then exploded in with the force of the shot.

I screamed again, throwing my arms around my stomach and hunching in on myself around my baby.

The deafening silence that followed was probably due to the ringing in my ears from such earsplitting sounds. I came back to the man kicking in some of the glass that remained and entering the house.

I ran into the kitchen, looking around for anything I could use as a weapon. Realizing I still had the phone in my hand, I rushed around the island, putting it between us, and scrambled to dial 9-1-1.

He stalked toward me, wearing the standard killer uniform of all black. He had a rope tied off around his torso and a clip of some kind dangling from it.

Dear Lord, had he repelled down the side of the house to get onto the balcony?

He lifted the gun and pointed it at me. I picked up a large block of cheese and chucked it at him. He batted it away, so I picked up the steel bowl that went on the mixer and threw that instead. It hit the gun and made a ringing sound, which muffled the man's curse. The gun fell out of his hand and skittered across the floor.

In the back bedroom, Charlie was going crazy, and in the back of my mind, I prayed to God he didn't come right through the door.

The attacker and I glanced at the gun at the same moment. I saw the flash of challenge in his eyes. I lunged like I was going for it, and at the very same time, he did, too.

Except I wasn't going for the gun.

Instead, I closed my fingers around a large chef's knife I'd been using. I got to it before he did the gun, and I used the two seconds of extra time to leap close and bring the knife down into his shoulder.

He howled and stumbled into the counter, the knife sticking out of his back like this was a horror movie and I was an ass-kicking heroine.

He gripped onto the edge of the sink, trying to keep his balance as sounds of pain vibrated his throat.

I kicked the gun away, and it slid under the refrigerator, out of sight. I went back for the phone I'd dropped on the island, not putting my back to the man at all.

The operator was calling out, so I yelled the address of the house and that there was an intruder.

Angry, the man straightened and reached out to yank the knife right out of his back. He gave a hoarse shout of pain, and the black shirt he was wearing seemed to grow even blacker in the area I'd stabbed him.

He glanced between me and the knife, whose blade was coated in blood, and threw it on the ground with a roar.

I screamed and took off toward the stairs, hoping to make it out the front door. I made it to the second step when meaty, sweat-slicked hands grabbed me and lifted.

"Get off of me!" I screamed. "Let go!"

He yanked the knife I was still clutching out of my hand, slicing my palm as he did. Sharp, stinging pain cut into me, but I refused to let it distract me.

I scraped at his arms and kicked him wildly as he towed me back into the kitchen. Thinking fast, I reached up, going for the gaping wound on his shoulder.

"I wouldn't if I were you," he intoned, and the sharp prick of a blade pushed against my stomach.

I nearly swooned with panic. "No!" I shrieked, going slack instantly. "Don't you hurt him!"

"I will cut that kid right out of you, you bitch." He snarled, pushing the knife a little harder against me.

I tried to twist away, then cried out in pain. "Ow!" I yelped.

Instantly, I looked down, reaching for my stomach and the small slice he'd made through my shirt and against my skin.

Rage unlike anything I'd ever known before lashed through me. I went slack, giving him every ounce of my weight. It was hard to let my head fall forward, but I did, wanting him to think I'd passed out.

"Fuck," he spat. "Damn women. *My baby, my baby.*" He mocked.

My heart was literally tearing its way out of my chest. It hurt so much that I didn't even breathe. My hands shook so violently I was scared they wouldn't work when I needed them to.

He dragged me near the sink and laid me on the floor. The urge to curl into a fetal position to protect myself until help arrived called to me, but again, I resisted. The knife that I'd put in his shoulder was lying half under the island, its bloody blade sticking out like a savior.

He straightened with a grunt, and I watched him reach for a towel, the towel my mother gave me, to press against his wound. I felt him move toward me, so I shut my eyes and went slack.

"Killing you is going to be a pleasure."

He glanced away, and I seized the moment. The blade cut my skin when I grabbed it and went for the handle. Since the man was standing over me, his feet were in perfect range. Using everything in me, I rose onto my knees and plunged the knife down through his boot and into his foot.

His scream was one that would haunt me for the rest of my days.

His back arched, and he buckled. The keening sounds he made echoed into the stainless sink where he fell.

I scrambled back and watched as he tried to lift his foot and come forward.

He couldn't. I'd pinned him right to the floor.

"That was for my baby, you nasty son of a bitch!" I screamed and lurched up. Wrapping an arm around my middle, I ran forward, fully intending to escape this time.

I almost made it.

My long, flowing hair that Liam loved so much was like a billowing curtain that the man was able to grab and yank me back.

"When that husband of yours comes home tonight, he's going to find pieces of you scattered all over this kitchen," he vowed. "But first, perhaps I'll cut out that kid and lay him on the island like some kind of sick Thanksgiving turkey."

A sob ripped out of me. Dear God. That was the most heinous thing anyone had ever said!

I kicked him, and he grunted but didn't let go. The timer on the oven started going off, reminding me the bread was done.

"Looks like dinner's ready. But you won't be alive to eat it."

I tried to lunge off again, but he pulled me back, making it feel like the hair on my head would come out at any second.

Another horrible, grinding sound went off through the kitchen.

I jerked around, the twisting motion causing more pain in my scalp, but I pushed it away. He was standing there maniacally staring down into the sink, in the direction of the noise.

The garbage disposal.

Oh shit, he'd flipped the switch to the disposal.

My eyes widened in pure horror when he palmed the back of my head and shoved my face into the sink. The scent of the disposal rushed up and hit me in the face. The grinding sound of blades against blades made chills break out over my entire body.

Even as I panicked about being somehow cut up by that… death trap, I shoved backward, trying not to put all my weight on the baby as he forced me over the sink.

"No!" I begged. "No…"

He laughed and shoved me closer. My long hair fell over my face and around me, reaching into the sink like dead octopus arms.

"Shall we start with a hand before we move to anything else?"

The hole of the disposal was so close I could almost touch my nose to the rim. In one last desperate attempt, I lifted my foot and stomped down.

Thankfully, I hit my mark, forcing the knife a little bit farther through the man's foot.

He roared and let go.

I lunged away but then felt pain that threatened to rip my skull in half. "Aghhh!" I screamed and reached around to see what was happening.

My hair!

My hair was caught in the disposal, winding tighter and tighter around the blades! Even as I realized it, I was pulled in, closer and closer to the sink.

The man choked out a laugh because he didn't even have to hold me anymore. I was trapped.

I tried to run off, to pull my hair free. All I got for it was severe pain. A warm sensation trickled over my head, and I fell against the counter. My head was bleeding.

I grabbed the length of my hair with both hands and tried to take the pressure off my scalp while at the same time backing away from the man as much as I could.

He reached out a bloodied hand and wrapped it around my neck. Bending me backward over the sink, he squeezed, choking me.

I slapped at him, tried prying away his hands, but it was no use. My strength didn't match his, and my hands were slick with blood from the two cuts I had.

I started to wheeze as my mind scrambled for another way.

I thought of my unborn son, my brand-new husband… After everything, was this how it ended?

After all the fighting I'd done, I was going to die anyway.

46

Liam

The sound of a grinding motor, a spastic dog, and the beeping oven slammed into me when I burst open the downstairs door.

I didn't say anything, just ran full speed across the room and took the stairs three at a time.

Rushing into the kitchen, I took in a scene that could belong to a cult-favorite horror flick.

A huge bleeding man was bent over Bellamy, who he was holding into the sink while he slowly choked the life out of her.

I didn't even hesitate. I didn't even think.

With a roar, I lunged into the room, grabbed the man by the back of his shirt, and pulled him off my girl. He made a surprised sound as I yanked, and then a crippling yell. I didn't care or pause. I kept pulling, slamming his back onto the island and dragging him across it. Everything in our path scattered and flew as he skittered over the top and I flung him off the end.

He hit head first into a bank of cabinets, landed on his stomach, and barely moved. I noted the large wound in his back, so I stomped on it with my boot, and he jerked in pain.

I glanced around me to Bellamy, who was still scrambling away from the sink. She was caught somehow, struggling to get free.

Blood smeared all over her, hair wild, and her eyes… Holy shit, her eyes were dilated so much they were almost black.

"Bells," I said, starting forward.

"Watch out!" she shrieked, focusing behind me.

I spun and kicked the man, who was rushing me, in the center of his chest. He fell back, but it wasn't enough. I went forward and rained blows upon him until his body turned to jelly beneath mine. I hit him still.

Blood coated his face, and his head lolled to the side, but all I saw was the image of him strangling Bellamy and the blood all over her hands.

I was going to kill him.

"Liam," Bellamy said from somewhere close by. "Liam!" she yelled, snapping me out of it.

I stopped and turned. Bellamy stood just behind me, her hair kind of hacked off at uneven angles, blood on her face, hands, and smeared on her shirt.

I glanced over her body, my eyes stopping on her stomach, on the tear in her shirt and the blood trickling out the side.

"Is that…?" I intoned, pointing.

Her hand covered the tear, and her face fell. "He tried to hurt the baby," she whimpered.

A beastly roar filled the kitchen as I spun, lifted the passed-out man by the front of his shirt, and dragged him over to the sink.

I tossed his body over the side and grabbed his hand.

His eyelids started to flutter, and I pushed my face close to his. "You threaten my kid?" I asked, utterly calm and low.

His eyes popped open, and he tried to scramble away.

I laughed.

"Did you come into my house, attack my wife, and then try to hurt my son?"

"I'm sorry," he whimpered.

I shoved his hand into the still-running garbage disposal. The sound of flesh grinding coupled with his shout of pain fueled my anger. I pushed his arm inside farther.

"Please, staaahp!" he begged, gurgling.

Blood splattered around the inside of the sink. I liked the sight of his blood far better than the sight of my wife's.

"This is nothing," I said, leaning into his ear. "This is nothing compared to what I'm going to do to you. You come after my family… and I'll rip you apart."

"Crone sent me!" he wailed, his body beginning to jerk as though he were having some kind of seizure. I didn't feel bad for him.

I felt nothing in that moment but insane anger and the bitter bite of frost.

"Perry Crone sent me to kill her. He hates you!"

The garbage disposal shut off, making a horrible choked sound. I glanced around at Bellamy, who was pale and wobbly on her feet. "The police are here," she whispered, swaying.

I let go of the asshole and reached for her, scooping her against my chest and hunching around her.

Behind us, the man slumped to the floor, his hand mangled and half missing.

I carried her to the top of the steps, and the door was forced in. Police with drawn weapons surged into the house, and Bellamy's head fell against my shoulder.

"I need a medic!" I bellowed. "Now!"

The EMTs rushed past the police officers, and I carried Bellamy over to the couch where they could look her over.

"She's twenty-three weeks pregnant," I told them. "He tried to stab her stomach, and it looks like he stabbed her hands."

"No, I grabbed the knives," Bellamy said, coherent.

Oh. She grabbed the knives. Rage flushed over me again, and I wanted to race back into the kitchen and inflict some more damage.

"Liam," she said as the paramedics basically rushed her.

"I'm right here." I promised, glancing behind me as the cops filled the kitchen.

"Jesus," one of them spat, and another started to hurl.

I turned back to Bells. "How are you? How's the baby? How bad are you hurt?"

"We're going to be fine. We're all fine." It was more like a mantra she was saying to reassure herself.

"What the hell happened here, Mattison?" the chief of police yelled, barging through the door.

I pulled out my cell and dialed Frost. When he answered, I said, "You better get here. Now. Crone sent someone to kill Bellamy again, and you will want to get his confession before he bleeds out."

"Bleeds out? Jesus, Mattison, I told you to let me do my job!"

"You weren't fast enough."

"Where are you?" he asked briskly. I could tell he was already on the move.

"My mom's place."

"She needs to be moved to the hospital," the EMT said, standing.

All that numbness I felt when I was grinding up asshat in there? It all went away, and the brutal sting of too much emotion nearly took my breath.

"Mattison," Frost yelled in my ear.

"We'll be at the hospital," I said, then disconnected the call.

"I need a stretcher," the one EMT said to the other.

Bellamy looked at me with panic and exhaustion in her eyes. I went forward and gently lifted her into my arms. "Where to?" I said.

They looked as if they were about to object, but I gave them a look.

"This way," one of them replied and led us out of the house.

The sound of Charlie barking and growling erratically made me look back.

"Charlie!" Bellamy cried, hearing him.

As I was lifting her into the ambulance, the dog leapt up and sat beside where she lay, gently laying his large head on her belly. He was protecting her. Her and my son.

"No dogs," the EMT said.

I turned and glared at him.

"Just this once," he muttered.

Sirens blazing, the ambulance drove away, leaving behind a busted house, crowds of police, and a half-dead killer on the kitchen floor.

47

Bellamy

The baby was healthy. Of this we were absolutely sure.

Liam stood over me at the hospital like a WWE wrestler (the kind that was super grouchy) and pretty much scared everyone that came in the room to look at me.

At one point, one of the doctors suggested we have the officer outside my room come inside.

Not for our protection.

No.

For the protection of the staff.

Needless to say, I had an ultrasound (yes, Liam took all the pictures and then demanded more), a panel of blood drawn, an IV, and I was still currently hooked up to a monitor so they could keep a close watch on the baby overnight.

Yep, I got to spend the night.

I guess being the wife of an Olympic medalist with crazy eyes had its perks.

Um. Not.

Regardless, I was happy that my little boy was getting all the care and attention he deserved. I would spend a thousand nights in this hospital if it would make sure he was safe.

Knowing he was okay made everything else easier to bear. Like the twelve stitches in my hand. The four stitches in my head. The bandage covering the cut on my stomach, which was the most minor injury I had but the most traumatizing.

And then there was my hair.

"I look like someone took a weed whacker to my head!" I wailed when Liam finally helped me into the bathroom and I glanced in the mirror.

"Your face is still real pretty." Liam consoled me.

How rude!

"I can't even do anything with it until these stitches come out!" I said, reaching up to tenderly finger near them. When Liam was beating the crap out of the criminal, I was so desperate to get free, I got a pair of scissors out of the drawer and cut off the length trapped inside the disposal.

Needless to say, some of it was still very long, and some of it was... well, not.

Liam pulled my hand away, gently scolding me. "Don't touch that."

"It hurts." I pouted.

"I know, sweetheart," he said, leaning in to kiss my temple.

"I have to pee," I declared.

He gestured toward the toilet.

I was horrified. "Get out."

"No."

"I can't pee in front of you!"

He rolled his eyes and turned his back.

"Liam," I whined. He seriously wasn't going to get out? This was absurd!

He reached over and turned on the faucet, allowing the water to run. Like that made this totally acceptable. This was stupid, but I was genuinely exhausted. I had no energy to argue with him. So I peed, glaring at his back the entire time and sneaking glances at the mirror to make sure he wasn't watching me through it.

When I was done, I washed my hands and reached for him. He was there, lifting me and carrying me and the large IV pole attached to me back into the bedroom.

One of the nurses was waiting patiently and smiled when she saw us. "I knew your bark was worse than your bite," she said, and I glared at him, just daring him to say something I would want to kick him for.

Wisely, he didn't.

When I was back in bed, she went about strapping the monitor around me again and making sure everything was registering correctly.

"I'll be back in a while to check on you," she said.

"Thank you," Liam told her.

When she was gone, I held out my hand to Liam, and he sat on the edge of the bed, caressing me with his eyes. "You scared the shit out of me tonight, Bells."

"It was terrible," I said, feeling a rush of panic fill me.

"Shh, shh." He soothed and scooted farther up on the bed with me. I wanted him closer, but I knew he wouldn't because of the monitor.

"Thank God you showed up when you did."

"I seriously wanted to kill him," Liam said darkly.

"I thought you were going to." I admitted.

"I might have if the cops hadn't showed up when they did, and he started squealing Crone's name like a pig."

"Do you think that matters?" I puzzled. At this point, I didn't even know.

"I sure as hell hope so."

As if on cue, Agent Frost walked into the room, followed by a few of his agents, the Caribou chief of police, and one of his uniformed officers.

I sank into the bed a little farther.

"Can't this wait?" Liam asked, standing to move between the bed and the men. "She's been through enough."

"It really can't," Frost replied.

"It's fine," I said, rallying. "I won't let him get away with trying to hurt Shaw."

"Who's Shaw?" Frost said, and everyone's eyes sharpened as though they missed some giant piece of the puzzle.

"Shaw is my son," Liam said, gesturing to my belly.

"Mine, too." I corrected softly.

He glanced over his shoulder and smiled. "Yes, sweetheart, yours, too."

"I just came from your house," Frost said, rubbing a hand over his jaw. "That was quite a scene."

"Try living through it," I muttered.

"I need you to recount everything that happened," Frost said, and everyone had their notebooks poised and ready.

I recounted. Twice.

Both times, Liam paced the floor. After my turn, Liam went. His turn was much faster because he hadn't been there as long.

"The man who assaulted you," Frost said when all the questioning was done, "is in ICU. He was airlifted to a hospital in Denver because of the, ah, limb loss."

I squeezed my eyes shut, thinking of the horrible grinding blades. Subconsciously, I touched my hair—or what was left of it. Liam brushed a hand gently over my face, and I opened to see him watching me with a frown.

"Is he going to make it?" I asked.

"Too early to tell," Frost answered.

The chief of police cleared his throat and spoke up. "I did manage to question him when he came to as the paramedics were with him."

"What did he say?" Liam asked.

"He corroborated what you said about Crone hiring him. He seemed more than happy to spill all of Crone's dirty secrets."

"Blood loss will do that to you," Liam quipped, ice nipping at his words.

Frost glanced at Liam. "He alleges that you were going to kill him."

"If I was going to kill him, he would be dead," Liam deadpanned. "I was just doing what I had to do to save my wife and child."

"No one blames you for that," the chief said instantly.

Liam inclined his head. "I appreciate that."

I steered the conversation back to where it needed to be. "Crone specifically ordered that man to break into our house and kill me?" I asked.

"He said he is willing to testify to it."

I made a noise. "If he survives."

"Which is why we are getting sworn testimony in writing and recording right away," Frost said. "And of course we will have guards on him twenty-four-seven."

"Can Crone go back to prison for this?" I asked, hopeful.

"It's a possibility."

Liam made a rude noise. "That means no."

"No. It means we will do everything we can to put him away again."

"So he can buy his way out *again*."

"I'm choosing to ignore your disparaging remarks about the ability of the FBI because I know you've been through quite an ordeal tonight," Frost told Liam.

Liam opened his mouth to say something utterly stupid, so I made a sound of distress. He flew to my side and was leaning over me in record time.

"Get a nurse!" he bellowed before even asking if I was okay. "A nurse, goddammit!" he yelled when no one moved.

I felt kind of guilty for making him stress this way, but it was the only way to get him to shut up. Besides, I wasn't lying. I was just being a little dramatic.

"What's wrong?" Liam asked, his tone much gentler toward me. "Is it the baby?"

"The baby is fine," I said quickly. One thing that was not okay was him thinking our child was somehow in harm's way. "See." I pointed to the monitor, which showed a healthy, strong heartbeat.

"Okay, then tell me." He cajoled, leaning over me a little more.

"My head hurts," I replied. That was the total truth. I would not recommend getting stitches there. "So does my hand." I held up the hand with bandages covering the stitched areas.

"Is everything okay in here?" the nurse asked, rushing into the room.

"She's in pain," Liam told her. "Fix it."

"I can get you a mild pain pill—"

"No pills!" we both said at the same time.

"How about some ice?" she suggested.

I nodded, grateful. "That sounds good."

The nurse nodded and then turned toward the men crowding the room. "She needs her rest, gentlemen. Can't this wait 'til tomorrow?"

They all turned sheepish and mumbled various replies. The nurse bustled out to get some ice, and Liam brushed some wild, hacked hair out of my face.

"Time to go," he said, gesturing for everyone to get out.

"We're sorry to have kept you for so long, Mrs. Mattison," the chief of police said. "If you need anything at all, just call."

"Thank you," I said, offering him a grateful smile.

"I'll be in touch," Agent Frost declared, and it sounded ominous. I looked forward to the day when the FBI wouldn't "be in touch."

Liam escorted everyone out into the hall, and I listened to the low timbre of his voice. It was soothing, and I yawned.

The nurse came back in, clucking her tongue and carrying two cold packs. "Poor thing," she said, checking the monitor before facing me.

"Thank you," I said when she placed one of the packs around my hand with the stitches, then the other near the wound on my head. I winced when the pack touched me, and she nodded in understanding.

"Head wounds are tender. And you have some swelling yet. I'm not sure what happened to you, but from the looks of your hair and scalp, I'd say you're lucky all you needed was some stitches and this ice pack."

"Very lucky." I agreed. It was one of the reasons I hadn't totally fallen apart tonight. What happened was horrible, and I knew once it fully set in, I would be dealing with the effects for quite some time.

But right now, all I could feel was grateful that I was okay, as was my husband and son.

The nurse passed Liam on the way out and pulled the door around as she went, closing out the bustle in the hallway and leaving us blissfully alone.

"Lay with me."

He stopped beside the bed and frowned. "I don't think—"

"Please." I felt the fresh prick of tears behind my eyes and blinked them back.

"Don't cry." He soothed and kicked off his boots. The shirt he was wearing had blood on it, and I found myself fixated on it, wondering if it was my blood or the blood of the man who tried to kill me.

Liam followed my gaze and swore. He ripped the shirt up over his head and tossed it on the chair he'd dragged close. "I didn't think about it," he explained.

"I know," I said softly. "I didn't either, until just now."

He climbed on the bed, gingerly moving up to my side and settling down as if he were holding a scalding, overfilled bowl of soup and he was terrified of spilling.

I turned my face toward him and smiled. He adjusted the ice on my head and kissed my nose. Since he couldn't wrap his arm around my waist, he settled for laying a hand over my heart and resting one of his ankles over mine.

"Thank you," I murmured, settling a little bit closer to him. My eyes drifted closed, and I laid the hand without stitches over his where it rested on me.

"If I could take your pain away, I would," he whispered.

I opened my eyes and smiled at him. "You are."

48

Liam

The man I grinded up in the garbage disposal died in the hospital. He managed to come through a lengthy surgery, only to die during the night.

The official ruling was that his heart wasn't able to withstand all the trauma to the rest of his body.

The unofficial ruling and my personal opinion? Someone slipped into his room and injected a little something into his IV to make it look like his ticker gave out.

Considering Agent Frost could neither confirm nor deny the theory just proved I was right.

It was just too fucking convenient that the only man who could provide damning testimony to potentially put Crone back in the slammer was no longer alive to give it. He died before he could give his sworn testimony to the FBI—also very convenient.

And now here we were, almost two weeks from that hell night, and the FBI had bupkis in building a case strong enough to put Crone away.

Bellamy had nightmares. She'd wake up screaming and holding her stomach, begging for the baby to be spared. Even though the kitchen had been entirely cleaned, the sink replaced, and the garbage disposal completely removed, I'd still find her periodically staring down the drain as though that man's pulped-up hand was down there.

I had to do something.

Waiting around for Crone to strike again was just not an option. Expecting the FBI to do something was laughable.

Alex cautioned about what it might cost me to kill Crone. From where I stood, knowing that asshole was dead was priceless.

It was our only way out. Even if the FBI could make the case against him for what happened, it wouldn't be over. He'd keep sending people, even from his cell. As long as Perry Crone breathed, my family was at risk.

We drew closer to the arrival of my son, and this wasn't the kind of world I wanted him to be born into. He deserved better.

My wife deserved better.

I had to kill Crone.

I couldn't go to him, though. Getting close to a notorious crime boss would be next to impossible. Even if I managed, there would be too many people who could possibly place me at the scene of his murder.

That left one option.

Lure him out. If Crone himself came at us and I killed him, I wouldn't need an alibi. Self-defense would stand.

And we would finally be free.

"I thought you said you wanted to keep it quiet as long as possible that you were returning to the pros," Bellamy said quietly, glancing around warily.

"Joiner says we need the press. It keeps sponsors happy. It brings in a bigger paycheck."

Bellamy frowned. "If this is about the house…"

I spun to fully face her and palmed her shoulders. Bending so I was eye level with her, I spoke. "This isn't about the house, sweetheart. I could never make another paycheck again, snowboarding or from the resort, and we would still have more than enough money to live on for the rest of our lives."

"Then why are you doing this all of a sudden?"

"It's not sudden. I've been training for months."

She didn't seem convinced, and I didn't want her to worry. Dragging my hands from her shoulders to clasp her fingers, I answered, "You said you followed my career while we were apart?"

She nodded. "For as long as I could."

Just the reminder of why she stopped was enough to strengthen my resolve to do this. "Then you know I did interviews and press all the time. It's part of the business, part of being a pro athlete."

Her teeth sank into her lower lip as she thought it over. "Tom said this would help you?"

"Yes, sweetheart."

She nodded, making her hair sway around her shoulders. After her head healed enough, she'd gotten her hair cut so it was all the same length. She came home in tears because she'd lost so much length and was worried I would hate it.

Like I could ever. The honey-colored locks were just past her shoulders now, and I thought it was beautiful. Hell, I would think she was gorgeous even if she was bald, and I told her as much.

"Are you up for this today? After everything that's happened, is it too much?" I asked, worried.

She made a dismissive sound. "I'm fine. Being almost murdered so many times barely fazes me anymore."

"Bells," I said, partly shocked and totally horrified.

She rubbed a soothing palm over my scruff. "Sorry. That was a bad joke."

Joke or not, part of it was true. All the more reason I had to do this. I didn't have a choice.

She sighed. "We have to live our life, Liam. Crone took a lot from me. From you. We can't let him take any more." After a slight pause, she cocked her head to the side. "Besides. Maybe all the extra press attention will make it harder for him to get to us. With them camped out everywhere to get a shot of you, sending hitmen will be a lot harder."

Maybe. But I was hoping like hell it actually drew him in. Perry Crone was a smart man, but he was cocky. No doubt, after buying his way out of prison, he was feeling pretty untouchable right about now.

Good.

Cocky men made mistakes. I was hoping he would see this interview and know I was calling him out.

I seized her face between my hands, marveling at how they swallowed up her cheeks. She was so small… but so *big*. "I love you so goddamn much, Mrs. Mattison. You got balls bigger than most of the men I know."

She smiled as I said the first part, but then she blanched and wrinkled her nose. "Thank you?"

I threw back my head and laughed.

"You're right, though," I said, a teasing glint in my eye. "This interview will draw attention, and people will be curious about you. About us. After all, I'm returning as a married man."

"Whatever will your groupies say?" she exclaimed, sarcastic.

Joiner approached, calling my name. "They're ready for you."

"Be right there," I called.

"Go stand with Alex," I told her, gesturing toward him with my chin.

She rolled her eyes.

"Give me some sugar." I leaned down for my kiss, but she turned her cheek, and my lips grazed her ear.

"You're gonna pay for that later." I promised.

A spark of desire lit her blue eyes, and she smirked.

Instead of kissing her, I leaned down and held her stomach. "Daddy has to go to work. You stay here with Mommy."

"Where else is he going to go?" Bellamy wondered above me.

Caressing her stomach, I whispered, "Love you."

He kicked right into my palm. My stomach flipped with the action. I guess he really did know my voice.

I pulled back to head toward the interview, but Bellamy caught my hand. "I changed my mind."

I raised a brow. "Did you now?"

She nodded once. "I want my kiss."

I pursed my lips, considering.

"Mattison!" Joiner yelled, impatient.

I swooped in and planted one on her, then jogged off toward the television crew. I had a comeback to announce and, hopefully, a hook to bait.

49

Bellamy

This television interview was sudden. The decision to announce his return to the pros and his intention to compete in the Olympic men's halfpipe next winter seemed kind of abrupt.

There'd been whispers about his return for months now. He never acknowledged them.

Until now.

And boy, he wasn't just announcing on a local channel or calling the newspaper. Nope. Not my husband.

He had the biggest news channel on TV out here to interview him *and* a few other networks to talk to as well. One of them being a huge entertainment show that mostly covered celebrity news.

To the extreme—that was Liam.

Still. I couldn't help wondering why today. Why the sudden change of heart?

I stood off to the side next to Alex (God forbid I stand alone!) and watched Tom Joiner bounce around like a golden retriever, smiling like a car salesman, and laughing at every joke.

"Kiss-ass," I muttered under my breath.

Alex cackled. "Ain't that the truth? But hey, he's only doing it for our boy. He does all this so Liam can concentrate on boarding."

"He does a good job."

Alex grunted, which I took as an agreement. Watching Liam's coach, I was more convinced that maybe he had been pushing for this. Maybe he was the reason for today.

The director, or whoever, yelled for everyone to be silent, and then the cameras and lights were on. Liam, standing next to some anchor wearing a buttload of makeup, looked relaxed and comfortable as if he were with friends and not about to be broadcast on television.

"I'm here with Olympic medalist Liam Mattison who, up until an unfortunate injury, was considered the best snowboarder in the world. In fact, Liam still holds many records for the men's halfpipe." The anchor introduced him. "Liam, we are thrilled to have you with us today in what is your first interview in nearly two years."

He shifted and smiled, his good looks nearly melting the camera. "Thank you for coming out to talk to me today. It's been a long road, but it's good to be back."

"Are you back?" the interviewer pounced. "Is that why we're all here today?"

"I thought you came 'cause you missed me," he quipped, smiling.

People around laughed lightly, and the journalist giggled like a school girl.

I suppressed an eye roll.

"I think I can say with full authority that we have all missed you. Not only were you the best, but you were always very well loved." Liam chuckled, and the interviewer continued. "That's why we are so anxious to know. Is Liam Mattison returning to snowboarding?"

"I am." He confirmed. "I've been training for a while now. You're going to be seeing me on the halfpipe real soon."

The woman beamed as though she'd just unearthed some magic cure for something horrific and turned toward the camera. "You heard it here first! Liam Mattison is coming back for his title."

"I definitely have a lot of work to do before I can even think about that," he replied humbly. My husband was a confident man, but he wasn't so arrogant to declare he would be the best once again.

"You were forced out of competing when you suffered a serious knee injury that required surgery, physical therapy, and a long recovery time. It was rumored that you would never return."

He nodded. "That's right, and to be honest, I didn't expect to."

"So why now? What's brought you back?"

"Besides the fact that my knee has been cooperating?" he asked, smiling. When he shifted, a lock of his hair fell onto his forehead and shielded part of his gray eyes.

The woman laughed, and he pushed the hair off his face and continued. "Life is short, and I decided I didn't want my career to end the way it did."

She nodded thoughtfully. "I think most of our viewers have seen the headlines about the tragic death of your father, Renshaw Mattison."

Liam nodded, all traces of charm wiped from his face as a sober look took over. "He was murdered."

I gasped lightly and started forward. This interview was about snowboarding, not an excuse to exploit something infinitely painful to my husband!

Alex slid an arm around my waist and pulled me back. I made a sound and glanced over my shoulder. "What are you doing?"

"Let him do this," he whispered against my ear.

"You can't possibly think this is good for him," I whisper-argued back.

"I think Liam is doing exactly what he needs to be doing."

I paused and started to turn at whatever it was I heard in his voice.

Alex made a sound and touched my stomach. "Damn, girl, you've put on a few."

I pulled away, gasping. "I'm pregnant, jackass!"

Someone nearby shushed us.

Alex snickered, and I glared at him. "You just wait until I tell Liam you told me I'm fat!"

His amusement faded, and his icy eyes nearly bugged out of his face. "You wouldn't."

I smiled.

Behind us, the interview continued.

"By an overzealous fan that came to stay at the resort you own and broke into your home, correct?"

"I wouldn't call him overzealous. Or a fan," Liam said darkly.

"What would you say, then?"

The intensity Liam portrayed so easily slipped into his silvery eyes as he stared at the camera. "Obsessive. Sloppy. Cowardly."

"Interesting. You think he's a coward?"

"I do," he said right away. "He came to my home when I wasn't there to defend it."

"Your girlfriend came home and interrupted him, is that correct?"

"She's my wife now." Liam corrected. "But yes, she did. Me and my father as well."

"And your father was shot and killed. You were shot, too, weren't you?"

"I was." He stared into the camera. "It will take a lot more than that to keep me down."

I shivered and glanced at Alex, silently asking if he still thought this was a good idea.

He patted my head like I was a dog.

"How have you been since those events?" the woman asked seriously.

"It's been tough," he said honestly. "My father didn't deserve what happened to him."

"Renshaw was a big supporter of yours. Was his death a factor in your return?"

Liam looked past the camera crew, beyond the lights, and found me where I stood. I smiled at him, hoping he knew I was here supporting him.

"My father believed in me. Probably more than I did at times. But coming back, that's something I'm doing for me."

My heart squeezed. Pride overcame all other emotion I felt just then because I knew how hard it was for Liam to do something solely for himself.

The interview went on. He talked about our marriage and the Olympics. About his knee and training. It seemed to last forever, and when it was finished, he did a few other shorter interviews for the other networks.

By the time he was finished, I had long since retired to a chair and was daydreaming longingly of taking off my pants.

I had to face it. They were all too tight. It was uncomfortable. Not even the hairband looped through the button hole and around the button helped anymore.

Alex was right. I was getting fat.

A pair of very familiar, sexy jean-clad legs appeared before me, and I glanced up.

"Looks like you could use some Raisin Bran."

"Mmm."

He held out his hand, and I surrendered mine so he could tug me to my feet.

On our way to the Extreme, I said, "How do you think it went today?"

His reply was almost menacing and definitely strange. "Time will tell."

50

Liam

I was too subtle. Something no one had ever accused me of before. Guess there was a first time for everything. I just wished this wasn't it.

Another week passed without a peep out of Crone. I wasn't relieved. I knew he was just lying in wait. But I was tired. Tired of hoping he would come to me.

According to the FBI, he was still in New York, lying low since the incident with the murderous repeller.

And just FYI, I was having bulletproof glass installed at our new house. Next time someone wanted to shoot through a window to get at my wife, he could think again.

I was beginning to wonder if maybe Bellamy was right. Maybe all the extra attention and press did deter Crone.

Or maybe, as I said, I'd been too subtle. I thought calling him a coward for coming at me when I wasn't home would do the trick.

I'd been wrong. *Fuck.*

I was going to have to go to him.

My phone went off, and I glanced at the screen.

"Is Joiner giving you a hard time for staying home today?" Bellamy worried from her place in my lap.

Absentmindedly, I rubbed over her growing stomach. Beneath my hand, the baby rolled. "No. It's Alex," I answered. "He's outside."

"Does he want you to come out and play?" she teased.

No. I want him to come out and play. "Ha. Ha," I said as we got up from the couch. "He wants me to let him in."

"Or he could just come in?"

"You know he won't do that, sweetheart." I reminded her.

She sighed. "I feel stupid."

"You aren't stupid," I said, firm. "You've been traumatized too many times. I can't really blame you for jumping every time someone knocks or rattles the door handle."

"I'm working on it."

"I know." I agreed, leaning down to kiss her. "It's going to take time."

"Stay with Bells," I told Charlie and went down to open the front door.

Alex was standing there waiting, a box in his hand.

"For me?" I said, acting surprised.

"It was on the steps," he said, his voice low and serious.

All humor and sarcasm evaporated, and I scanned the area behind him and around the house. The snow was pretty much melted now, the ground beginning to thaw from its frosty state.

"There's no one here. I checked the perimeter before I texted."

I cursed. "You know who it's from."

Alex's face was grim.

I took the small white box from him as a sick, nervous feeling wormed inside me.

This was it. This was what I was waiting for. Whatever Crone sent in this box would determine my next move.

Both of us glanced around, making sure Bellamy wasn't standing nearby. I pulled off the lid and looked inside. There was a note with a single line.

Watch this alone.

It wasn't in Crone's handwriting. It didn't have his signature.

I held the note out to Alex and then reached in to pick up a small black flash drive. There was nothing else inside the box.

"Liam?" Bellamy called. "Is everything okay?"

I jammed the drive and note into my pocket and shoved the box at Alex. "Yeah, baby." I spun around. "Everything is good. Alex was making me look at the new rims on his Hummer."

Bellamy appeared at the top of the steps. "Hi, Alex."

"Hey, girl," he said, sounding like his usual relaxed self.

"Aren't you going to come in?" she asked, wrinkling her nose.

We moved as a unit into the house, me staying slightly in front of Alex so the view of the box was obscured. When the door was closed behind him, I said, "I gotta piss."

"And you felt the need to announce this?" Bellamy quipped.

"I didn't want you to miss me," I said, winking.

She shook her head and laughed low. "Alex, I made pumpkin bread!" she called, going into the kitchen.

Alex slipped around me, slyly stuffing the box in my hand. "Girl, you better break me off a piece!" he hollered, running up the steps after her.

I went down to our bedroom and quietly shut the door. Pulling out my laptop, I booted it up and plugged the drive into the side.

It felt like I waited years for whatever was on this thing to show on the screen.

And then it did.

White, grainy static filled the screen, along with a bunch of white noise. "What the fuck?" I muttered and smacked the side of the laptop as if that would somehow fix the issue.

The picture blinked on, and I stared at the grisly scene.

It looked like a bad home movie taken on a jumpy camera with bad audio and lighting. Still, the quality was good enough to know exactly what I was seeing.

I sank beside the bed and pulled the laptop close to watch the unfolding scene.

There was a man tied to a chair perched in the center of an empty concrete room. His hands were bound behind him, and his feet were bound to each leg of the chair. He was bloody and beaten, his head lolled to the side, blood leaving a trail from the corner of his mouth all the way down his ripped-up and dirty white dress shirt.

There were what looked like knife wounds in his chest and one in his side. There was so much blood I might not know his shirt was white if it wasn't for the collar.

I watched as someone moved from just beyond the frame of the camera, tossing a bucket of what I assumed was frigid water all over the man.

He gasped and lurched up, unable to go far because of the binds.

It was Perry Crone.

Someone sent me a video of Perry Crone being tortured.

It was sick and wrong, but I kinda wished I had some popcorn to enjoy the show with. I also wished I was there, landing a few punches of my own.

As he sputtered, someone moved in the frame again, and white static covered the screen. I grabbed the laptop and shook it, wanting the screen to clear.

The audio worked fine, though, because the blood-curdling scream that Perry let loose filled my ears.

Seconds later, the screen cleared. Perry was still there, alone, and he was crying. His ear hung off the side of his head, only attached by a thin band of skin.

"You're going to pay for this!" he vowed. "My family will avenge me."

"No." A distorted voice came out of the dark. "No, Crone. We will not. You've brought shame and heat on this entire organization, and when you die, all of this ends."

He sat up, his ear swinging as he stared off to the side of the room. "You!" he growled. "This was you! My own—"

"No." The voice cut him off. "This is on you. You've made too many enemies. The FBI watches like a hawk. This was too good of an opportunity to end all of this. To end you."

He started to rock back and forth, trying to dislodge the chair. It fell over, and he hit the ground, crying out.

Someone covered from head to foot moved forward. The screen went fuzzy again, but I heard the groans of Crone coupled with the sound of flesh hitting flesh.

When the screen came on, Crone was upright again, bloodier than before. And his ear… it was completely gone.

"Please," he groaned, sounding pathetic and terrified. I had a moment of pity for him, and then I remembered what he'd done to my father. To my wife.

"Rot in hell, you son of a bitch," I whispered.

"Just let me go—" He didn't get to finish because the sound of a gun going off cut off his words.

I jerked when the bullet slammed into his head and watched as brain matter and blood splattered everything. The person holding the camera moved, walking close to the body, looming over him while filming.

Blood seeped out around him like a black halo, and his eyes stared, glassy, into hell.

The camera zoomed in, giving a grisly up-close and personal view of the bullet hole in the center of his head.

"Confirmation of elimination." Another distorted voice spoke, the one I assumed was holding the camera.

It was indeed a confirmation. Perry Crone was dead.

A victim of his own making.

I stared at him a moment longer, and then the picture blinked out, white static filled the screen, and then everything went black.

I hit a few keys, trying to call up the video again. I couldn't. It was gone. Erased.

Just like Perry Crone.

51

Bellamy

I was beginning to wonder if Liam fell in.

Surely it didn't take this long to pee.

Maybe I should stand in the bathroom with him while he did his business, too.

He'd probably enjoy it. Perv.

Alex was plowing through the generous serving of bread and coffee I'd set before him. He paused long enough to say, "This bread is the shit."

I cut off another hunk and slid it onto his plate.

"Bless you," he said, shoveling in more.

"How long has it been since you've eaten?" I asked, horrified by his manners.

He shrugged. "I've been busy."

"Stay for dinner." I offered.

"Don't mind if I do."

"Bellamy!" Mom called from the other room. "Bellamy!"

Alex stopped chewing, and we looked at each other, alarmed. "Mom!"

"Come quick!"

I started to rush forward, but Alex moved in front of me, blocking me with his body and reaching behind him to keep me there.

His hand brushed against my stomach, and the baby kicked.

Her jolted and spun around. "What was that?"

"The baby moved," I said and tried to rush by.

"Hell no you don't," he quipped and moved back in front of me. "Stay behind me."

I made an impatient sound, but he moved, and I followed along, racing out to where Mom was standing in the living room.

"What is it?" I asked, worried.

"Look!" She gasped, pointing at the TV.

Moving from behind Alex, I stepped up to stare at the wall-mounted flat-screen.

Mom turned the volume up as I read the large headline at the bottom of the screen.

Crime boss Perry Crone found slain.

I gasped and threw out an arm. Alex grabbed it and pulled me into his side.

"Perry Crone is dead?" I asked.

"Seems so," Alex answered, watching the unfolding story. The view was aerial, and it appeared the camera crew was filming overhead Crone's estate. Below, I could see a ton of police officers and government vehicles, along with an ambulance.

The front door opened, and the camera zoomed in as several EMTs filed out pushing a gurney with a zipped-up black body bag lying atop. I watched as they loaded it into the waiting ambulance with CORONER written on the back.

"Liam!" I screamed. "Liam!"

He pounded up the stairs in record time. "What! What is it?" he demanded.

I pointed at the TV just as Mom had. "Perry Crone is dead."

His eyes flickered and then went to the screen. The four of us listened to the anchor go on about how he was found early this morning by his housekeeper, who called 9-1-1. His body was said to be in bad shape, and he was pronounced dead on arrival.

Liam came farther into the room and pulled me out of Alex's side and into the circle of his arms.

"There is no news or leads at this time about those responsible for this grisly murder, but police will be investigating. The director of the FBI released a statement earlier today stating they will be looking at the case from every angle and there are many. As we all know, Perry Crone is the most notorious modern mobster of our era and was not too long ago released from prison, having his life sentence reverted to time served for good behavior.

"Sources speculate that this could be the work of any number of his enemies, as he had many. Some also hypothesize that this could be the doing of his own organization because of all the unwanted press and heat he'd brought to organized crime in the past few years.

"Either way, it seems like we might never know what actually happened to this crime lord, and as hard as it is to say, this is one murder that I don't think many people will be losing sleep over.

"Back to you, Bob."

"Well, I can't say I'm sorry." My mom was the first to break the silence. "I, for one, am glad that monster is dead."

Liam and Alex both made sounds of agreement.

I stared at the screen a few more minutes, shock still rippling through me.

"Bells." Liam nudged me gently, stepping around so he could stare at me directly. "Are you okay?"

My eyes fixed on his. "It's over," I whispered, relief flooding my entire body. "It's really over."

He nodded, his eyes glimmering. "Yes, sweetheart. It's really over. We're free."

I collapsed against him and cried. I couldn't even begin to voice the way it felt to know Crone would never be coming after me or my baby ever again. That he finally paid for what he did to Ren and our family.

In the middle of sobbing all over Liam's chest, I gasped and pulled back.

"What if his family comes for us? What if they blame us?"

It was hard to actually believe this all ended here. Now.

"That's not going to happen," Liam and Alex both said at the same time.

I glanced between them, my sight blurred with tears. "How do you know?"

"You heard it yourself," Liam explained, brushing away the wetness on my cheeks. "They said on the news his own organization is who likely did this to him."

"They're the only ones with enough ability to get close enough to kill him." Alex reasoned.

"You think so?" I asked, wanting so badly to believe.

"I know it," Alex said, his voice ringing with certainty. I couldn't help but notice that iciness he usually hid was back in his eyes. That calm, deadly air around him was on full display.

I looked at Liam, wondering if he saw it, too.

He was watching me, reassurance in his face. "It's over, Bellamy. You can believe him. Trust me."

I did trust him. More than anyone. Liam had risked everything time and again just to make sure I was safe. If he said we didn't have to be scared anymore, then I believed him.

I fell into him again with a relieved cry as more tears soaked into his shirt.

Holly came rushing into the house, up the stairs. "Did you hear?" she cried. "He's dead!"

"We just saw it on the news," Mom answered.

I pulled back and looked at Holly. She was crying, too.

She held her arms out to me, and I went into them. We clung to each other and cried. "The man who killed my husband has finally paid for his crimes," she said into my ear.

I pulled back and stared into red-rimmed eyes. "The man responsible?"

She touched my face and smiled. "Yes, honey. The man. Not you. Him."

I hugged her again, feeling a million times lighter than before. Between us, Ren's namesake kicked. I pulled back and put a hand to my belly.

Holly reached out, and I nodded.

She felt her grandson move, and more tears fell.

"He's happy, too," I told her. "Renshaw William Alexander Mattison can be born into this world without any fear."

"You're naming him after my husband?" Holly gasped.

I nodded. "After the man who saved his life. After all the men who protected him."

Holly started crying again and went to Liam to hug him. "Your father would love that."

"He would," he said, hugging her back.

"Alexander?" Alex exclaimed. "You giving that baby my name, too?"

"First I've heard of it," Liam muttered.

I glanced at him and smiled. "I think it's fitting."

He smiled back. "Me, too."

"This calls for champagne!" Mom proclaimed. "And cider for the pregnant lady."

I never thought I'd be toasting to celebrate the death of a man, but here we were.

And I wasn't sorry.

52

Liam

I was standing on the balcony, gazing out over the kingdom that was left to me. A kingdom I fully intended to earn.

The champagne in my hand was forgotten because I didn't need to celebrate the death of my enemy. It was good enough for me that he was dead.

Alex walked out across the deck and took up position beside me, both of us staring over the place we ruled.

"I don't have to go after him now," I said.

"You belong here with your wife and kid."

"You did this."

"I don't know what you're talking about," he replied, tipping his glass to his lips.

That box on my steps wasn't sitting there when he showed up. He'd brought it with him. He hadn't been anxious to see what was inside because he already knew.

"What did this cost you, A?" I asked, serious.

"Nothing."

I turned my head to look at him then. He looked back.

We did that thing Bellamy accused us of all the time, having a conversation without any words.

You aren't a killer, Liam.

I do what I have to do.

You didn't have to do this.

Neither did you.

I didn't.

But you know who did.

He glanced away then, our secret conversation over, and I knew we'd never speak of this again.

We didn't have to.

"Think Bellamy knows?" Alex whispered after a while.

"If she does, she'll never say." She didn't have to. Her adding his name to our son's was loud enough.

We drank the champagne, and Alex made a face. "This shit is for girls."

I laughed. Movement out of the corner of my eye made me turn. Bellamy was standing near the window, laughing at something one of our moms said. Her hand lightly rested on our child.

"Thank you," I told Alex.

He slapped me on the back, and we went back to overlooking our kingdom.

After a while, I exhaled, feeling like, finally, everyone could begin again.

Bellamy

Winter Olympics, Colorado

The massive crowd was hushed. The tension and anticipation filling the air was unlike anything I'd ever felt before. The sky was clear and bright. The sun shined down, reflecting off the snow and nearly blinding everyone.

But the games wore on.

This was it.

The final run in the men's halfpipe for this Winter Olympics. Liam was down just slightly behind the last boarder who'd just completed his run. I looked up to where Liam stood, readying himself for a run I knew he thought of as the defining moment of his career.

If he nailed this, he would win the gold.

He'd worked so tirelessly for this the past year. Him and Tom Joiner both put everything they had into getting him here. And he made it.

And it all came down to this.

The crowd began to rumble and cheer as Liam bounced around and adjusted his goggles, readying himself. Joiner was standing beside him, and they pounded it out before Liam turned back and a look of determination and concentration transformed him.

He pushed off, sailing down as people cheered and yelled. I watched with bated breath as he went down into the pipe, sailed up into the air, and nailed his first jump.

"You got this," Alex whispered beside me, and my stomach clenched.

I was so nervous and excited it made me nauseous.

The crowd went wild as he perfected another jump and then gracefully but powerfully went into the next.

When his board finally hit the ground, he pumped his fist in the air in celebration. Everyone went wild. I cheered and screamed, knowing I'd just witnessed his perfect run.

He slid across the snow a little farther and then stopped and unstrapped his feet. He would remain there in the center, separated from the crowed by colorful partitions, as we all awaited his final score.

The man who was slightly ahead stood nearby, also waiting to find out his fate. Liam paced, anxious to see if everything he'd done was enough, then stopped abruptly and turned to where I was standing in the crowd.

We locked eyes and smiled, nodding.

The scratch of the intercom came over everything and read off his final score.

Everyone erupted, and Liam jumped up before bowing to his knees in elation. He'd won. He'd reclaimed the title stolen from him before.

I cheered so loud my throat went hoarse. Tears streamed down my face, threatening to freeze where they fell. Around me, our moms and Alex went crazy as someone handed Liam the American Flag and he held it up to wave above him.

He was smiling the biggest smile I'd ever seen when our eyes locked again.

He took off, running across the snow, the flag waving with his momentum. From behind, Alex picked me up, lifting me over the partition, and I rushed forward, colliding into his chest. Liam spun me around, both of us laughing.

When my feet hit the ground, he put his arms around me, wrapping us both up in the flag, and claimed my mouth with a kiss that probably wasn't television appropriate.

I kissed him anyway.

This wasn't anyone else's moment but his.

When he pulled back, his eyes were bright.

"How's it feel to have another gold medal to add to your collection?" I asked.

"Damn good," he replied, grinning.

"I'm so proud of you, and I know your father is, too."

"Thank you," he said, pulling me close again. "Thank you for believing in me even when I didn't believe in myself. Thank you for loving me."

"Loving you is the easiest thing I've ever done."

Even though the crowd was going nuts and people were vying for Liam's attention, I still heard the familiar cry cut through it all.

Instantly, I turned toward the sound, my instincts sharpening. "Too much commotion," I said, reluctantly leaving Liam's embrace.

He pulled me back, lifted me into his arms, and the crowd went wild again. He carried me over to our family and reached into the baby carrier Alex was holding.

"Hey there, little man." Liam soothed, unstrapping Shaw and gently lifting him out. "No tears today. Your daddy just got something shiny."

Shaw stopped fussing and turned to the sound of his father's voice. The sun was so bright the baby recoiled, and I hurried to pull the thick hat on his snowsuit lower so it shielded his face.

Liam held his hand up, blocking the sun and smiling down at the baby who looked just like him.

"I love you," he said, cradling him close.

My heart turned over. I honestly never imagined I could have loved him more than the day we married. And then the day our son arrived.

During the last four months since little Shaw was born, Liam's interaction with his son melted my heart. Watching him walk the floors, cradle him close, and sing off-key in the middle of the night was literally the highlight of my life.

I truly couldn't ask for anything more.

And even though getting to this moment was so incredibly hard, I would do it all ten times over to end up exactly here again.

"Mattison, come get your gold!" Joiner hollered.

I laughed and took the baby, shifting him against me. Liam leaned down and carefully kissed his soft cheeks and then rose to kiss my lips.

"I love you, Mrs. Mattison. I love you more than any gold I'll ever win."

"I love you, too." I smiled. "But you should still go and claim it."

He laughed. Before running off, he pounded it out with Alex—who, I might add, was a giant softy when it came to babies. Or at least the one who carried his first name.

Although we never got around to talking about Alex's past with the army, I knew it was intense. I also knew, without ever asking, the reason Liam and I finally got free from the mob was because Alex used his self-proclaimed "skills."

I could live with that.

We would all live with it, happily.

Liam returned to us a short while later with an impressive, glistening medal around his neck. He pulled me and our son close, lowering to kiss me once again.

"Does this mean you're finally coming back to work?" Alex quipped.

Liam lifted his head and grinned. "I was thinking about it."

"I know you own the place and all, but this sense of entitlement has got to stop," Alex cracked.

"You own part of it, too," Liam pointed out.

"Which is why I'm telling you to get your ass back to the office!"

Liam flashed his teeth. "See you Monday?"

Alex nodded. "Wear sweatpants. It sure gets a rise out of the suits."

Liam snickered. "Can't wait."

"You two are terrible," I proclaimed, rocking the baby lightly.

"That's why you love us," Liam told me.

He was right.

I leaned up on tiptoes to kiss him again, and Alex made a sound. "Give me my nephew. You all are gonna traumatize the kid."

Carefully, I placed Shaw into Alex's arms, smiling at the way he always seemed to concentrate so hard when he held my son.

As soon as Shaw was secure with his uncle, Liam picked me up and spun me around, people close by cheering once more. We kissed in the center of the crowd, the gold hanging from his neck and the sun shining down.

Even though we were standing in the snow, the bite of frost was gone. All that remained was a lifetime filled with joy.

THE END

Stayed tuned for Alex's story in BearPaw Resort #4…

AUTHOR'S NOTE

Let me share a little secret with you. I'm seventy-two thousand words into this book, and I still have no idea how to end it. That's right. I'm skipping ahead to write this because I don't know what else to write.

Here's hoping the end of this book is not lame.

Up until this point, the story came along fairly well. I focused on putting their relationship back together after things sort of went to hell at the end of *Blizzard*. I actually was kinda surprised at how long it took to do it, as in how much of the book I dedicated to it. There was a lot to mend and a lot to reveal. I think it was good, though, fleshing out Liam and Bellamy's relationship. They've really been tested, so it was good to see them pull each other close again.

I also felt it was important for Liam to work out some of his demons. Maybe not slay them totally, but put them back in their place where they belong. Having him go back to boarding and go out on *his* terms was important to me. He does so much for other people and carries the weight of everyone he loves so intensely. I really wanted him to have something for himself.

I'm pretty happy with the way Bellamy evolved as well. Going from a paranoid woman on the run to standing tall and staring down death (numerous times) and not letting it force her out of her life again. I liked that she grabbed for her dreams (going to work at The Inn) and then discovered that maybe her dreams weren't what she wanted after all. Maybe in the midst of all her life-changing trauma, she discovered another side of herself. I think it's relatable that she changes her mind, and not because people are mean to her, but because she evolved and so did her life. In my own life, I've often felt like changing course with a dream is a little like throwing in the towel or admitting defeat, but it's really not. It's about following a winding path that hopefully leads to exactly where you should be.

Wow. For someone who can't seem to write an ending to a book, I'm sure full of thoughts and wisdom, aren't I?

Geez.

I hope that you as a reader enjoyed this last chapter of Liam and Bellamy's story. They were quite the challenge to write. They burn hot, love fiercely, and barely stop between all the suspense. As a writer, it was hard to keep up with. Hard to maintain to its full potential (if I was even able to!). Several times while writing these three books, I felt as if I wrote myself into a corner and have struggled to get out. Writing the mob is no joke, people. I honestly can't think of anything harder to get out from beneath that doesn't involve death.

And for those reading this and thinking, *Oh no, it's the last BearPaw book… I want Alex!* slow your roll, as he would say. I'm writing a book for Alex. That will be the last BearPaw book. Hopefully, he will be easier to deal with than Liam… Ha.

Thank you for reading, thank you for leaving a review, and thank you for all the support. Now I guess I should scroll back up and actually finish.

Edited to add: I've come back now that I have finished this book at a little over ninety thousand words. This was tough. I would like to add a GIANT thank-you to Adrienne Ambrose, because if it wasn't for her, I would likely still be sitting here trying to figure this thing out. Either that or I'd have killed everyone off and ruined my career. Seriously. Adrienne is a hero.

See you next book!

XOXO,
Cambria

ABOUT CAMBRIA HEBERT

Cambria Hebert is an award-winning, bestselling novelist of more than forty books. She went to college for a bachelor's degree, couldn't pick a major, and ended up with a degree in cosmetology. So rest assured her characters will always have good hair.

Besides writing, Cambria loves a caramel latte, staying up late, sleeping in, and watching movies. She considers math human torture and has an irrational fear of birds (including chickens). You can often find her painting her toenails (because she bites her fingernails) or walking her Chihuahuas (the real rulers of the house).

Cambria has written within the young adult and new adult genres, penning many paranormal and contemporary titles. She has also written romantic suspense, science fiction, and male/male romance. Her favorite genre to read and write is contemporary romance. A few of her most recognized titles are: *The Hashtag Series*, *GearShark Series*, *Text*, *Amnesia*, and *Butterfly*.

Recent awards include: Author of the Year, Best Contemporary Series (*The Hashtag Series*), Best Contemporary Book of the Year, Best Book Trailer of the Year, Best Contemporary Lead, Best Contemporary Book Cover of the Year. In addition, her most recognized title, *#Nerd*, was listed at Buzzfeed.com as a top fifty summer romance read.

Cambria Hebert owns and operates Cambria Hebert Books, LLC.

You can find out more about Cambria and her titles by visiting her website: http://www.cambriahebert.com. Please sign up for her newsletter to stay in the know about all her cover reveals, releases, and more: http://eepurl.com/bUL5_5.